OMEGA

CHILDREN OF THE SPEAR: BOOK FIVE

RHETT GERVAIS

Omega
Children of the Spear: Book Five

Rhett Gervais
Editor: Paula Grundy
Cover: Jake Caleb, J Caleb Design

Published January 2020

FOLLOW and LIKE:

https://rhettgervais.com/

PROLOGUE: THE NORFOLK INCIDENT

His mind was quiet now; the voices were gone. For a long time, he couldn't be sure what was real and what was not, but now, watching the waves rising and falling on the Atlantic, he felt grounded, like himself. He just wasn't sure who that was yet.

He caressed his face, wiping away cool ocean spray dripping down his square jaw, a jaw like his father's. He could remember him now: tall and strong with dark brown eyes and skin.

He blinked at the brown, freckled flesh of his hand, still amazed at its softness. How odd it made him feel, touching skin to skin. Standing on the prow of the drone carrier, with the hot sun on his face, he could almost pretend the nightmare of the last two years had never happened, that he was a normal young man, looking forward to officer training, maybe meeting a girl or even arguing with his little sister, but he only had to look down at the jagged crystal plates covering his body to disavow himself of that fantasy.

The memory of Rowen wrenched his mind back to the night in the park, the night he woke from the nightmare. After, when he was alone, memories drifted through his fractured mind in fits and starts, odd flashes of emotion, anger, rage, and sadness. His most profound memory was the day of his mother's funeral, standing above her grave: tiny snippets of the man he used to be.

The deep rumble and hollow whine of jet engines roaring to life brought him back to the present. Glancing over his shoulder, he could see hundreds of Apex drones preparing to launch, the triangle-shaped aircraft were black and sleek, giving them a narrow radar profile, making them seem to vanish when looked at horizontally. The weapons formed the backbone of their attack for this mission. They were built for speed, with small swept-back wings and a single turbine that made up most of its body, a single rotary cannon protruding from just below its nose providing enough firepower to annihilate anything in its path.

Looking back at the rest of the carrier, he was glad that the flight crew was minimal, no more than a dozen men and women running rudimentary inspections before the drones launched, his commanders watching it all from the bridge. Being around people made him uncomfortable, their wide-eyed panic and half-hearted excuses to be elsewhere whenever he appeared, had taught him to avoid them if he could. He knew he looked strange, almost seven feet tall, clad from head to toe in heavy-plated, crystal armor that was mostly a dull green now. Being no longer in contact with the tower had muted the colorful glow and shifting colors. It still happened when he was emotional, out of control, but those occasions were rare now.

A deep thrum passed through him as the Apex drones rumbled in their launch catapults, lifting off on pillars of white-and-blue flame that stained the deck black as they climbed, hundreds of them filling the air, machines precise, rotating in unison, locking on their target. Looking out toward the shore he couldn't yet see, he imagined the base suddenly going on high alert, klaxons screaming, men scrambling; not that any of it would make a difference. They might be able to stop the drones, but they would not be able to stop him.

As thinking about it caused it to happen, he suddenly felt a vibration pulsing through his entire body, pushing him, compelling him. In the old days, he would have leapt into the air without question, a hound let off the leash chasing the scent of prey in its nose, but now he held his ground firm, simply turning around to look at his commanders who watched him from their safe perch on the bridge. Even at this distance, he could see Kolov frantically pushing buttons on a tablet, trying to force him to dance to their song. He smiled grimly to himself watching the old men argue with one another, raising his chin and frowning in disgust at their weakness, knowing how desperate they were now that they had lost the tower in New York and lost full control of him. "Commanders, would you like me to join in the attack?" he asked in a measured tone, his own deep voice still strange to his ears.

After a moment of frantic button pushing, Kolov burst onto the comms, his mild Russian accent making him sound like he was an aristocrat of some kind: "Yes Negry, attack! Destroy the base entirely."

He shook his head, slowly and deliberately, making sure the old men in their safe space saw him. "Jonah. My name is Jonah," he growled before turning away. Drinking in a deep breath of salt air, he bent his knees, leaping with enough force to warp the metal beneath his crystal heels as he took flight, ocean air screaming in his ears as he departed on his mission of destruction.

It took him only heartbeats to reach the ceiling, the base of the lowest clouds. From his vantage point, he could see the Americans had two full carrier groups stretched out across the Atlantic, the base at Norfolk just at the edge of his field of view. His forces had managed to hide their approach, and now that the Americans scrambled to respond, the two groups lined up like ancient medieval armies facing one another on a field of battle. The Americans were just now launching predator drones. Like most of their weapons, the propeller-powered machines were outdated, archaic, no match for the speed and maneuverability of the Apex drones bearing down on them, presenting little real danger, and in reality, their only real threat was the chance that one of the rockets they carried could slip past and hit a Russian carrier. The predators acted mostly as fodder, soaking up fire that allowed their destroyers to close in and do real damage with their heavy artillery.

None of that would happen today; Jonah would see to that. The men who commanded him called him Rystar—knight. They treated him as such, like a piece on a chessboard to be moved under their discretion, limited in what he could do, but whatever his sister had done to him had freed him. He no longer had to play the game: now he would smash the board.

Jonah plunged from the sky just as the drones engaged, filling the salty ocean air with greasy, choking smoke. He aimed for a missile carrier at the vanguard of the battlegroup. His impact at the prow of the boat echoed like a god's hammer pounding on an anvil, lifting the bow out of the water before crashing down again with a titanic splash. In a heartbeat, his crystal-clad body tore through the steel-plated hull like it was made of wet cardboard, breaking through each deck, going deeper and deeper, never once slowing before finally exploding from the keel and plunging into the ice-cold waters of the Atlantic. Without missing a beat, he adjusted his course just slightly, taking aim at an outdated Virginia-class sub that should have been retired decades ago. Just as he reached the round-nosed tip of the darkened hull, torpedoes blasted out from the two forward hatches, moving past him with enough force to send him tumbling in their wake. Jonah hesitated only for an instant, looking back and forth between the sub and the torpedoes before racing after the weapons. Time moved at a sluggish pace as he chased after them. For some reason, his ability to fly diminished exponentially in water for reasons no one in the Rystar Program could explain. They only knew that the magnetic fields the crystals generated for flight were greatly damp-ened by water.

It took him only moments to catch the tail of the slower torpedo, the water in its wake boiling hot from its thruster, driving it toward the drone cruiser his commanders were on. Ignoring the blistering heat, he crushed the propellant nozzle with his crystal-covered hand, causing the weapon to go dead in the water. Then accelerating with all his might, he caught the tail end of the second torpedo, wrapping himself around the weapon and bending it in half.

Dropping the now-dead torpedo, he surfaced, emerging from the water on a massive geyser, returning to the clouds deck where he had begun his attack, ready to strike once again. The world above the water was one of pure chaos, with black smoke blotting out the sun as hundreds of Apex and predator drones circled one another, careening back and forth in a waltz of destruction. Jonah was deafened by a series of explosions as the carrier groups, still lined against one another across the ocean, hurled volleys of missiles back and forth, the deadly strikes countered by 50mm flak cannons filling the air with burning steel. Jonah shook his head, sure that this could go on forever: strike and counterstrike with neither fleet gaining ground.

Accelerating to his top speed with a growl, he plummeted to the ocean surface once more, leaving a massive wake of giant waves behind him as he tore into the keel of a destroyer. Then when he was done, he continued, never slowing, flying like an invisible missile through hull after hull, ship after ship, filling the air with the gut-wrenching sound of steel and iron being torn asunder, like a clarion call of death for the hapless sailors trapped inside and up on deck, the men panicking as they were swept like ants into the unforgiving sea. Pausing to look back at his work, Jonah smiled to himself. Having thrown the entire fleet into chaos, he could see the crews of the vessels scrambling to put out fires or simply abandoning ship as boats began to list from taking on too much water.

The only ship left untouched was an aircraft carrier, almost invisible behind a swarm of point-defense flak cannons, filling the air with dark smoke and bright explosions as the rapid-fire weapons annihilated swarm after swarm of incoming drone attacks.

Gathering his strength with a deep breath, he was about to charge and puncture the hull when the ship was suddenly shrouded in a bright cobalt glow. Then just beside it, standing on a glowing platform, appeared a stern-faced, middle-aged man, with a receding hairline, dressed in a long crimson coat that showed his hidden bulk everytime it fluttered with the ocean breeze. He wore form-fitting trousers that tapered into knee-high boots and a golden cross drawn neatly over his heart.

The man watched him through dark, hooded eyes. Wrinkling his nose as though he smelled something rancid, he began, "I am Lieutenant Gabriel Cornwall of Divinity Corps. I am here to negotiate terms of surrender."

Jonah raised an eyebrow as the man spoke, looking him up and down, wondering how he could be here before surmising the truth. "You are not really here," said Jonah in a halting tone. "You are just a hologram stalling for time."

Gabriel shook his head despite not being there. The thinning, dark curls on his head blew out with the wind, lashing at the sides of his round face. "Yes, and we would like to have a cessation of hostilities while we negotiate surrender,"

Forcing himself to calm, he kept his features steady as he watched the other man. "Does that mean you want to stop fighting because you don't think you can stop us, stop me?"

"Yes."

"Then, no," he barked. "My mission is to see this base and everything around it reduced to ash; negotiation is not an option."

Jonah could tell it was not the answer the lieutenant wanted. His lips compressed into a thin line and cocking his head, he continued in a raised voice. "There are families on that base: civilians, innocent people not involved in this conflict, you can't—"

"You're wasting your time," said Jonah, raising a hand to stop any further discussion. "War is cruel. Nothing can stop us, and none of you will be spared. You are a weak nation full of foolish people. You have proven this time and time again with your losses to us. It is time to remove you from the field."

Ignoring Gabriel's pleas, Jonah waved him off, returning his focus to the carrier, drifting just below the deck, and feeling his way along the cobalt shield that covered the entirety of its surface. While the barrier looked like pure energy, it felt smooth, almost metallic to his hand. Jonah drew back his fist to test its strength when suddenly an incandescent beam slammed into him with enough force to knock him back from the boat, sending him plunging into the Atlantic, the power of the beam boiling the water, forming a geyser of steam and fire. Shrugging off the heat, Jonah found his bearings, leaping from the water with a growl, only to see Gabriel and two others blocking his path. The three were dressed almost identically, with long crimson coats fluttering in the breeze, emblazoned with golden crosses over their hearts. Each of them stood on platforms similar to the shield that covered the carrier. Gabriel stood radiant in shades of blue and cobalt, looking at him with disgust. The others, a brown-skinned man, with a nose that looked like it had been broken more than once, wore a sour look on his face, the other a small Asian woman with harsh features that looked like she was often angry.

Jonah dove forward, teeth bared, intent on ripping the three limb from limb, only to find himself narrowly dodging twin beams of light, thicker than his wrists, shooting out from the woman's hands. Looking back where she struck, he could see the water turning to steam, hissing like a boiler under too much pressure.

"You can't fight us all" shouted Gabriel as the three of them dispersed suddenly, the platforms they were on flying off in random directions. "Surrender and withdraw, and we can end this."

Frowning, Jonah shook his head, not caring to waste his breath on fools. He took off after the woman first, spinning like a dervish to avoid the blinding beams of light that she wove from her palms, each miss sending pillars of steam high into the air when they struck the water, giving him cover to avoid her teammates. He was just about to grab her neck when Gabriel appeared, his shield absorbing the blow and knocking him back, forcing him to dodge a new barrage of white-hot beams shooting erratically from the woman's hands, the three of them turning to give chase. Ducking low, he skimmed just above the water's edge, creating a massive wave of ocean water following in his wake, obscuring him just enough that the woman shot wide with each blast of light.

Flying by a group of terrified sailors floundering in the water, Jonah had a flash of insight, slowing down enough to effortlessly pull the terrified men out of the ocean, their ear-piercing screams fading in the distance as he hurled them bodily at the approaching defenders, forcing them to scatter after the flying men.

Jonah smiled to himself as the three of them broke off their attack, desperately chasing after the hapless men and women. He could see the wide-eyed panic in the sailors as he plucked them up one by one, throwing them in random directions, forcing his attackers wider and wider with each throw. Satisfied that he had them sufficiently distracted, he shot off in pursuit of the Asian woman, a shockwave exploding behind him as he accelerated past the sound barrier.

Jonah let his speed do the work for him, grabbing her by her dark hair as he flew by, the sound of her neck snapping echoing like the crack of a whip.

He slowed, raising her flailing corpse high so her allies could see her, Gabriel and the other faces frozen in masks of fury, incandescent beams of light spraying in all directions as life faded from her body. This one was weaker than the one he fought in the park, he thought, letting it fall with a heavy splash. Jonah understood now that he had been holding back, limiting himself. Now that his mind was his own, and he was much stronger, he would crush these idiots and destroy the base, then he would work to test what he could truly become, and God help anyone who stood in his way.

ONE

THE BURDEN OF KNOWLEDGE

Rowen danced back on her heels, swinging wide with her escrima, forcing the much bigger man to step back or take a punishing blow from the hardened wooden sticks. She followed with a flurry of cross blows, aiming for his hands and neck, only to have her father counter by locking her weapons with his, knocking them high and following through with a heavy boot to her chest, sending her roughly tumbling to the floor. Breathing hard, sweat dripping from her thick mane of wild red hair, Rowen punched the floor in frustration. Her arms felt like lead, and she wanted nothing more than to lay down on the gym's padded floor forever. They had been practicing this series of attacks and parries for the last hour, with her father making aggressive attacks, trying to break her guard, and Rowen dodging back, nimbly deflecting his strikes and trying her best to keep her much bigger attacker at bay, so far, without much success.

Her father offered a hand, which she grudgingly took as he effortlessly pulled her to her feet. "You're wasting too much energy. You have to let your opponent tire themselves out: a tired attacker makes mistakes, mistakes you can take advantage of because you're still fresh."

"I would have shot you...so many times, by now," grunted Rowen through clenched teeth, suddenly throwing down the fighting sticks in disgust. "This would never happen in real life. There's a reason I have a gun, many guns. It's so I don't have to fight like a dumb caveman."

Her father narrowed his brow, lowering his batons to his side, his thick chest heaving. "You think you'll always have a gun?" he asked, wiping away the sweat from his forehead using a cloth off his belt. "What happens the day someone catches you by surprise, or you run out of ammo? You have to be prepared for every scenario."

Blowing out her cheeks, she scratched at the jagged scar on her head, the sweat rolling down her face making it itch. "I think I'd just let them kill me; it would be less annoying."

"Okay, I hear you. You've been working hard. Take a break."

"Damn right," whispered Rowen under her breath, taking a deep pull from her water bottle. "Anything new from Cardinal Washington, or are we still in limbo?"

Her father shook his head, the frown on his face matching the frustration she felt. It had been almost eight months since they had escaped New York, evacuated to central command buried deep in Western Pennsylvania's Iron Mountain complex: officially, to Rowen, at least, the most boring place on earth.

The walls of the training area, where she spent most of her time, were a depressing shade of gray and roughhewn, like someone couldn't be bothered to finish the job of putting them up properly. The place was gloomy on the best of days, with fluorescent lighting barely keeping the shadows at bay, making everyone look washed out and pallid. What was worse was that while they were not forced to stay inside, she often did. The world outside the massive stone doors was little more than gray rock, highlighted with the occasional tree, covered in runways that never seemed to have any aircraft. When they first arrived, they had been grilled on a daily basis about what happened in New York, about Arthur, about poor Gwen and Uriel, who had given their lives to put a halt to the war, which, so far, seemed to be working. With the strange tower in New York gone, the Russians had halted their advance, their command structure falling into chaos in some cases. Then from one day to the next, Rowen and her father were left to their own devices, quietly forgotten. Even Cardinal Washington, who had threatened a court martial for her father, had stopped coming by to offer threats.

Given that they had nothing but time now, her father had decided that it was well past due that she learn to fight beyond the basics he and her mother had taught her years ago. Rowen still didn't know what to make of the mixed assortment of Brazilian jiujitsu, judo, and kumerica he was teaching her. All designed, he said, for someone like her, who would often be at the mercy of much larger opponents. She had spent the last few grueling months learning to keep people at bay, practicing grapples and how to escape them. It felt like she had learned more about fine joint manipulation, leg locks, armlocks and choke holds than she ever wanted to.

She found it all very annoying, and she would rather avoid the mess of throwing punches and just shoot people! Shooting people was easier, made even better by the fact that her father would admit she was good at it. Her training with Mary Beth had only made her better.

With a deep sigh, Rowen picked the escrima sticks off the floor, twirling each of them in hand until they felt like they were part of her. "Okay, let's try this again," she said, readying her weapons and falling into the stance he had taught her, with her feet close together to give her maximum mobility. Her father gave her a brief nod before crouching deep, leading with his strong arm and leg to maximize striking power. He was about to begin when he raised a hand for her to stop, nodding at something over her shoulder. Rowen turned to see Captain Young coming toward them faster than a man his size should, red faced and wheezing all the while. Gibbs was nipping at his heels, his clear-blue eyes full of worry. She gave the bulky captain a questioning look and got a tight-lipped smile for her efforts. After their rough start a few months ago, she had gotten to know the big man well, even liked him a little. The things she knew most about him were that he loved to eat and hated exercise with a passion she had never seen.

Her father frowned at the pair, crossing strong arms across his chest. "You gentlemen look like you've just been ordered to take Normandy beach. What's got you guys up in arms?"

"Josh, you gotta see— Holy shit, you're not gonna—" began Gibbs, words spilling from his mouth so quickly, she barely understood him. Captain Young silenced his verbal diarrhea with a stern look over his shoulder before shambling over to her father, his pudgy hands racing over a tablet then tossing a portable holoprojector into the air with a deft twist. "Shit just went over a cliff; bad times are a comin," he said in his Kentucky drawl while mopping sweat off his brow.

Her father nodded, running a hand along his jaw. "They attacked? Where? When?"

"Norfolk, the whole damn thing is a clusterfuck, not much left. The holovid is from our satellite feed," said Captain Young as the projector hummed to life, and the utilitarian gray of the training room was suddenly overlain by white-capped blue ocean, warships on fire in the distance. Rowen felt like she was a giant overlooking the burning naval base and sinking fleet from high above, the Atlantic Ocean churning as entire carrier strike groups sank, destroyers, gunboats, and their escorts slipping into the depths, the sky dimming as thousands of drones circled one another, exchanging volleys of fire.

"How is this even possible?" asked her father, shaking his head. "Norfolk is the biggest naval base in the world. There are never less than two full carrier groups in house, more most of the time, not to mention hundreds of aircraft. What the hell did the Russians attack with? They don't have the drone power to even come close to doing this kind of damage."

"It wasn't the drones. It was him, Rowen—the thing from the park," said Gibbs, earning another stern look over the shoulder from Captain Young.

"Goddamn, son, you gonna get my boot in your ass if you keep blurtin' shit out and slow down when you talk; you ain't running from hounds in the dark...goddamn Northerners."

Rowen's entire body went numb. She blanched in horror, watching sailors who were lucky enough to escape their sinking ships, attacked by Russian drones strafing the water, rotary cannons spitting out white-hot fire and turning the ocean a sickening shade of red. Then she saw him, tearing through the hull of an aircraft carrier, barely slowing before moving on to the next and the next. His crystal armor was a dull-gray green, but she would know her brother anywhere just from the way he moved.

"He tore through the entire fleet as if it was nuthin': doubt if he even broke a sweat."

"What about Divinity Corps, kids like Gwen and Uriel" asked her father, his deep voice echoing off the rough-cut walls. "There must be others."

"The recording didn't catch the first part of the encounter but... Just watch," said the captain, shaking his head.

While they watched the hologram zoomed in from behind, tracking Jonah's movements as he skimmed across ocean surface, racing toward a man in a crimson leather coat, standing on the keel of a sinking ship, uselessly firing some sort of machine gun at him. Jonah stopped short suddenly when a blue shield appeared, blocking him from his target. A moment later another man dressed in red appeared, thick bodied with thinning hair.

"That's Gabriel and Winston; they were last active duty members of the Corps," said Captain Young quietly. "Gabriel can make shields and platforms that can fly, has a bit of flare for the dramatic. Winston, well, his abilities were classified above my pay grade for some reason, first time I ever saw him in the field.

"Were?" asked Rowen, mesmerized by the image in front of her.

Captain Young nodded toward the battle, pursing his lips. As Rowen watched the two men attacked in unison, Gabriel creating barriers around her brother each time he was about to strike, sparks cascading wildly with each blow, Winston continuing to fire his useless weapon. Each time Jonah moved to strike either of them, another barrier would appear. Knowing her brother, Rowen could almost hear him growl in frustration.

Then it happened so fast, she almost missed it, Jonah darting away suddenly, Gabriel and Winston twisting and turning, trying to see in all directions at once, then suddenly there was a burst of air, and both men were careening head over heels like thrown rag dolls, their bodies falling dead in the roiling water.

"I gotta make it run like molasses if you wanna make anything of it."

Captain Young replayed what had happened in slow motion. The satellite only catching the tail glimpse of Jonah's flyby. Rowen covered her mouth in shock as an expanding cone of air blocked part of her view, followed by a massive shockwave, which pummeled the two men, crushing and stretching them out in the blink of an eye.

"We couldn't get sound off the satellite, not that it would make a lick of difference, but if our math is right, he flew by them a little faster than Mach three. At that speed, that close, with a shockwave of that magnitude, it don't matter if you're just a regular asshole or some ascended, blessed by a god type, you're dead as dirt."

Rowen couldn't look anymore. Turning away from the image, she began to walk out of the holoprojector area when she heard her father's voice. "Stop, stop it now. Roll it back, expand!" he said almost screaming. She turned back to see him watching wide eyed at a giant image of Jonah's face, frozen in time, shards of crystal still protruding from the jagged edge from when she shot him. "Jonah," he whispered, locking eyes with her as the words spilled from his mouth.

"What? You mean Jonah your son, he died in New—" started Gibbs in a rush, only to be silenced with twin looks of anger look from her father and her.

"You knew," he said, his eyes darting back and forth between the image and Rowen. "You shot him, broke the mask, saw his face. You knew Jonah was alive, turned into that monster, and you didn't tell me." He stormed over to her, his massive frame casting her in a frightful shadow.

Rowen wrapped her arms around herself, quickly looking away. "I didn't know how to tell you. I didn't think—" she began, stumbling over her words.

"That's right, you didn't think, like always. That's my son, your brother," he screamed, balling his hands into fists, towering over her, "You let us sit here for months knowing he was alive, knowing we could do something to save him, stop this slaughter from happening, all those deaths! This is on you, Rowen!"

"All that time we were in New York, you didn't spend a minute looking for him, did you?" said Rowen in a flash of anger, feeling like she'd been slapped. "I was the only one looking. You spent all your time with your new son, Scotty, over there! Doing like you always do, ignoring your family, putting strangers before us. Go to hell," she finished with a shriek, her entire body trembling as she stormed away.

"Don't you dare turn your back on me. Where the hell do you think you're going?" Ignoring his shouts, she walked faster, his screaming growing more faint as she left the gym in a fury, slamming the door shut with a loud echo, stomping her feet on the polished granite as she wandered aimlessly, cursing herself because she knew he was right. She wished she could go back and have the courage to do the right thing. If they could have stopped this attack today, all those soldiers would be alive; it was her fault, and she didn't know how to fix it.

TWO

ONE DAY AT A TIME

The lady behind the counter rolled her eyes, a frown of disgust marring her too-pretty face. She was the type of girl that Gwen hated. With perfect blond hair falling in waves, framing her face, and makeup that looked like she just walked out of a holovid of some kind.

"You been living under a rock, honey?" said the cashier in a hurried tone, looking back at the long line of customers. "The city banned American money months ago. Everything's N-coin now —digital."

"But I need these," said Gwen, holding up her empty pill bottle. "Besides, I've been using cash since I got here." Gwen rung her hands in front of her, her pulse racing. She was down to the last few hits, and her usual hookups were nowhere to be found, so she was forced to use legitimate sources to deal with her cough, the pain in her chest. She would not usually go to a pharmacy. She tried to avoid people altogether these days given how she looked, dressed in a ragged hoody and torn jeans. Her skin was pale and waxen, and for the life of her, she couldn't remember the last time she washed her hair. But she didn't have much of a choice unless she wanted to be coughing up blood, barely able to breathe until she got a hit. As if to confirm her thoughts, the man behind her in line coughed into his hand, constantly sighing and tapping his foot.

"Cash is only good for dope, sex, or cheap liquor that'll make you go blind. If you don't got money, sister, move along."

Gwen ground her teeth, her hand twitching to reach over the counter and just take the pills. It wasn't like anyone could really stop her. "Screw you, lady," she said with a snarl. She gave the much-too-pretty cashier a sidelong glance before storming out of the pharmacy, nearly ripping the door off its hinges. She managed to walk a few feet before she stopped in the middle of the sidewalk, a numb sense of hopelessness overwhelming her. Burying her head in her hands, she put her back against the wall next to the storefront, half falling, half sitting on the pavement. Gwen had promised herself that she would stop crying. She spent too much time doing that every day, but the tears came anyway, wracking sobs mixed with snot that soaked the sleeve of her dirty, gray hoody. Already she could feel the tightness in her chest, the small tickle in the back of her throat. The pills were a synthetic morphine, strong as hell and not sold over the counter, and while they were nowhere as potent as Diomoxin, they were the only thing that worked...if she took enough of them...

"Hey, kid, you okay?"

Gwen looked up to find the man who had been in line behind her at the pharmacy giving her a tight-lipped smile, looking her up and down, judging her. "How about you take that Big Boy haircut and keep walkin', asshole," spat Gwen, not having the energy to deal with his type. He had that look, like he ironed his jeans and listened to soft rock. People like him always had that polite, condescending smile plastered on their faces that said they were better than you.

"Whoa, relax," he said, backing away, palms out. "You just look like you're having a rough go of it. Look, you can go to New York Central Services and register for the N-coin app. Last I heard, Arthur has authorized the city to deposit a few bucks into an account when people register, sorta like a Welcome to New York kinda thing, and you look like you could use the money."

At the mention of Arthur, Gwen's hackles rose, anger replacing tears. There were some days she could almost forget him and the things he'd done, the pain in her lungs, her cough. But then she would see his face on the news, or he would appear on her phone, bragging about this or that, about how great his leadership had made the city, how safe. Not long ago, she had promised that she would end his pathetic life, and she meant to keep that promise. The last thing she needed was for him to find her before she got the jump on him.

With a grunt, she used the wall to push herself up, ignoring the guy with the Big Boy haircut. Without another word, she grabbed her earbuds out of her pocket and shoved them in her ear, increasing the volume enough to drown out the noise of the city and everything else. Pulling her hoody up, she lost herself in the crowd, shoving her hands deep in her pockets. Keeping her head down she made her way down the avenue, thoughts on ways she could get a new supply of pills.

All of her usual contacts had dried up over the last few weeks, most of them having found regular work that paid better than slinging dope. She had Arthur to thank for that too. With all the new projects in the city, money was free flowing, and people had no problem finding well-paying jobs, not to mention, because he had banned many of the major corporations from doing business in the city, many people with the smarts and the guts to branch out on their own were starting their own companies. She supposed she could take the idiot's advice: go to city hall; maybe give them a fake name; try and get into the system, but she was almost sure they would run her DNA, but that was how she got into this mess to begin with.

It had been almost two years since that fateful night that she had fallen asleep at the bus shelter, high as a kite and her head bleeding from a nasty fall. The Ann Arbour Police had picked her up, and to her dismay, they had followed procedure, fingerprinting her and running the usual genetic tests. Her blood had revealed her potential for Ascension, and that had brought her to the attention of Arthur and the major bishop, changing her life forever. Now, she found herself far from home with nothing and no one. New York would have been a cool place to party in the old days before the war, but now, with Arthur rebuilding the city to his vision, the place was one giant construction site filled with people who cared too much about work and not enough about having a good time.

A low roar, like the air being sucked out of a room, shook her from her thoughts, Gwen looked up just in time to see a contrail cutting across the cloudless summer sky. Before she could register what she was seeing, the entire area was rocked by a violent explosion as something struck one of the towers under construction, black smoke and flame billowing from the gaping maw in the brick, throwing Gwen from her feet.

Within moments, the placid crowd transformed into a wild stampede, with people pushing and shoving in all directions, a living mass of humanity driven by pure chaos, without direction. Rising to her feet, Gwen pressed herself against the wall of a nearby building, avoiding most of those fleeing. Up above, she watched as whatever had struck the building continued to burn, flames licking the exposed steel girders and wood framing of the tower under construction.

Gwen was about to turn and run, follow the surge of humanity, when the horrible sound of twisting metal and grinding steel pierced the screams of those fleeing. She could see that parts of the building framing were no longer intact, the structure weakened by the explosion and flames. The building would collapse, sooner rather than later. Gwen felt the familiar tickle in the back of her throat as panic set in, her chest growing tight with each breath. She could just run; it wasn't her problem; she would be fine, and no one would judge her but her. "Son of a bitch!" she muttered under breath, shaking her head. Blowing out her cheeks, she closed her eyes, desperately searching for deep vibrations that once came easy to her: waiting, fumbling, failing.

Opening her eyes, she found herself still on the ground, rooted to the same spot. Gwen cursed herself. It had been months since Uriel died, and she had done nothing except feel sorry for herself, wallowing in self-pity. All around her, debris started to fall, flaming steel and concrete smashing on cement, bits of razor-sharp shrapnel scattering in all directions among those trying to escape. Steeling her resolve, she pulled out her near-empty pill bottle, dry swallowing the remaining contents in a single gulp. Without another thought, she shunted the volume of her Mp3 player to maximum, just as Ozzy Osbourne's mad laughter echoed in her ear, the ripping guitar chords of "Crazy Train" almost deafening her. She bobbed her head to the ebb and flow of the guitar, the high-pitched whine of his voice she knew so well. Gwen felt the vibrations then the hum she hadn't felt since that day when her world changed. Suddenly the wind whipped through her hair and stung her face, and like a bullet, she surged from the ground, finding herself high above the city street next to the blazing inferno that was leaning precariously toward the ground. From her vantage point, she could see New York spread out before her, its towers of glass and steel reflecting the afternoon sun.

Down below, the streets were jammed with throngs of people and vehicles, some paralyzed by fear, others racing to escape the falling building. Above the burning sections, she could make out construction workers, many of them dangling freely from harnesses still attached to anchor points. Without missing a beat, Gwen bolted for the first worker, tossing him a wink and a smirk when his jaw fell open. She tore the harness from the hardpoint that had saved him from falling but now kept him from escaping. She flew from man to man, holding on to the hapless workers by their harnesses so that they trailed behind her. She had almost a dozen in tow before she returned to the ground a few blocks away with only seconds having gone by. She was grateful for the music in her ear as the men all crowded around her, their lips flapping but their words falling on deaf ears.

Without another word, she shot off again, arriving at the burning building just as the upper portion was teetering like a drunkard, threatening to fall to the street below.

Assessing the situation, Gwen flew around the structure, trying to figure out a way to stop it from collapsing onto the street. Part of her was confident enough to think she could lift the entire structure, but she knew that was probably the dope that had given her a head rush, everything around her suddenly hazy and glowing softly. She decided it was a bad idea, sure the entire thing would collapse under its own weight anyway, but the thought of the building collapsing under its own weight gave her an idea. She flew directly into the inferno, tearing through metal and concrete like it were made of paper mache, dust and grit nearly blinding her. It took her only a few moments to find one of primary support beams, spotting the others in short order.

Taking a deep breath, Gwen sped off like a meteor, punching through steel without slowing, using her body like a scythe forcing the building to collapse under its own mass, tumbling straight down-ward. Exploding finally from the crumbling mess, she watched with grim fascination as layer after layer fell in an almost perfect line, plumes of dust and dirt, choking the flames under tons of debris.

Landing on the sidewalk next to what was left of the building, Gwen fell to one knee, breathing hoarse, her throat feeling like she'd swallowed shards of glass. She clutched her chest as a fit of coughing began, a short, sharp whooping that wracked her entire body, bringing the taste of copper to her mouth and staining her teeth red, spots of white dancing in her vision.

A hand on her shoulder brought her back from the abyss. Opening her eyes, she found a small crowd around her. In front of her on one knee, like he was proposing, was the man with the Big Boy haircut from the pharmacy, holding up a bottle of water to her mouth. She nodded to him, closing her eyes and shuddering as the cool liquid ran down her throat, soothing her ache, if only a little. Sitting back on her heels, she turned off the music, the sounds of the city filling her ears.

"That...That was amazing, how—" stammered the man, his eyes wide as he leaned in close.

Pushing him away, Gwen rose on legs that felt like lead, her face twisting into a grimace as she swallowed. She pushed herself too far, and now she would pay the price. "Are you stalking me, dude? What the fuck!" she said, rubbing her chest.

He shook his head, his brows coming together. "No, just a coincidence, I guess, but that doesn't matter right now. You need to get to a hospital."

Gwen's heart sank, and around her the crowd began to murmur, people reaching out to touch her, phones held up to record her, take her picture. Someone off to the side mentioned Divinity Corps. People knew her face, knew who she was even if she looked like shit. She had worked so hard to stay out of sight, be invisible, but now because she couldn't keep enough to herself, Arthur would know she was here. He would find her, and there would be hell to pay.

THREE

CONVERSATIONS WITH THE DEVIL

Arthur's heart sank as he watched black smoke rise from the fallen tower, his brow creasing with worry for those hurt by his failure to stop the missile attack. A hail of incoming fire snapped his attention back to the cockpit of the small VTOL he was using to defend the attack high above his city. He strained against the harness that held him in place as he banked hard and dove to avoid another wave of attacks. Arthur held his breath, wiping away the sweat rolling down his temples as the small craft rocketed toward the ground, every alarm in the small VTOL screeching like a banshee in his ear. The small transport was normally limited to short hops in local airspace. It wasn't considered fast or maneuverable, but Arthur needed something, anything to get close enough to use his abilities and stop the incoming attacks. Due to their limited resources, the little craft was the best he had at the moment. Pushing his powers to the limits allowed him to use it far past its capabilities. He just hoped it could hold together long enough to survive the day.

The early warning drones patrolling the airspace around the city had confirmed what he already knew—Cardinal Washington had sent another wave of Reaper drones to test him. The old man considered himself the commander in chief from sea to shining sea and took it as an insult that Arthur had turned New York into its own city state, independent of his rule, and he was relentless in his desire to take it back.

Finally close enough, Arthur closed his eyes for a moment, taking full control of the air wing of sleek Russian drones that flanked him, overriding their programming so that the triangular machines would cover his approach and take the brunt of any incoming fire. Arthur flinched, raising a hand to cover his eyes when the drone that flew on point was cut to pieces by a hail of incoming stinger missiles, disintegrating the matt black aircraft into a ball of white-blue flame. Wanting to avoid the same fate, he pulled up hard, sending the Peri clawing for altitude. Below, he watched with grim satisfaction while his drones opened fire, snub-nosed rotary cannons filling the sky with red tracer rounds, shredding titanium like paper, and two enemy Reaper drones were suddenly no more.

Glancing down at the controls, he could see almost a dozen more enemy Reapers closing in. He had half as many of his own drones engaging them in a strange dogfight of machine against machine. The Apex drones the Russians had left in the city, were deadly but in short supply, and since he no longer had the tower to control them at a distance, he had to be nearby for them to be of any use to him.

Leveling off the Peri to face the incoming attack, Arthur took a deep breath, steeling himself for another pass, knowing that each time he did this, he might not be fast enough. With a flick of his wrist, his small craft leaped forward, engines straining with the high-pitched whine of jet fuel exploding through turbines pushed beyond their limits, leaving a trail of white-blue flame behind him. He had only a heartbeat to prepare. Up ahead, a swarm of stinger missiles erupted once again from hardpoints below the Reaper's wings, approaching at speeds well beyond Mach 2 according to the limited sensors he had on the transport. Arthur gritted his teeth, counting down the milliseconds. He was quicker once again...only by a heartbeat. Using all his might, he deflected the missiles with a wave of his hand, forcing his will onto them when they streaked by. He delved deep into their electronic guts, his mind taking complete control of their guidance systems and driving them back around in a wide loop toward the Reaper formation.

Arthur's hand shook, knowing how close he had come to being on the losing end of the exchange. The stinger missiles annihilated the Reapers in a storm of death, filling the sky above Manhattan with red and orange flame, burning metal and plastic raining down from the sky. Leaning back in the cockpit, he glanced down at his screen, letting out a deep sigh now that the threat had passed. Exhausted, Arthur rubbed the grit from his eyes, feeling overwhelmed by the constant attacks: they came at all hours of the day, and he couldn't remember the last time he'd slept a full eight hours.

A shudder ran through his small body as he turned to Peri back to base and reprogrammed the drones to resume their patrol, so far being able to keep the engagements away from Manhattan, away from the people starting new lives full of hope, but not today. Today was the first time an attack had penetrated their defenses.

"You've been lucky so far, boy, but luck runs out," said Cardinal Washington's disembodied voice through the Peri's comm system.

Arthur's nostrils flared, his face going from caramel to a deep shade of red. "Your attacks have done nothing, Cardinal. My city is safe and free. If you had any courage, you would come yourself instead of hiding in that bunker," he said, trying to keep the heat from his voice while his mind delved into the controls of the small transport, examining every system, every circuit, still unsure of how the cardinal communicated this way.

The cardinal's deep-throated laughter reverberated throughout the cabin, setting Arthur's teeth on edge. "We're all a little busy right now, boy, but I promise you that I've left you a little gift today, and after we've crushed the Russians, I'll do as you ask and pay you, and those fools who follow you, a visit."

Arthur shook his head. He still couldn't understand why the cardinal hadn't nuked the city and carried out his threat. "We'll be

ready," said Arthur, banking the VTOL back toward the fallen building. It would be smarter to send someone to look over the site while
he got some much-needed rest, but part of him knew it would be
important for the public to see him, for them to know he was there for
them. There had been, and still was, a barrier between the people
and their leaders in the old version of America. He didn't want that
here. He would be accountable to the people: he could do that much.

Arthur landed not far from the destroyed building, smoothing his
simple black service uniform as he exited the craft. He scrubbed his
hand through his curly hair, hoping he looked somewhat presentable.
Emergency services had sealed off the area, but there was still a
significant crowd when he arrived, and after so many months of
running the city, most of the people who lived in New York knew
him well enough, and they moved aside once they noticed him
pushing through the crowd. A loud gasp spread through the crowd as
he neared the front, with some people jeering and pushing, others
shouting. By the time Arthur reached the front, the wave of astonish-
ment had passed, and he found himself face-to-face with what looked
like some of the construction workers from the site, most of the men
with their safety harnesses at their feet. Behind them, the building
had collapsed on top of itself perfectly as if it had been destroyed by a
proper demolition crew. "What happened?" asked Arthur to one of
the workers when no one came forward to offer an explanation.

"A girl," said a gangly construction worker who had a short beard
and shaved upper lip that was covered with beads of sweat. "It was a
girl." All around him the crowd murmured in agreement, whispers of
amazement reaching Arthur's ear.

Arthur shook his head, confused. "Is someone trapped in there?"
he said in a panic, tensing, and about to charge into the smoldering
wreck.

A neat-looking man with a crew cut stepped forward, his lips
pressed into a thin line. "There was a girl, a street kid," he began,
looking back toward the building when he spoke. "After the explosion, she appeared out of nowhere, flew in, and pulled everyone out."

The small group of construction workers behind him nodded in agreement.

Arthur locked his arms behind his back, his stomach churning. "Did you see any of this?" asked Arthur, turning to one of the policemen taking statements.

The officer frowned and shook his head, raising an eyebrow. "No, sir. I would say they were all nuts, but then I've seen what you can do...so, who knows?"

"I saw her before it all started," continued the man who had spoken before. "She was at the pharmacy. She looked like she needed help, so I tried talking to her."

"What did she look like?" asked Arthur, swallowing hard.

"Blond hair, small build. Wearing a dirty hoody and jeans."

"Pretty?"

The man with the crew cut made a face, his eyes darting around at the women in the crowd. "She looked like she had a rough go of it," he said finally. "Had a hell of a mouth on her too. Ran off in a hurry when people started taking her picture."

Arthur bowed his head, tasting bile in the back of his throat, feeling like he was about to vomit. Gwen, whom he loved, who he tried to murder, who hated him. She was alive. She had survived that horrible day in the park. And now he had no clue where she was, or what to do.

FOUR

PATRIOT

Rowen rewound the projection again. She had lost count of how many times she'd watched it, her mind still reeling from the brutality of the attack. Jonah had murdered without hesitation, destroyed an entire battle group like it were nothing. And when they had taken their best shot, and counterattacked with the remaining active members of Divinity Corps, he made short work of them as well. From everything she could see, he had grown stronger since that night in New York, much stronger.

She was about to restart it one more time when there was a knock on the door of her small room. With a sigh, she turned off the holo-projector and scrubbed a hand through her tangled mess of red hair, rolling her eyes when she caught a glimpse of herself in the mirror as she made her way to the door. Someday, she would have nice hair, easy and manageable.

She opened the door to find Captain Young filling its frame, his beige uniform showing dark stains of sweat down the front. "We need to talk," he said, pushing his way into her tiny room without waiting to be asked in.

"Ya, know, you don't have to stay in this little pissant of a room," he said, glancing around and realizing the only place to sit would be on the small bed shoved into the corner. "God damn, now that I think about it, why aren't you with your daddy. He has a full officer's suite on base."

Rowen shrugged, crossing her arms across her chest, grumbling to herself that her breasts still hadn't made an appearance and probably never would. "The last time I lived with my father, we were a real family: my mother was still alive, and my brother wasn't a monster. I'll stay here, if you don't mind."

Captain Young snorted, rubbing a thick finger under his bulbous nose. "Well, shit, I'm sorry if I brought up a sore spot. You can stay where you want," he said, his Kentucky twang making his words sound like a song.

"Thank you, sir," said Rowen with a nod. Without waiting, she returned to her bed, scooching into a corner and raising her eyebrows, giving the captain an expectant look that he should sit. She felt the bed raise like an unbalanced seesaw for a moment as he settled in, his face flushed red as he gave her an apologetic look.

Clearing his throat, he began. "I'm not one to beat around the bush, so I'll be straight...we're screwed six ways from Sunday," he said, his eyes fixed on the holoprojection of Norfolk burning. "We were just hangin' on by a thread before, but now...With your brother racing up the coast destroying everything in his way and Divinity Corps gone...If the country is gonna survive, we're gonna have to take some drastic measures," he continued, turning to look her in the eye.

"I'll help anyway I can," said Rowen, scratching at the scar running from the top of her skull to her chin. "But I'm not sure what one person can do."

"When you gave me your report, we talked about my kin," he said, putting a pudgy hand up to silence her as she moved to speak. "You were close to my girl, Mary Beth. You were the one to put down my boys, Ariel and Augusta."

Rowen felt the heat in her cheeks as they flushed a bright red, and pressing her lips together, she bowed her head and looked away. "Yes," she said in a small voice, not daring to look up.

"I'm sorry you had to do what you did. It wasn't fair, but hell, life never is," he said. "You were one person, untrained against three Ascended, all with years of experience and abilities beyond what most people could imagine. I say one person can make a big difference."

Rowen pulled her legs in close, wrapping her arms around herself. "It was just dumb luck," she mumbled. "Mary Beth told me they were near the end, that they only had a few months left, and let's not forget—they wanted me alive."

"No such thing as luck with those odds. Gibbs and your old man told me how it went down. You shoulda been dead along with everyone else in that room."

"I don't see what this has to do with the situation we're in now," said Rowen. She still woke up some nights in a cold sweat, reliving that horrible day in her dreams over and over. She didn't do anything except protect herself and the people she cared about: it had cost her more than she cared to admit.

"It has everything to do with it," said Captain Young with a sigh. "You play chess, Rowen?"

"My parents used to play together; they taught me a little, but I could never find anyone my age to play with."

The fat man shook his head, his jowls flapping. "Kids, these days, don't know what's good for 'em. Don't matter, anyhow. Chess at its heart is about war, two sides moving, countering, attacking, and defending. Right now, our enemies have outplayed us at every turn, cleaned our clock. The only way we can beat 'em now is to cheat— put new pieces on the board that they don't expect. We need someone who can counter your brother, and that my dear, is you."

Rowen scrubbed a hand through her tangled mess of hair once again, fighting not to laugh in the captain's face. "Last time we faced him, we had Gwen and Uriel, not to mention that psycho Arthur; we barely slowed him down," said Rowen, pausing the playback and pointing to the hologram of her brother rampaging through Norfolk. "He's only gotten stronger since."

"But he knew who you were. He stopped attacking and ran off when you shot open whatever it was coverin' his face. You said so in your report."

Rowen tensed, her hand clawing at the sheet on her bed. Captain Young was the only person she had told about what had passed between Jonah and herself, that he had spoken to her. Not even her father knew that part, and she intended to keep it that way. "I think he was in shock, confused. But it doesn't matter; it's been months now, and he hasn't come home. He's still with them. Lost."

"But you managed to hurt him, get his attention, and slow him down."

"I don't see how it matters," she said. "If you heard his voice, saw the look in his eye, he was like an alien. I don't think I'll be so lucky next time."

"You will be, if you go through with the Ascension process."

Rowen was taken aback. For long moments, the only sound in the room was the captain's heavy breathing. Finally, she shook her head. "No! No way."

The flimsy springs on the tiny bed screeched in protest as the captain stood, straightening his uniform. "You and me, we may come from different parts of this great country, but we got more in common than you know," he said, turning to face her. "We come from good stock: hardworking, loyal, patriots."

Captain Young's eyebrows drew together, a look of confusion on his face as Rowen began to laugh, a half smile on her face. "Did I say sumthin' funny?"

"Mary Beth and I were close," said Rowen, sidling a hand under her pillow, comforted to find her SIG there. "She told me you told her the same thing word for word when you convinced her to give up childish things and do her duty for her country."

The captain pursed his lips, shaking his head. "It wasn't like that. It—"

"I find it funny that everyone has to make sacrifices but you, even with all of your kids dead and buried—"

"Now, you wait just a goddamn minute. No one has given more for—" he began, his face turning an ugly shade of red.

"Mary Beth gave a hell of a lot more, so did Uriel and your other boys. I'll do my duty and serve my country, and I'll do just fine without any of your bullshit," said Rowen, gripping tight to the butt of her gun under the pillow.

"Rowen, please, you gotta see you're wasting your potential, girl."

"Not a chance in hell!" she said, shaking her head. "We're done here. Get out, and find someone else to be your guinea pig."

Captain Young's shoulders slumped as he let out a deep sigh. "I was hoping it wouldn't come to this, but I am well within my rights to order you to take the procedure. So that'll be the end of that. Do as you're told, and everything'll be right as rain."

"I don't think so," said Rowen, sliding her SIG out from under her pillow and leveling the weapon at the captain in a single, smooth motion.

"Are you out of your goddamn mind!" he said, his entire body shaking, nostrils flaring.

"Hands up and not another word," said Rowen, sliding off the bed and motioning for the captain to stand in front of the door. Without taking her eyes off him, she opened the small footlocker at the end of her bed, pulling out the tactical goggles Gibbs had made for her and shrugged on her gray duster.

"What's the plan, girl? You think you can just walk off this base whistlin' 'Dixie,' and no one'll do shit to stop you? I thought you were brighter than that."

"I've been here for eight months; you don't think I have a plan?" said Rowen. "Turn around, and put your hands on your head —slowly."

"Okay, let's do it your way." Cocking his head, the heavyset captain turned around slowly, doing as he was told and putting his hands on his head. Moving quickly, Rowen kicked him in the backs of the knees to force him to the floor. She found a set of zip ties, the kind used by military police when they wanted to restrain someone, and was about to slip them around his wrists when her world exploded—blinding-white light and ear-shattering sound sending her tumbling back against the small cot in the corner. She cursed herself for not thinking Captain Young would have had contingencies in place. Temporarily blind and deafened, she rolled back to the wall, holding her SIG defensively in front of her. "Take another step toward me, and I empty the clip into Captain Young over there," she bluffed, praying that she looked threatening enough to make anyone coming for her to think twice.

A short, sharp shock pierced her chest, and thin metal prongs buried themselves in her flesh. Rowen ground her teeth as electricity coursed through her, her small form rocking back and forth, tensing and spasming all at once. After what felt like an eternity, the waves of electricity stopped, her body still twitching from the aftereffects of the electrical shock.

She opened her eyes to find a bloodied Captain Young looming above her, flanked by a pair of burly soldiers, dressed in full tactical gear, aiming Tasers at her. "I'm truly sorry to do this, Rowen. You deserve better, but I would sacrifice a hundred of my kin to save this great nation, so yeah, I'm gonna force you to do your duty, and I'll try and live with the consequences." He gave a brief nod to the men beside him, and they dragged her up from the bed, prying the gun from her hand and flanking her, holding her in an iron grip.

"I'm gonna kill you," promised Rowen through gritted teeth, fighting against the soldiers as they took her away. Glaring at the captain as they entered the hall, the rational part of her brain understood: it made sense. But in her heart, she raged, knowing that her life would be over—freedom would be gone.

FIVE

BRAVERY

They met with little resistance after the carrier groups were sunk, with only the occasional wave of drones attacking them while they secured the rest of the base, not that anything would have been able to slow him down. Knowing his father's level of skill and having planned to join the service not so long ago, Jonah expected more from the American military and felt a tinge of disappointment as he strolled through the burning streets of Norfolk. He had visited once with his parents, and the base hadn't changed very much. Its streets and clean boulevards were home to many military families, ordered and quiet...until today.

They had attacked the base and surrounding city with wave after wave of Apex drones. Along with himself, they had reduced the outer limits to rubble, and it was not long until the city and the base were theirs.

The sound of gunfire drew him from his thoughts, and with a start, he realized that bullets were bouncing off his armor, the flattened balls of lead falling at his feet like rain. Just up ahead was a barricade of burning cars and SUVs, the source of the attack. With a grunt, he charged ahead, moving at the speed of thought, his feet never touching the ground. Jonah shattered the makeshift barricade, slicing through an iron-gray SUV like a scalpel through soft flesh. He found a pair of young enlisted men clinging to their weapons with white-knuckled hands, wide eyed at seeing him appear in front of them, the flames from the burning car still licking his armor. Jonah found it odd that he thought of them as young—they weren't much older than him—and if he'd followed the path he was destined to, it could have been him standing there about to die. He raced forward, the poor soldiers appearing to be standing still. Before they could blink, he tore the assault rifles from their hands, tossing them far behind him.

He was pleasantly surprised when neither man ran, each of them nodding to one another in turn, then crouching low and coming at him from each side with bare fists. Ignoring the man to his right, Jonah stiff-armed the charging soldier to his left, throwing him to the ground with enough force to make him slide back half a dozen feet, clutching his chest, his face a shade of purple. With a sigh, he turned to face the other, who was pounding futilely on his back with heavy downward chops, doing more harm to his own hands than Jonah's armor. Seeing his blows have little effect, the soldier's face went pale, and he backed up, holding his palms out defensively.

"Brave, but stupid," said Jonah, lashing out, grabbing the other man's collar and pulling him in close enough to smell his sour breath. "It would have a better chance if you ran, lived to see another day, instead of dying for a lost cause: nameless, forgotten."

Jonah heard a scraping against his side. He glanced down to find the soldier had unsheathed a blade of some kind and was attempting to slice into him. Staring deep into the young man's eyes Jonah caught glimpses of rage...and something else. "Why fight? You can't win."

The soldier's face contorted in twisted fury, and without a word he spit. The warm spittle running down Jonah's cheek. "Fuck you, asshole; just kill me already," he said.

Jonah cocked his head, a warm feeling bubbling in his belly, a sense of pride washing over him. "It would be best if you ran," he said, frowning down at the soldier. "I won't be the one killing you today," he said, letting go of the hapless soldier, who stumbled back and fell on his behind, a look of confusion on his face.

Looking up at the sky, he bent his knees, and Jonah pushed off with enough force to leave deep cracks in the concrete, leveling off seconds later when he hit the cloud deck. He hung there motionless, like an anchor in the sky, questioning why he simply didn't kill the idiot; it would have been for the best. If it he didn't do it himself, there were enough Russian troops on the ground that getting away with their lives would be lucky at best. He supposed that's why they attacked him in such a stupid way. Better to die in battle than be caught like a coward trying to sneak out the back door.

From high above in the clouds, the base looked mostly intact, only the burning in the harbor, flicking orange and red reflecting on crystal-blue waves, that told the story of what happened. The greatest navy in the world had been crushed, and the way forward was clear, all because of him. He should have been proud, but he only felt nothing. It was all too easy, only the girl in the park and his sister had made him feel something, and that made him hurt. He would find them again, finish what they started, and see who was truly stronger. Having a goal, Jonah felt better suddenly, a sense of purpose uplifting his spirits. Nothing would stop him: he was sure now.

He was just about to return to base when a resonance ran through him, like an extended note from vibrating crystal. Jonah looked down to see his crystal armor pulsing once more, shifting from amber to jade, cobalt, and crimson all in a rapid sequence. Somewhere, another tower was active, and he had no clue what that would do to him.

SIX

SPILLING THE MILK

Gwen didn't know how long she stood in the dark facing the shuttered pharmacy, running her hands along the cool metal gate that covered the fragile glass windows. The last day had been a blur, with nothing feeling real, except the pain. Her lungs felt like they were filled with shards of glass every time she took a breath. She didn't know how much blood was in a human body, but she was sure that she had coughed up most of her own. The red stains on her clothes and lips, not to mention her rasping voice, had turned away most of the clients that would give her a few dollars for her affections.

This was her last resort. She bent over, gripping the base of the roll-up door before she lost her nerve. In a single swift motion, she ripped the steel from the moorings buried in the concrete, the screech of the door rising, breaking the silence of the night. Having committed herself, Gwen tore the metal frame of the main door from its hinges, the glass shattering as she casually threw it behind her. She rushed into the store and leaped over the counter, hunting for what she needed: pills to suppress her cough, pills to dull the pain, pills to get through the day.

Somewhere in the back of her mind, she registered the wail of the alarm, the flashing of red and amber lights in the dark. When she found what she was looking for, Gwen cheered, dancing in a small circle with her hands above her head. Wasting no time, she dry swallowed three pills at once, each of them feeling like nails being pounded into her throat.

Blowing out her cheeks, she began shoving bottles into her backpack, not bothering to read the labels, knowing that she could use them or sell them later. By the time she was filled to capacity, the sharp pain in her chest and throat were muted, all the hard edges of reality had vanished, and it was as if she were seeing the world through a lens that gave everything a soft glow.

Gwen slipped her earbuds from her pockets and stumbled out of the shop, a wide smile on her face as she scrolled through her old iPod to find something she could dance to. The night air was fresh and cool, smelling of pepperoni and cheese from the pizza shop that was still open just down the street.

The flash of red and blue, along with the wailing of sirens, pulled her attention from the list of music she was scrolling through.

She looked up to find a policeman slowly exiting from a patrol car, drawing a nightstick. The officer, like most people who lived in New York now, was not much older than her, well muscled and square jawed with swarthy skin and dark eyes, and hair bleached so pale it looked white. "Hands up where we can see them," said the officer, his voice deep and commanding.

Gwen did as she was told, a smile plastered on her face while she raised her hands, swaying a little. "At least the cops in this city are cute. You should have seen the cows we had back home in Detroit, ugh, just gross."

The officer shook his head and returned his nightstick to his hip, a frown creasing his face. "Freaking junkies," he muttered. "Look at this mess! How the hell did you get in there?"

Looking back at the missing door and ripped-up concrete, she cocked her head and gave him a shrug, her head spinning from moving too quickly. "I don't feel so good," said Gwen, her words starting to slur.

"Yeah, no kidding, by the looks of you. I'm gonna take you in, so I need you to follow my instructions exactly. Do you understand?"

Gwen staggered back, her hands falling a little. "I'm a little fucked up, so I don't really feel like hanging now, but you're cute. Maybe we can hookup later."

The policeman raised an eyebrow, pulling out a pair of cuffs. "You're being arrested. It's not like you've got a choice how it goes down. Now, get on your knees, and keep your hands on your head."

Eyeing the silver cuffs in the officer's hands, she shook her head, letting her hands fall. "Last time I got arrested, really bad things happened," said Gwen, slumping down in place, bowing her head. "I met an asshole who was supposed to be my friend—bastard tried to kill me when I didn't wanna be his girl. People who hurt me alot. On the bright side, I also met a great guy, but he died. It's been a pretty shitty ride lately, if I'm being honest."

The officer squatted down beside her, patting her awkwardly on the shoulder. "I'm sorry you've had a rough time of it. I was homeless for a while too until Arthur drove the Russians out, saved the city," he said, putting his cuffs away. "I don't know who broke in before you, but you still can't just take whatever you want. Anyway, I'm gonna take you to the hospital. It looks like you need that way more than a trip to lockup." The officer slipped a strong hand under her, helping her to her feet.

"I can't go to the hospital; he'll find me," mumbled Gwen, staggering to the patrol car like a drunken sailor, leaning hard on the officer.

"What? Who, who's gonna find you?"

Gwen stopped in place, raising a hand to block the light of the police strobe. "He didn't do it alone, you know. We all helped...paid the price, while he takes all the credit. You smell really good, by the way."

"What are you goin' on about?" said the officer, wrinkling his nose like she had just reminded him of something. "And I'm gonna be totally honest here: you really need a shower."

"That little shit...people keep thinking saved New York. You know I used to think he was awesome too, thought he loved me...but he only loves himself: selfish prick."

The officer leaned her up against the patrol car, narrowing his eyes. "You mean Arthur. You gotta be kidding me. Don't get me wrong, but I doubt he would associate with someone like you. I mean he's a stand-up guy and all, but he's a hero. Hell, my parents who live in Kentucky want him to come in there and take over. Everyone knows the system has been screwing them over for a long time. We're all just glad that someone's doing something about it."

"He did this to me; he's an asshole," said Gwen, shoving the policeman back. "On second thought, I don't wanna hang. I'm out." Closing her eyes, Gwen found the subtle vibrations that were always in her mind, resonating, pulsing in tune with her heart. For an instant, she felt the cool rush of air, and she leaped skyward, the roar of wind in her ears. Then just as quickly, she hit something hard, her breath fleeing from her lungs. She blinked away the dirt in her eyes and turned over, realizing she had only managed to fly a short distance, finding herself not far from the patrol car and the officer who was trying to help her. His shadow falling over her was the last thing she saw before everything went dark, and she surrendered to the abyss of unconsciousness.

SEVEN

DEALMAKER

"You'll thank me for this later," said Captain Young over his shoulder as they hurried down the dimly lit corridor, the big man huffing and puffing.

"Did Mary Beth thank you, or Uriel?" said Rowen in a bitter tone, struggling against the burly soldiers on either side of her, dragging her along.

Captain Young stopped short, turning to face her, red faced with nostrils flaring. "I ain't past giving you the back of my hand, missy," he said, shoving a finger in her face. "Sacrifice is messy, and I did what I had to do. You think I wanted to lose my kin! Those kids were my entire life, and I gotta live with the pain every day now that they're with the good Lord."

Struggling against the iron grip of the men at her side, Rowen could almost hear her father's voice telling her that she needed to learn to fight, more precisely against opponents bigger than her. "Good initiative; bad judgment," she said with a smile as the veins in Captain Young's neck throbbed. The phrase was one her father taught her for when a marine did something for a good reason but with awful results.

With a snort, he turned on his heel, motioning for his men to follow. Watching his back, Rowen's hands itched for her SIG. It would have been easy enough to finish this and execute her plan to escape the Iron Mountain... And then what? Would she go on the run forever, hiding out from the military and the government until they gave up or caught her? Was she willing to spend the rest of her life putting herself, her friends, and family in danger. Living like a criminal who never committed a crime?

"Captain Young—" began Rowen, just as the lighting shut down, plunging the corridor into pitch darkness. By instinct, she ducked down as best she could, flinching a moment later when the sharp crack of gunfire exploding in the narrow corridor, nearly deafening her, the acrid smell of propellant burning her nostrils. The soldiers at her side fell away, and an instant later, she heard Captain Young grunt in pain, his heavy body slapping onto the hard floor. Rowen crouched to one knee just as the lights came back, revealing her father loaded for bear with an MP5 in one hand and a Beretta 9mm in the other, dressed in dark camo tactical gear with a full comm suite built into his helmet.

On either side of her, the burly men who had been holding her lay unconscious, a vicious set of bruises on their heads and necks. Up ahead, Captain Young sat back on his oversized haunches, clutching his gut and breathing hard.

"Nonlethal rounds. They'll be out for a bit," said her father by way of explanation when Rowen raised a questioning eyebrow. "I'm not gonna kill these men just because Angus here decided to be an ass. Are you okay?"

Nodding, she sprung to her feet, scrubbing a hand through her tangled mess of hair to give it some order. "I didn't need anyone to save me."

Her father came closer, towering over her. "There's no shame in accepting help, Rowen. You'll learn that as you grow up. The men and women I've served with over the years have saved my ass more times than I can count," he said, holstering the 9mm and glancing back over his shoulder. "Okay, we're clear."

"You sure?" said Gibbs in his hurried tone, poking his head out from around a corner just up ahead. "Yup, yes. Looks like it." With a smile plastered across his face, he hurried toward her, looking her up and down before wordlessly giving her a tight hug.

Rowen accepted it all with a shrug, mouthing a thank you to her father while Gibbs held her like he would never let go. "Thank you," she said, finally pushing him away. Looking at her friend she could see pieces of dull crystal crawling down the side of his neck, vanishing just behind his ear. Since the destruction of the tower in New York, the mysterious shards of glass had gone dark, no longer pulsing with color, and Gibbs seemed like himself...only smarter. "I'm guessing it was you who hacked the lights," said Rowen, eyeing the tablet in his hand.

"The network security is really flimsy. You'd think the military would spring for a decent fire wall and countermeasures," said Gibbs quickly. "Oh, here, I managed to get your equipment." Reaching into the bag on his shoulder, pulled out her armored duster, along with her SIG Mark II and the tactical glasses he had made for her. Giving him a grateful smile, she happily shrugged on the coat and holstered her gun. The weight on her hip calming her nerves.

"We should get moving," said her father, glancing worriedly up and down the corridor. "Gibbs, find us a way out of here, one that won't attract too much attention."

"That'd be a pretty dumbass thing to do," said Captain Young, glaring at her father. "Didn't think you'd be the type to abandon your country when it needed you the most, Josh."

Her father's eyes shot open like he'd been slapped. With a quick stride he grabbed the bloated captain by his collar, shaking him for good measure. "You gotta lotta balls talking to me like that right after you just tried to force my daughter into this chamber of horrors you people got going here. I'm the one who signed up to serve, not her."

"Yeah, well, just where do you think you're goin'? You gonna spend the rest of your days runnin' like some coward?" said Captain Young.

Hearing her thoughts reflected back to her, Rowen blinked hard, tracing a finger down the deep scar on the side of her face. A coward was the last thing she was, and in her heart the thing she wanted most was to be a soldier: Special Forces, like her parents. To free the oppressed.

"You're the coward, Angus, and it cost you everyone you ever loved," said her father. "I'd rather be called a coward a thousand times over than let you hurt my kid, so unless you want me to switch over to live ammo, I'd keep my mouth shut."

Captain Young frowned up at them, raising his chin. "That's the difference between us, Josh. I know freedom ain't free; you gotta—"

"What was the plan?" said Rowen, brushing past her father to stand in front of the captain while crossing her arms under her flat chest. "What was supposed to happen if I went along with this crazy scenario here."

Captain Young narrowed his eyes at her and then shrugged. "You an' Gibbs here would be the heart of a new Divinity Corps unit. Your genetics are off the charts, and Gibbs here, he's a smart son of a bitch. He's modified the algorithm we use to find kids like you, kids with the right stuff."

Beside her, Gibbs cleared his throat, a sheepish look on his face. "Okay, I've found us a path, reassigned guards, and put the cameras on our route on a loop. We should be able to just walk out."

"See what I mean?" said Captain Young, blowing out his cheeks.

Rowen bowed her head, looking back and forth between her father and Gibbs. "I don't want to spend my life on the run, and I don't want to be some freak waiting to die," she said, nodding her head as her thoughts came together. "And someone has to stop Jonah."

"Rowen, we can't. You saw what he did at Norfolk," said her father.

Rowen didn't look at him, instead locking eyes with Captain

Young, who sat stock still on his haunches, watching them all with an intense gaze. "You don't need powers or abilities to be a hero, Captain," she said. "My parents, and the people they served with, proved that to me every day when I was growing up. With courage and the right tools we can stop the Russians...my brother too."

"Do you really want to do this, Rowen?" said her father in a low voice. "I agree, but—"

"There has to be a way to get to Jonah," she said, looking up at him. "And we can't do that on the run. Gibbs, what about you?"

The pale man's head bobbed up and down, a smile creasing his face. "Way better than going home and facing my father. I've been avoiding his calls for eight months. I'd like to avoid my ass whooping for as long as possible."

"That's it, then. As long as no one tries to kidnap me and turn me into a living weapon again, Gibbs, my father and myself will build your team and make sure we win this. Deal," said Rowen sticking out a hand to the fat man.

Captain Young stared hard at her for a long time, his eyes darting back and forth. Finally, after what felt like an eternity, he shrugged and took her hand. "Let's hope we all live long enough to find out if you're right or wrong. God help me, but you gotta deal."

Just as she took the captain's hand, Gibbs let out a gasp, clutching at his neck and staggering against the wall. Rowen rushed to him, taking him by an arm to stop him from falling. It was then she saw it, the long, dulled crystal that protruded from his collar, the crystal he had gotten that fateful night when they had attacked the Russian base in New York. That had been dormant since the tower had been destroyed but suddenly it was active again, a swirling pulse of color and light.

Captain Young's wide shadow fell over them, his jowls shaking as he shook his head. "Well, good thing we gotta deal, 'cause it looks like we just ran outta time. And God help us all."

EIGHT

MISSED CONNECTIONS

"They've found the girl."

Arthur flinched as the Italian's bold features emerged from a pool of rippling shadow in the corner of the room. He stared, fascinated as the rest of him shimmered into existence like moonlight reflecting on a smooth lake, at first, and then coalescing into a man of flesh and blood. The way he traveled still gave Arthur the creeps, and he had to still his face whenever Rodrigo appeared from the nearest shadow. Arthur's parents had told him never to judge someone by their appearance, but it was hard with Rodrigo, his aquiline nose and high forehead made him appear to be looking down on everyone, and the more Arthur got to know him he realized that most of the time, Rodrigo was. It had been months since the handsome Italian had promised to serve him in return for his protection, fearful to return to Cardinal Washington, and despite all the time they spent together, Arthur hadn't warmed to him. But given his ability to transport himself and others almost anywhere, he put up with his arrogance.

Tearing his eyes away from the holographic overlay of the city, Arthur stood, straightening his plain black uniform and focused his attention on Rodrigo, fighting to keep a smile from his face despite the news. "Where?" he said with a calm he didn't feel, his heart pounding out of his small chest. For the second time, Gwen had come back from the dead. After the rocket attack in the city a few days ago, he allowed himself to hope, but without proof, it was just that—hope. But now she was where he could find her, see her...touch her, explain.

"Bellevue hospital," said Rodrigo, narrowing his eyes, scanning the display of the city's defenses. "She collapsed outside of a pharmacy, coughing up blood. The patrol officer who found her said she had stolen a bag full of painkillers, enough to kill a horse."

Arthur locked his arms behind his back, sucking in a deep breath through his nose and releasing it slowly. Knowing full well why she needed the medication, a wave of guilt washing over him. "I need you to take me, now. I need to see her."

"Are you sure? It is not your favorite way to travel," said Rodrigo in his Italian accent, making his words sound almost musical despite their thoughtlessness. "From all accounts the girl is unconscious. Why do you rush to see this whore?"

Arthur raised his chin, giving Rodrigo a hard stare. "Last time you called her a whore I removed your head from your neck. Are you sure you want to test me again?"

Rodrigo bowed his head, a frown coming to his handsome face. "Scusa, I forget my place." The tall Italian rubbed his temples, squeezing his eyes shut before continuing. "I do not know why I say such things. It still feels like someone who is not me is in my head."

Arthur nodded, pressing his lips together. "Cardinal Washington really did a number on you. He removed so many of your memories that it fundamentally changed who you are."

"I spend so many hours wondering who I was before or if I was ever a real person at all and not some monster he concocted in the lab," said Rodrigo, looking away.

"You're real, and you're certainly not a monster. You've proved that. A lot of people in this city wouldn't be here if you didn't join us in throwing out the Russians and getting things back to normal," said

Arthur, moving to stand beside him, giving him a small pat on the arm. When Rodrigo had come to him after the battle of New York, the man had been tormented by memories he couldn't explain, feelings that threatened to overwhelm him, but mostly he was terrified to return to Cardinal Washington, knowing what the man had done to him. Uriel, before he died, had opened the door, revealing that he and Arthur had fought and killed a version of Rodrigo at Iron Mountain weeks before and were shocked to see him alive and well not long after.

"But can a copy be a man? A real one?"

"You can be whatever you want," said Arthur. "We've managed to remove most of the nanites that he'd used to alter or change your memories, to program you. Now, you're a mostly blank slate, but given time, you'll become whatever you want to be. You get the luxury of getting to choose who you become."

"Si, gratzi, you are wise for a black."

"Let's just get going, and forget about all this," said Arthur, keeping his face still despite his irritation at the comment. Most of the memories Rodrigo had were from growing up in a small village somewhere in Italy, and from what he'd gathered there was not much diversity back then or tolerance. But something told him that no matter what, Rodrigo was destined to be an asshole.

Nodding, Rodrigo put a hand on Arthur's shoulder, and he suddenly felt as though he were being immersed in icy water, the world fading to a dim, moonless night. Trapped in the dark, Arthur locked his arms behind his back, and he fought for breath, his lungs burning from lack of oxygen. Wherever it was that the tall Italian took them to teleport, the air was beyond alien, icy cold, and impossible to breath. They shifted forward, moving without moving, and then as quickly as it had begun, it was over, and he found himself on an elevated crossway overlooking a large atrium, bright-colored sunlight streaming in from a glass mosaic high above that served as the ceiling.

Rodrigo stood at his side with a bored look on his face, waiting for him to catch his breath. Each time he traveled this way, he swore the next time he would control himself and not succumb to the lack of air and icy cold, but each time felt worse, not better.

"Part of me thinks you enjoy watching us struggle and gasping like a fish out of water."

Rodrigo said nothing, merely giving him a tight-lipped smile before turning away, motioning that he should follow. "I thought it wise to transport us to a quiet part of the hospital. I know how much you try to avoid attention. The girl is in the emergency ward a few flights down."

Arthur nodded as he followed, wrinkling his nose at that odd mix of antiseptic and soap that gave every hospital he had ever been in *that smell*. The corridors in this section were mostly empty, with only the occasional staffer who gave him a polite nod or warm pat on the shoulder. "I wish they wouldn't do that," he muttered to himself, the attention making him uncomfortable. He has happier just being normal, someone who was quickly forgotten, not some hero for everyone to ogle. He kept thinking he would get used to it or that people would stop staring with their jaws hanging open every time they saw him, but for now he would bear it and grin.

"This way, they are missing beds, so she is still in the emergency ward," said Rodrigo, leading him to an elevator that smelled of mildew and made an awful racket while they descended to the main floor of the hospital. They rode down in silence, Arthur's thoughts focused on what he was going to say to her, knowing he had to find a way to fix things. She was like this because of him, and he needed to make things right. Staring down at his shoes, he wished he could go back in time to that day in Iron Mountain, that he could have been a better man and controlled his temper, not hurt her.

The shudder of the elevator coming to a halt pulled him from his thoughts, and Arthur smoothed his shirt, his stomach fluttering. When the doors slid open, his eyes went wide at the pure chaos of the emergency ward. They gave each other confused looks as they forced their way past shouting hospital staff and patient beds that clogged the wide hallway, their ears assaulted by hacking and coughing, people moaning in pain.

"Was there some sort of accident in the city that I wasn't aware of?" he asked Rodrigo, eyeing a blond woman sprawled on a narrow cot shoved up against the wall, for a moment, thinking it might be Gwen.

Rodrigo shook his head, frowning at the mass of people hurrying about. Without a word, he fished out a handkerchief from his sleeve and covered his large beak of a nose, a look of disgust on his plastic face. Wanting answers, Arthur forced his way to the nurses' station and grabbed the first person he saw, a tired-looking doctor in stained light-blue scrubs that looked even brighter against his dark skin. "I'm so sorry, but what's going on here? Was there some sort of accident?"

"Influenza of some kind," said the doctor, scratching his balding scalp, not bothering to look up from a tablet he was reading, irritation in his voice. "We had a few cases yesterday, but it hit us really hard today, and we're short staffed as it is."

"I'm looking for a girl who was brought in not long ago: blond, slim build. Her name is Gwen, Gwen Parker, but she may be going by a different name—"

"Listen, buddy, I don't have time to help you find your girl. The shit is really hitting the fan here, so go do like everyone else and go to the front—Oh shit! You're *you*! I mean, Arthur—sorry, sir, I'm Dr. Fillipo. I'm attending on duty today."

Arthur shook his head, pressing his lips together. "Don't worry about it, Dr. Fillipo. I didn't know what was going on here. Do you need me to bring in more medical personnel from other hospitals?"

The doctor shook his head. "No, it's better that we keep additional contact to a minimum, have the infection contained here. It seems limited to this neighborhood, for now, anyway," he said, flinching at a loud crash from the other side of the ward.

Rodrigo stepped forward, still holding the cloth to his nose. "The girl, she would have been brought in by the police not long ago."

"Let me see, here," said the doctor, raising an eyebrow at the tall

Italian while he scanned the tablet, mumbling names under his breath. Knowing he could probably find her faster, Arthur closed his eyes and took a moment to focus. His ability to control machines had come with the strange power to sense the world around him in the fundamental forces of nature, energy and light, the motion of atoms and electrons. It used to take a great deal of effort when he first learned to do it, but now it was like flicking a switch, easy like blinking. When he opened his eyes, the mundane world had vanished, and he could see the currents of electricity surging through the machines in the ward and the wires above them. The living were little more than shadows, dark outlines animated by small arcs of cobalt-blue energy. But Ascended like him or Rodrigo were different; they practically glowed with a golden halo of light, making them easy to spot among the muted outlines of everyone else.

Scanning the crowded emergency ward, Arthur cursed to himself, his lips turning down. "Doctor, what did you say these people were sick with?"

"Influenza, the flu," he said absently. "Here she is. Yes, she is in a secure room they use for people in custody. She was brought in by a local patrol officer a few hours ago. He found her robbing a drugstore. The chart says she was coughing up blood then passed out...after trying to fly?? That can't be right; these new nurses are always messing up the charts...says there was enough oxytocin in her system to kill ten horses."

Arthur nodded absently forgetting about Gwen for a moment, his face creased with worry. The sick filling the ward were not glowing with the normal blue spark of life. They sputtered an ugly green with traces of silver, their energy looking like brackish water. Seeing the same strange energy in the doctor, he absently placed a hand on the man's chest without thinking, direct contact making it easier to figure out what was going on. With a start, Arthur pulled away when a wave of the strange energy immediately creeped toward where he touched the doctor. He pulled his hand away, shifting his vision back to normal to find the doctor tilting his head, giving him an odd look. "Something wrong, sir?"

"Have you managed to isolate the virus, take samples?" asked Arthur, locking his arms behind his back.

"I'm not sure, but I think someone on the team has. What does that have to do with the girl?"

"Nothing. I want this ward locked down—no one in or out. Anyone else who comes in with these symptoms, keep them here, understood? Now, take me to the patient, please," said Arthur, ignoring the doctor's look of disappointment, the poor man probably realizing that the order included him too. With a sigh, the doctor nodded, keying the orders into the local network. When he was done, he waved them on through a series of security doors into a quieter section of the ward, finally coming to a closed door with a police officer sitting in a plastic chair, half asleep. Hearing them coming, the security man perked up in his chair, blushing slightly. Arthur gave him a short nod, motioning that he should open the door.

"Wait here," he began to Rodrigo and the doctor. He placed a hand on the door, about to go in when it hit him. He continued in a low voice. "Rodrigo, I want you and the doctor here to speak to everyone in the ward. Find out who they spoke to and when. Then I want anyone who's come into contact with these people isolated, understood?"

Rodrigo raised his chin, a plastic frown on his face. "Sei un pazzo?"

"No, Rodrigo, I'm not crazy. Something Cardinal Washington said to me last time we spoke. He said he was leaving me a gift. This infection is not natural—it's mechanical. I can feel it, like every other machine in the world. Whatever it is, I'm sure the cardinal is behind it, so just do as I say," Arthur finished, turning his back on the pair of confused-looking men.

Stepping into the darkened room, he had a strong sense of Deja vu, his mind going back to that day at Iron Mountain, after he and Uriel had hid her in one of the old bedrooms. Closing the door gently behind him, he undid the top buttons of his plain black uniform, removing the medallion that he wore beneath his clothes, a medallion she had given him for his last birthday. Moving deeper into the dim room, he could see Gwen was unconscious. A breathing tube down her throat was attached to a ventilator in the corner that hissed ever so softly every few seconds. Just above her, floated a holographic projection of her vitals: her pulse, blood pressure, and in orange was a ragged image of her lungs, looking more like shredded meat than human organs.

Arthur put the medallion, she had given him as a gift so long ago, in her hand, remembering that she had given it to him because she thought he was a good person, better than her parents, but like them, he had betrayed her too. He'd asked everyone to wait outside so that no one could see him like this. He squeezed his eyes shut as hard as he could, trying to hold back the pain, the tears, but they came anyway, deep, wracking sobs that he couldn't control as he held her hand as tightly as he could. He had done this, in his anger, for not getting what he wanted and had nearly killed her. When she had rejected him he wanted her to be in as much pain as he was, and it was too late when he realized what he'd done.

"I'm so sorry, Gwen, so sorry," he whispered, falling to his knees, no longer holding back the pain, sobbing, and gripping her hand tightly. "I'm going to do everything I can to save you. I promise. I promise. Even if it kills me, I will fix you."

NINE
PURPOSE

Laying in his regeneration crèche, Jonah felt like ants were crawling over his skin. It grew worse every time the crystals from the armor pulsed or changed color. He didn't remember feeling like this last time, but then he was little more than a mindless drone, a monster meant to do the bidding of his superiors. But now, with his mind intact, he knew who he was, and he remembered small details of his life before: the auburn of his mother's hair, his father's deep voice, even his sister's bratty little smirk she always wore when she got the better of him. He could feel it slipping away again, little moments quietly fading from his memory. He couldn't lose control of who he was. He wouldn't go back.

Running his fingers along the controls, he keyed in the sequence to open the clear glass cover, the viscous blue fluid draining from the tall metal cylinder that housed him when he was at rest.

The pair of guards standing duty to his chamber flinched to attention when the door opened, and his heavy boot hit the grated floor, clutching their rifles tight as his seven-foot-tall frame loomed over them. "I need to see Dr. Kolov," he said, his deep voice loud in the narrow corridor.

The pair glanced at one another. "But...it's the middle of the night," mumbled one of the guards in a broken Russian accent, rubbing the sleep from his eyes.

"You do not have to speak in that broken tongue," said Jonah, switching to Russian, and he heading down the corridor, ducking every so often to avoid the occasional exposed steel beam or lose wiring. The drone cruiser they were on had been converted from an unfinished aircraft carrier back from the cold war almost a century ago and was spartan at best, its only real advantage was its drone fleet, which they depended on for almost all of its defenses.

The pair of soldiers hurried after him, babbling behind him that it wasn't time for him to be active, that Dr. Kolov should not be disturbed. Ignoring them, Jonah climbed the short flight of stairs that led to the launch deck, drinking in deep the salty ocean air as he raised his face skyward, smiling in awe at the infinite number of stars filling the night sky.

"Dr. Kolov gave orders that you are to remain here!" shouted one of the soldiers, a hand pressed against the side of his head while he listened to some unseen voice in his ear giving orders. "That under no circumstances are you to leave this ship unless he calls for you."

Jonah took a step forward, leaning down, nose to nose with the soldier. "And under what circumstances do you think you can stop me?"

The soldier's hand dropped away from his ear, and he swallowed hard, fumbling with his rifle then stepping back. "I have orders to shoot if you don't return to your regeneration crèche."

Showing them the whites of his teeth, Jonah spread his arms wide. "Then shoot," he said, leaping for the stars. In a heartbeat, he was suddenly high above the drone carrier, flying in the inky blackness of night. From high above he could just make out slack-jawed amazement plastered on the men's faces, their bumbling confusion as they tried to figure out what to do now that he defied them. Forgetting them, he turned, facing west, heading toward the base at Norfolk, the wind screaming past his ears.

Once the Americans had been slaughtered, Dr. Kolov had been quick to abandon the spartan furnishings of the drone cruiser, preferring the comforts of the officer housing on base. The flight from the carrier to the base lasted only moments, and Jonah landed in front of a state-of-the-art building with two-story-high panes of glass that served as their command center, a large fleet of tanks and drones spread out in front. While large parts of the base had been burned to the ground, Jonah had been ordered to keep this building intact and had spent a few hours here on the first day they had taken Norfolk, standing guard over Dr. Kolov and the officers while they brought in the necessary equipment to establish their command center here.

The men standing guard moved to intercept him as he strode to the door, rifles at the ready. "This is a secure area, Negry. You are not supposed to be here," said one of the guards with a cough.

"My name is Jonah, and I am the one who secured it," he said, his nostrils flaring. Part of him knew the men were just following orders, doing their duty, so he gave them a chance. "I need to see Dr. Kolov, so clear a path, or I will…"

The soldier glanced at the men behind him, who only shook their heads. "Yes, of course… Jonah," he said. "Apologies. I never saw you, okay?"

Jonah snorted as he walked past them into the brightly lit building, his heavy boots echoing like thunder on the hard tile. He was about to storm the building, tearing everything apart to find the doctor when he had a flash of insight. "Where does the doctor hold his meetings?" he asked, turning back to the guard who'd spoken to him.

The soldier shrugged, coughing again, his face pale. "There is a communication room on the second floor. Dr. Kolov uses it as the war room."

"Good," said Jonah, heading for the stairs. "Tell the doctor to report to me there; tell him I am waiting for him."

———

"Negry, what is the meaning of this?" said Dr. Kolov, storming into the war room, his Russian accent so subtle you could almost miss it. "What was so important that it could not wait for morning?"

"This," said Jonah, raising a glowing armored forearm, locking eyes with the doctor, "Every time it pulses, it's like ants crawling on my skin."

Dr. Kolov nodded absently, his focus on a tablet in his hands. "We are aware of the problem. Now return to the ship until I call for you. We are still in the planning stages of our next attack, and I cannot afford such distractions," he said, brushing down his moustache with a thick finger.

Eyeing the doctor up and down, Jonah could see that the man was not himself. He had never seen the man not perfectly dressed, even when surprised, but now his suit was rumpled, the pristine white lab coat he always wore was stained and creased. "You don't know why, do you?"

The doctor looked up from his tablet, frowning. "What do you mean, Negry?"

Jonah balled a fist at his side, his pulse quickening. "I have told you, my name Jonah."

"What you were is in the past, this boy Jonah that we found in the ruins of New York is long gone," said Dr. Kolov, his voice taking on a lecturing tone. "We have made you more than he ever was. Stronger, faster, invincible! No, you are Negry, now. Nothing can change that, so forget your past. It does nothing for you."

"My father is Captain Joshua Macdonald. My mother was Major Sarah Macdonald. I have a sister, Rowen. My past defines who I am, and I won't forget it, not for you, not for anyone," said Jonah. "Now, tell my what's happening to me, to the armor?"

Dr. Kolov looked up from the tablet, pursing his lips. "We are running tests, trying to improve—"

"You're lying!" said Jonah, clutching his skull, as another pulse ran through him, setting his mind on fire with the urge to itch his armor-covered skin. It felt like the crystal was growing at a snail's pace, digging ever so slowly into his flesh. "There is another tower out there somewhere. Like the one from New York. I can feel it. It's the only thing that makes sense."

The doctor raised an eyebrow in surprise, looking like he hadn't considered that somewhere out there was another tower of pulsing crystal. "I cannot help you if you are not open with us. Tell us where you think it is," said the doctor, keying a sequence in the tablet.

A pulse ran through Jonah's body, like something was pressing against his brain, telling him he should stand down, return to the ship. Jonah shook his head, slowly breathing in and out until the feeling passed. "That...will...not...work anymore," he said in a low voice, stepping close enough to the doctor that he could smell the man's musky odor, and something else that he couldn't place.

"That is close enough, Negry. Step back," he said, pushing back against Jonah's chest with his palm then pulling it back with a grimace when he felt the razor-sharp lines on Jonah's chest.

"No," said Jonah, leaning in close enough that he could smell that Dr. Kolov had been drinking—scotch of some kind. "There is no barrier between us now," said Jonah suddenly, his thoughts going back to the night he had met the doctor. It had been in New York, and he had been locked away in a lab for months, feeling like they had forgotten him.

"I don't understand," said Dr. Kolov, again keying in a sequence on the tablet.

The vibration ran through him again, and he found it easier to resist this time. "When we met, I was in a cage. You came to me, and gave me a new crystal, Anton's crystal. You told me he was dead, and that you would be in charge of the project, of me."

"Yes, Anton suffered...an unfortunate accident," said Dr. Kolov, running a hand across his forehead.

"I liked Anton; he was honest," said Jonah. "That's the same tablet you used the night you gave me his crystal, isn't it? I don't remember much after that, not until the moment my sister shot me in the face, blew off part of my helmet."

"That does not matter; what matters is our plan to conquer this land, bring order to its shores."

"Right now, I don't care about your plans," said Jonah, not removing his eyes from the tablet. "I just want this pain to end. I don't want to be this monster you have made me."

"You are no monster; you are the future," shouted Dr. Kolov, puffing out his chest.

"The future of what? What is my purpose? Am I supposed to spend the rest of my life as your weapon, a dog only let off his leash when it's time to kill?" said Jonah, plucking the tablet from the man's hand and staring at the screen.

Dr. Kolov blew out his cheeks, his pale face flushed a deep crimson. "You need to learn your place, Negry. How dare you!"

"You didn't answer my question," said Jonah, absorbing the details on the small screen, trying to understand the information on his physiology presented on the screen. "If I do as you wish and help take control of this country, what will be my purpose? What happens to me when there are no more worlds left to conquer?"

"I will fix you," said the doctor, eyeing the tablet in Jonah's hands, then raising a hand to touch his chest, ignoring the cuts to his flesh. "I *can,* you know, make you whole again."

Baring his teeth, Jonah's hand shot out, grasping the doctor by the throat and lifting him from his feet, pulling the flailing man in close. "From the day I met you, you have tried to control me. Why should I believe you? Why shouldn't I just rip your head from your pathetic shoulders and be done with you!"

Dr. Kolov kicked and scratched against Jonah's iron grip around his throat, blood flowing freely from his hands as the razor-sharp armor sliced into his soft flesh while he clawed for breath. "I...can...make...the...I can make...the pain stop," he rasped, his entire body shaking as Jonah held him aloft.

Jonah loosened his grip by a hair to let him breathe. "You're a liar, and you would say anything in this moment to save your pathetic life."

"No," said Dr. Kolov, shaking his head. "If you kill me, you lose your only chance to make the pain stop, to one day be normal again."

He searched the doctor's clear eyes for hints of deception. Part of him wanted nothing more than to close his hand and crush his fragile throat. It would be nothing to kill him, effortlessly, but if there was even a small chance. "Tell me how."

"Put...me...down...please."

Grinding his teeth, Jonah tossed Dr. Kolov to the ground, stalking away from the man before slamming his armored fist through the circular table that dominated the war room, the fine wood splintering and scattering like dust on the wind. "You have one minute: make it good."

"We must come to an agreement first, a pact," said Dr. Kolov from his knees, wincing when he touched his bloody hands and throat.

Jonah rounded on the doctor, his blood boiling. "Are you insane? Give me what I want or die. Right here. Right now!"

Dr. Kolov nodded, putting his hands up defensively. "The solution I will give you will be temporary at best, but you must promise to work with me; help me take this pathetic country, and when we do, I will have the resources to fix you permanently."

"Go on," said Jonah, his entire body tensing as another wave went through him, his skin on fire. "I'll do whatever you need; just make it stop. I can't take anymore."

"Da, good. The pain you feel, the itching. This comes when the crystals are growing, expanding. Right now, they are burrowing into your flesh, nesting. The crystal I gave you the night we met reduced your higher brain function, so you would be able to withstand this. I did not think it was possible, but somehow that crystal was destroyed, and now you can feel everything that is happening to you."

Jonah buried his face in his hands, wanting to claw off his skull, "I was meant to be a mindless thing, Frankenstein's monster."

Dr. Kolov swallowed hard, a wide-eyed look of panic appearing on his face before he bowed his head, his voice a whisper. "Yes, but I did not...I wish I could have—"

"Don't try to excuse what you did," said Jonah, waving off his attempt to apologize, thinking of his father and the harsh lessons he'd taught him about what happens to soldiers who are captured. "War is war, and I was a prisoner, but right now you are the prisoner, and you will do as I say."

"Yes, of course," said Dr. Kolov, rising to his feet, holding on to the table to steady himself. "May I ask how the crystal on your skull was destroyed, along with the mask?"

Raising an armored hand to his skull, he was careful not to cut himself as he touched the spot where the crystal had been seated, thinking of Rowen, and her wild shots from the strange weapon she had. "That night, it was so strange. My sister was there, but she was nothing like I remembered her. She had a small army with her, and people, like me—people with powers."

Dr. Kolov cleared his throat, running a thick finger under his moustache as he began, "Yes we are aware. They call it Ascension. They turn children with the proper genetic markers into superhumans. They are nowhere near as powerful as you, but they are impressive. And it does not last, the children, well, there are consequences," he said, dropping into a leather-bound chair, letting out a deep breath before he continued. "And one of these superpowered individuals removed the crystal, along with the mask?"

"No," said Jonah, thinking back with a frown. "My sister, she had a weapon I'd not seen before. She shot me...a few times."

The doctor blew out his cheeks. "Impossible. No bullet could pierce your armor. You must be mistaken."

"It doesn't matter; just do what you promised," said Jonah, starting to pace.

The doctor pointed at the tablet that Jonah had haphazardly thrown on the table, slumping down in his chair as he did so. "At the heart of that tablet is a control crystal; it is the only one we have left. It is depleted and will only last a few weeks at best, but I can program it to halt the growth of the armor on your body: stop the pain, for now."

"What happens when it runs out of power?" said Jonah, eyeing the tablet as if it were a snake.

Dr. Kolov shrugged, his lips turning down. "We have no clue. We used it to raise the communication tower in New York and to control the small batch of secondary crystals we had. We had just found another one, another control crystal, but it was stolen by a group of insurgents. But I am sure that together we can find more, and with those, we can fix you permanently."

"What makes you think there are more?"

Dr. Kolov took the tablet and began keying in a series of commands, his voice taking on a lecturing tone as he spoke, "They resonate on a very unique frequency, almost like the Earth is breathing, and they are very difficult to pinpoint. All we know is that there are several on this continent, not to mention something buried deep under New York, something powerful that sets all of our instruments alight."

"So, what now?" said Jonah as the doctor handed him the tablet.

"Break it," said Dr. Kolov, pointing at the device. "Take the crystal embedded inside and place it against your neck.

Jonah flipped the tablet over in his hands, running a finger along the edge and eyeing the seams that held the device together. "And what happens when I put it on?" he said, bouncing the tablet in his hand in front of the doctor.

"The pain will stop," said Dr. Kolov with a shrug.

Jonah snapped the tablet in half, the twisting of metal and glass the only sound in the room. When he was finished, he plucked a tiny sliver of crystal from the heart of the tablet, raising it to the doctor's eye level. "These crystals made me!" said Jonah with a deep voice, "and this one controlled them all?"

"Yes," he whispered, staring at the tiny piece of glass.

Jonah did the same, unable to tear his eyes away from it. The crystal was different from the others that made him. It was clear, like a diamond, never pulsing or changing colors. When Anton had worn it, it didn't react, didn't grow into something else. It simply was.

"Those who risk nothing, do nothing, achieve nothing," whispered Jonah as he slipped the tiny crystal into a space between his shoulder and his neck. His entire body tensing in anticipation of the pain he experienced whenever he had a new crystal placed on him, but there was nothing, only a single low-pitched note running through his mind like a bassoon. He opened his eyes, and his breath caught in his throat. The pulsing, the itching was gone, his armor suddenly crystal clear, and he could almost make out his dark skin beneath. He was staring at his hand when the images began flicking through his mind, slowly at first, then faster with each passing breath, a kaleidoscope of knowledge pouring into his mind. In awe, he sat down, spending the rest of the day in silence: learning, understanding, growing.

TEN

LAZARUS RISING

Gwen gasped with wonder as she came awake, drawing in a lungful of cool air without a hint of pain. She wanted to cry when she took a second breath and realized it no longer felt like someone was sitting on her chest, and that for the first time in months she could breathe without feeling like there were shards of glass in her lungs. She was almost afraid to open her eyes, terrified that it was all a dream, and the pain would come roaring back the moment she was truly awake.

Gathering her courage, she cracked an eye open, finding herself looking up at a white ceiling in a very bright room, a large hologram of what she assumed were her lungs floating above her. It took her a minute to figure it all out. The image of her insides were a wild mix of colors, parts of it a soft blue, the bottom portion a bright red that was covered in tiny specks of gold and green. Curious as to where the hell she was, she tried to look around only to find she couldn't move her neck. Worried, she looked down her nose to see she was in a clear glass cylinder of some kind, covered in a white drape, her entire body restrained by an invisible force that held her in place. Gwen began to panic, flexing and fighting, her muscles straining against whatever was holding her down.

"Please, lie still. The restraining field wasn't built for someone with your strength, and if you move too much before we finish, it could undo days of work."

Gwen stiffened, feeling like she had just fallen into a pool of icy water that froze her to her core. She would know that voice anywhere. "Arthur?" she whispered, her eyes opening wide, fear churning in her belly, terrified of what he was doing to her.

"You need to calm down; your heart rate is spiking. We're at a critical stage, and I needed you awake, but I can't afford for you to panic right now," he said in a voice that was strained, tense.

"What are you doing to me, asshole!" she said, taking a deep breath to try and calm her pounding heart. Whatever he was doing was taking the pain away, so she would listen, but when it was over, she would kill the little shit. She had promised—for herself, for Uriel.

"I deserve being called an asshole for what I did. I accept that," he said, his voice steady. "But as to what I'm doing. I'm fixing what I broke, or at least I'm trying to."

Even though she couldn't see much more than the ceiling and the hologram of her lungs, Gwen could almost see the smug look on Arthur's face, that half smile he always had when he knew he had the better of someone. "What makes you think I need you to fix me. I was doing just fine," she said with a heat in her voice she didn't feel deep down.

He was quiet for a while before he began. "You were dying, Gwen," he said in a soft voice. "Maybe not in that moment, but from what the doctor told me, you only had a few days before what was left of your lungs filled with fluid and you drowned in your own blood."

"And you would have finally gotten what you wanted," she said, not falling for his fake sadness. "You did this to me. Don't pretend like you want to save me now."

"I know what I did, and I've been regretting it from the moment I left you on that floor," said Arthur. "And you have my word. I will save you, no matter the cost."

The conviction in his voice made her hesitate, and she could almost believe him for a moment. "The doctor's at Iron Mountain. The ones in charge of the Ascension program told me that I was screwed, that it would be impossible to fix the damage from the nerve gas you dosed me with."

"Well, I've got more tricks up my sleeve than those idiots, and with what I've learned in this lab for the last few months, I'm sure we can make the impossible a reality."

"And where exactly is here?" asked Gwen.

"The Rockefeller University," he said in a lecturing tone. "They did some of the most advanced research in the country here—nanotech that was cutting edge. Nasty stuff for biowarfare. When I took over the city, I repurposed the labs for medical research, carved out some space for myself. My abilities make me very well suited to repurposing the Nano weapons they were developing. And now, I'm using it to rebuild your lung tissue."

Gwen blinked in confusion; part of her wanted to believe him, wanted to hope. But he had taken so much from her. "How do I know I can trust you?" she said in a small voice. "How do I know this isn't some sort of trick?"

Arthur went silent for a few moments with only the soft hum of machines in the background. Gwen was about to call out when he piped up, his voice cracking when he began. "You don't. But this is a lot of work for a trick; what would be in it for me? If I really wanted to hurt you, I could have done it while you were passed out," he continued in a tired voice. "The control I need for the next step, for the nanobots to finish rebuilding your lungs is I need to remove the restraining field, and it will work best if I can touch you."

"So, now you're trying to cop a feel! You gotta be fucking kidding me," barked Gwen, instantly regretting her laughter when it suddenly felt like someone stabbed her in the chest.

"You have to keep still," said Arthur, appearing above her, his liquid-brown eyes wide with worry.

"Oh God, that hurts," said Gwen, taking a rasping breath. It took a few moments to calm down, and she couldn't help but stare at him. He looked different, older and mostly tired. The mischievous twinkle in his eye, like he was laughing at a joke only he could understand, was gone. "What happened to your hair?" she blurted out.

Arthur's eyebrows shot up, like he just remembered something. He ran a hand over his scalp, a wry smile coming to his face. He had shaved off the thick mane of hair that had once curled down to his shoulders, leaving only a thin layer of stubble. "People see me as a leader now, someone to look to. I need to look responsible."

"You don't owe anyone jack shit. Most of the people living in this city are here because you helped get the Russians out of the city; you got things running again, gave them their lives back. You can look any way you want," she said, not sure why she was defending him. "Besides, I liked your hair. It was the only cool thing about you."

Gwen swore under her breath as Arthur shook his head, an easy smile coming to his face before he caught himself and looked away, dragging a hand across his eyes. She was amazed at how easy they fell into old habits, him taking life too seriously, her teasing him, trying to show him how to have fun. When he looked back at her, she could see wetness on his cheeks.

"I'm sorry, but I need to touch you to make this work," he said, bowing his head, his eyes looking everywhere but at her.

"Okay," she said, not knowing what else to say. She wanted to be normal again, to breathe without pain.

"Here goes nothing," he said, placing a soft hand on her chest. Gwen shuddered at his touch, her stomach turning with an odd mix of revulsion and hope.

Arthur closed his eyes, a thin outline of white light, almost invisible appeared around him, making him look like a saint from an old painting. She took a deep breath and felt a tingle starting in her extremities. Her fingers and toes went numb as if she had spent too long out in the cold on a winter's day. The sensation danced up and down her legs and arms for a heartbeat before concentrating in her chest. She flinched as beads of sweat fell from Arthur's forehead, his face a frozen mask of concentration, the hand on her chest shaking with exhaustion, and his breath coming in short rasps like he was in the middle of a sprint.

Then as quickly as it had begun, Arthur fell to the floor with a shriek. With a gasp, she looked over the side of the bed to find him trembling, his simple black uniform he favored soaked in sweat. Sitting up she drew in a deep breath, a wide grin coming to her face. She had forgotten what it was like to breathe like a normal person, to not have to live with pain. A groan from the floor pulled her back to the moment, and she got off the bed and pulled him to his feet. "Are you still with me?" she asked, helping him sit on the bed she had just occupied.

"Always and forever," he said, opening his large eyes, giving her an odd look. "How do you feel?"

"Right now, better than you," she said, wanting to dance. "I keep thinking this is a dream, and I'm gonna wake up."

"It's not a dream; it's real. You've got your clear skies for now," he said, trying to use her own line on him and failing.

"It's clear horizons, moron!"

"Sorry, I guess. You know what? Never mind. You should be okay now though. Just take it easy for a few days, okay?" he said, sliding off the bed, locking his arms behind his back and looking her up and down.

She nodded, spinning in place. "I may party a little," she said with a giggle before she locked eyes with him, suddenly serious. "Don't think this makes everything okay between us. I still owe you a world of pain for what you've done, asshole."

"I understand," he said, walking away from her, waving a hand above his head. A hologram suddenly showing New York floated above their heads. "I will need something from you for this."

"Here we go again! Fuck you, Arthur," she said, rolling her eyes, angry that she didn't see this coming. He was always like this, even back when she didn't want to kill him for ruining her life. She should have known that everything he did came with a price. "What makes you think I would do anything more than not rip you limb from limb for the things you've done?"

"It's not what you think," he said, raising his chin, his words tumbling out like rushing water. "Cardinal Washington wants to destroy what we're trying to do here. There are constant drone attacks, by air and land. I've done my best to protect everyone, but I can't keep up. I'm holding on by a thread."

Gwen crossed her arms across her small breasts, raising an eyebrow. "What? You want me to help you stop him?"

"I want you to help me protect the city along with everyone in it," he said, raising his voice. "And don't tell me you don't want to do it. You risked your life last week to help those men from that collapsing building. No one asked you to do that; you just did it. It's in you to be a hero, Gwen."

She snorted at him, shaking her head. "That's not me. I just wanna chill. Listen to good music and have a few drinks. I don't wanna be flying cats out of trees and helping old ladies cross the street."

"Bullshit. I know you. You want to help people; you want to make the world a better place. Besides, you need a job, and the one I'm offering you pays pretty good."

"Really? You're gonna pay me to be a superhero? Are you on something? 'Cause that's the kind of idea you get when you're high."

"It makes perfect sense," he said, nodding at her. "You want a life where you can do what you want, hang out, and have a good time, well, there's no better place than New York, but that all costs money. If you become the hero I want, you get the money to afford it."

Gwen had to stop herself from nodding along. It would be cool to actual live like a real person and not some homeless junkie hunting for a fix constantly, but to work with Arthur. "I think I'm gonna take a hard pass, so if you can get me my shit, so I can put on some clothes and get out of here, that would be cool." Gwen held her breath, knowing him well enough to know an explosion was coming. He hated not getting his way, and it seemed like his head had gotten bigger in the months she hadn't seen him.

"Fine," said Arthur with a stiffness in his voice, his caramel skin flushing.

"Really," she said, half in shock and half laughing at him. "After putting me back together, you're just gonna let me go?"

He turned away from her, pointing to a dim corner of the lab that suddenly lit up. "I've had everything washed. Unfortunately, they were not able to get out all the stains—blood tends to do that."

She walked over to the table, surprised to find the ratty jeans and bloodstained hoody she had been wearing for the last few months, along with her backpack, which contained the rest of her meager possessions. A few old schoolbooks, along with her ancient iPod and a change of underwear. Beside it all was a neatly wrapped package with her name tidily written in Arthur's handwriting. "What's this?" she asked, looking back at him.

"I was hoping you would have said yes to my offer. I had it made just in case."

"Really?" she asked, watching for any hints that he would try and stop her from leaving, not that he could if she was fast enough.

"It was something I thought you would like," said Arthur, swallowing hard, "but it doesn't matter anymore. I should have realized there was no coming back from what I did to you."

Gwen ran a hand over the package, feeling something soft inside. She had received enough shitty Christmas gifts from her parents over the years to know it was some sort of clothing. Her mother knew how much she liked cool clothes, and since most of the year they couldn't afford much, she always went out of her way to apologize for the crap they lived through all year with new outfits at Christmas. With a small twinge of excitement she unwrapped the package, finding some sort of smooth, white leather underneath the wrapping. When she was done opening it, she shook it out, raising an eyebrow, impressed at the fine leather trench coat trimmed in gold along the shoulders and sleeves, along with pants and a top that looked like some kind or tactical armor. "What the hell is this supposed to be?"

"I found the plans for these in the secret archives," began Arthur. "When they first started the Ascension program, they all had these long leather coats in red or black. They were made of carbon nanotubes, designed to take a beating and not shred. I managed to add my own enhancements to the design, make it strong enough that no matter what you do, you won't end up fighting naked anymore. Your clothes won't get destroyed by your powers."

"You wanted me to wear this? Why? It makes me look like I'm some kinda virgin saint."

"I was hoping you could be a symbol, something for people to look up to. I mean, you love the spotlight, the attention. Me, I just prefer to slink around in the background doing what I need to do, but people would look up to you."

"Now, I know you're high," she said, scrunching her face at him. "I've spent the last couple of years as a junkie, man, not to mention all the bad shit I did in the back seats of cars."

"I know, and still they love you. I saw your news conference," he said, remembering the relief he felt when he saw she was alive, and the odd sense of pride he had when she stood up for herself. "People went nuts for you, and those guys you saved at the construction site couldn't stop talking about you. Face it, Gwen. People love you."

"Then why the fuck did you leave me like that?" she screamed suddenly, wanting to pummel him. "You were my friend! You should have loved me more than anyone else. You could have just left if you were pissed! That's what normal nonserial killer guys do! They just fuck off and disappear."

Arthur fell into a chair in the corner of the room, burying his head in his hands. "I didn't want to, but after what Cardinal Washington and his cronies did to me, I was so mad, so hurt. I was just going to leave, to find my parents. So I went down into the secret archives, the restricted ones where you found me. I found out that my parents knew all along that they were going to come and take me. They raised me like livestock; they'd done it before."

"What!" said Gwen, covering her mouth, feeling like she'd been slapped.

Arthur looked up at her, his eyes rimmed red with tears, "I felt like everyone I ever knew betrayed me. I closed myself off. I wanted to burn down the world and kill anyone and everyone, including myself...you just happened to be in the way...I loved you so much. I don't know what else to say. You can go if you want. I won't stop you, but know that I'm sorry."

"I'm so sorry, Arthur," she said. Not knowing what else to do, she walked over to him, taking him in her arms, holding him tight. They stayed like that for a long time, both of them sobbing, finding one another once again.

ELEVEN

TAKE IT EASY

Once upon a time, Winslow, Arizona was considered one of the nicest small towns in America, with a bustling main street high-lighted by classic brick brownstones and little shops that sold anything and everything. Situated along the historic Route 66, it was considered a must-see for anyone planning a road trip across the Midwest...at least according to the travel guide Rowen had read. But that must have been a long time ago, she thought as the Peri touched down just after dusk, its thrusters rocking the branches of half-dead trees lining the street and kicking up small dust devils of discarded trash from the grime-covered boulevard.

"This place looks downright scary," quipped Gibbs beside her, echoing her thoughts. From what she could see in the dark, the once nice small town was now mostly faded brick buildings with boarded-up windows that looked long abandoned, the only light coming from a flickering neon sign above a garish-looking bar called the Standing on the Corner Café, and a pawn shop whose windows were so covered in grime that it was impossible to see what they were selling.

"Corporate raiders screwed over places like these a long time ago," said Blake, looking at them over his shoulder from the pilot's seat. "They sent the local jobs overseas then shuttered and sold off the factories bit by bit for easy profits. To add insult to injury, when it was all said and done, they redirected the highway to avoid the small places like this, altogether. Most of these little places have pretty much turned into ghost towns over the last few decades. Not sure what made this place hold on, must be tougher than most I guess."

"I'm still not sure why my father insisted you come," said Rowen, frowning at the salt-and-pepper-haired man, not that she minded. Blake had been one of her first to answer the call when they were recruiting militia while still trapped in New York. He was a prepper who spent months playing hide and seek with Russian soldiers. He was a little rough around the edges, but she liked him. He was capable, not to mention resourceful.

"I told your old man I'd been cooped up on base for too long," he said, keying the engines of the small aircraft to stand by. "When I followed you guys out of New York, I didn't expect to be sitting around Iron Mountain doin' jack shit for months on end. So, this milk run is me just getting to stretch my legs."

"Let's just find our target and get this over with," said Gibbs, looking down at a tablet in his hands. "There's a reason they called these the fly-over states. I can only imagine how inbred these rednecks are."

Rowen punched Gibbs in the shoulder, shoving him back in his seat as she stepped out of the aircraft. "My mom grew up in a town like this," she said, adjusting her new body armor, flipping up her mirrored tactical glasses to hold back her wild hair. "These are good people, smart and hardworking. They get a bum rap because they like their lives the way they are; they don't want anyone bothering them, that's all—and I thought we had decided we weren't going to call them targets? This is someone's kid, maybe not much younger than we are."

"Yeah, they don't want anyone bothering them *while* they're inbreeding," said Gibbs, dashing around to the other side of the small transport to avoid getting punched again. "And you agreed to not call them targets. For me it's easier to process the data if I don't see them as anything but numbers"

Blake raised a hand to silence the both of them, his head on a swivel as he scanned the area. "Keep the chatter to a minimum. We probably drew more attention than we needed to land a military jump jet on a quiet street like this. Let's try and not rile up the locals any more than we have to."

Rowen nodded, dropping her hand onto the butt of her SIG Mark II, her nerves calming when she touched the weapon. "Okay, Gibbs, let's see if your number crunching works. Where did the parents say they would meet us with the boy?"

"The bar," said Gibbs, rolling his eyes, waving at the half-lit neon sign, "obviously."

"Don't worry, this will work," said Rowen, patting her flustered friend on the shoulder, walking past him. He was trying to show a brave face and be cool and confident, but she could see the worry in the way he kept checking the data on his tablet, his eyes darting in all directions. They were all worried, her near invincible brother had just decimated the 11th Fleet and had taken the base at Norfolk in a single afternoon.

He had also killed the few remaining members of Divinity Corps almost as an afterthought, made worse by having almost no way of recruiting more kids with the right genetic profile. Things were looking grim until Gibbs stormed into her father's office last week, claiming that he had figured out how to do it, how to find kids with the divinity gene that didn't require them sacrificing hundreds of young lives in the process.

"Okay, let's go," said Gibbs, nodding to himself, following after her.

Rowen walked into the bar and was hit by the stench of old beer and stale sweat that she could almost taste. She had expected to find the place packed given the number of cars in the parking lot, but strangely, the dimly lit bar was completely empty, the only sign of life coming from an old jukebox in the corner, blasting an old Eagles track that was the bar's namesake.

"Beers still cold," said Blake, walking behind the bar and sticking his head through a swinging door that Rowen could see led to a kitchen of some kind. "No one back there either. Whatever happened, they left in a hurry."

"The question is where the hell did they all go?" asked Gibbs, wrinkling his brow in confusion.

"Gibbs, do we have a way to contact the boy's family?" asked Rowen, resting a hand on her holster. "Or at least have a number for them?"

"I have a number; it's the first thing I tried, but there's no response," said Gibbs, falling into a rickety chair, hunching over his tablet. "I'm just gonna ping the number, and see if I can find out where they went off to."

Seeing that Gibbs was immersed in finding the boy, Rowen circled the room, wrinkling her nose in disgust at discarded piles of food on the floor, doing her best to avoid the sticky, stained parts of the faded wood. Shaking her head at the scarred tabletops that had seen better days, she said, "I think the subway in New York, even abandoned for twenty years, was cleaner than this place," she said, wondering how people could eat and drink in such filth.

"Well, the subway had the flood of the century to clean up before it was shut down," said Blake, standing by the door with his arms folded across his chest. "But this place is worse, for sure."

"Part of me almost misses it," said Rowen, starting to pace. "It was simpler than waiting around Iron Mountain, waiting for the worst to happen."

"I don't," said Blake, glancing back at her. "I hated that freaking city, even when things were normal."

Rowen scratched the scar that ran from the top of her scalp to her chin, her eyes narrowing. "I thought you were a lifelong New Yorker?"

"Nah, I was born in Boston, Massachusetts. Living in New York was...a compromise for me," he said, rubbing his square jaw. "But even after ten years I couldn't stand the place, not to mention being around so many Yankees fans. Those guys are the worst sort of a-holes."

"Who cares? Nobody even plays baseball anymore. The league folded, like what, fifteen years ago, didn't it?" said Gibbs, not looking up from the tablet.

"Yeah, and Yankees fans are still bragging that they are the winningest team in all of sports. Imagine that."

Rowen moved to stand beside Blake at the door, running a hand through the tangled bird's nest that was her hair. "I know what you mean; my dad grew up in New York. Every now and then he would try to make us watch an old game, try and get us into it, but me and Jonah would just roll our eyes when he did: it was so boring! We grew up playing soccer, like normal people."

Blake shook his head, a frown coming to his handsome face. "You kids and your damn soccer. You don't know what—"

"What the hell is that!" said Rowen, catching a flash of movement in the corner of her eye. Not wanting to lose sight of what she saw, she elbowed past Blake to stand in the doorway, peering up and down the street, trying to catch a glimpse of what caught her attention.

"What did you see?" asked Blake behind her, a silver Beretta in his hand.

"I don't know, couldn't really tell," said Rowen, "but it looked like people. I think we should take a look; maybe get some answers as to where the hell everyone is. Gibbs, lock the door; stay here!" she said as she strolled out into the street, slipping her tactical glasses into place.

"Oh, sure. Leave me all alone in the scary bar in the ghost town. Good idea," he shouted after her, the pitch of his voice hitching up a few octaves.

Ignoring Gibbs and his worry, she cycled through the vision options on her glasses, setting night-vision mode, her entire world turning a sickly shade of green.

"Anything?" asked Blake in a low voice, walking out into the middle of the street with her.

"I can't make out much. It's too far away, but it looks like the whole town decided to go for a walk, a few blocks west of here," whispered Rowen, seeing a large crowd in the distance, moving slowly, like they were part of some silent parade. "Where the hell are they going?"

"Let's see what all the fuss is about," said Blake, shouldering his pack, leading the way.

Nodding, Rowen followed, drawing her SIG. By the time they arrived at the intersection, most of the crowd had already passed, with only a few stragglers left at the tail end, all of whom kept their eyes forward while they walked in silence. Not knowing what to do, she glanced at Blake, who only shrugged, frowning at the line of people as they went by. Annoyed, Rowen moved to block an older lady in a yellow sundress who was passing by. "Ma'am are you okay?" she asked. "Can you tell me what—"

The woman didn't slow, pushing past Rowen with a blank look on her wrinkled face, her eyes never blinking.

"Are they sleepwalking or something?" asked Blake, pulling Rowen out of the way of another man wearing a striped set of pajamas who was about to bowl her over.

"These guys better not be zombies. I'm gonna be pissed if it's zombies," said Rowen, a half grin coming onto her face as she stared off after them. "Maybe if we follow, we'll get lucky and find the kid we're looking for."

Blake chuckled as he fell in beside her. "This isn't some cheesy holovid, kid, but whatever it is, we'll figure it out...and if we can't, well, we've got lots of ammo, right?"

They followed the slow-moving parade of townsfolk for the better part of an hour, with Rowen poking or prodding one of the people every now and then trying to get them to react or at least fight back. Growing frustrated, she picked a lanky young man in a plaid shirt and ripped jeans and put out her foot when he walked by. He stumbled for a moment, waving his arms like a windmill in an attempt to keep his balance, then he fell hard on the pavement, face-first. Almost immediately, without a word or scream, he pulled himself to his feet. Rowen grimaced when she saw an ugly bruise on his cheek along with the blood dripping from his nose.

"Well, they're definitely not asleep," she said, frowning at the plaid-shirted man that continued walking as if nothing happened.

"I'm getting a bad feeling about this. It's too weird. Screw it. Let's get the hell out of here," said Blake.

"Aren't you curious? I mean, we've been following this for an hour. Let's see where this is going."

"I think I'd be happier chillin' with a cold beer, back at base with all my bits attached."

"Well, you were the one who got tired of hanging around Iron Mountain," said Rowen, giving him a smile. "C'mon, five more minutes."

"Whatever," said Blake, eyeing a dark-skinned woman stumbling along with her breasts out.

Rowen kept her head on a swivel as they continued following the trail of people down the dark highway, hoping that the low-light vision of her glasses would give her and Blake enough of a heads-up, so they wouldn't be caught off guard by whatever craziness they were being led to. She was about to give up when in the distance she spotted a tall spire where the sleepwalkers seemed to be converging.

"There's some kind of steeple up ahead. C'mon," she said, tapping Blake on the shoulder and breaking into a jog, her trench coat streaming behind her. It took them only a few moments to close the distance, and she found herself at the back of a large crowd of sleep-walkers who stood stock still around a steeple with a rusted cross at its peak. The place turned out to be a small church that had seen better days, overgrown with weeds and sun-dried brush, its windows little more than dark, gaping maws where stained glass once appeared, and chunks of mortar and brick having been worn away by the elements of time.

"Rowen, stop. Something isn't right," said Blake behind her as she pushed aside the people at the back, taking advantage of her small size to weave her way through the mass of docile bodies crowding around the old building.

"I gotta see what the hell this is," said Rowen, her curiosity driving her forward. Finding her way to the front, her jaw fell open, her stomach suddenly twisting in knots when she gazed up at the spectacle on display. Floating above the doorway suspended by some unseen force was the boy they had come to find. Taking a step closer, Rowen could see he was still alive, his eyes fluttering open and closed, his thin chest heaving, while sweat rolled off of him in waves. Balling her fists, she took a step forward, beads of perspiration forming on her temples. "How can you idiots just stand there! Why won't you help him?" she shouted, glaring at the motionless crowd.

She was about to climb up and pull him down when a thin metal filament emerged from the boy's side, covered in a clear viscous liquid that dripped onto the ground. Rowen watched, fascinated, as the appendage appeared to grow before her eyes, segmented metal sections sliding out of one another with soft clicks. Then another appeared, and another, the disjointed tentacles swirling like a clutch of snakes around the floating boy like they had a mind of their own. Rowen jumped in her skin, a yelp escaping her throat when a hand fell on her shoulder. She turned to find Blake behind her, his eyes glued to the boy.

"Time to go, kid. This shouldn't be happening, but we gotta get out of here before it's too late," he said, holstering his Beretta and reaching into his pack to pull out a curved cylinder wrapped in dark red leather about as thick as his thumb and the length of his forearm.

"What's that?" said asked, eyeing the object in his hand, backing away with him as more tentacles emerged from the boy's torso, his head suddenly snapping up, his gaze suddenly falling onto them.

"Time's up," whispered Blake, pressing a button on the weird object he was holding. A thin silver blade sprung to life, the color of liquid silver, a soft rasp of steel on leather vibrating through the air. At last when the blade was almost two feet long, an ornate crossguard of black iron appeared in place between the blade and the leather-bound hilt. "Guns don't work so good against this thing," he said, pointing the slightly curved weapon at the boy, pulling her behind him.

Rowen had seen a similar weapon in a holovid once, from a classic 2-D film from back when movies were made for the silver screen. The story was about a woman out for revenge after a group of assassins had tried to kill her. The blades were supposed to be extremely sharp, so sharp it could cut God if it had to. What Blake was doing with such a strange weapon, she had no clue, but given the look of wide-eyed fear on his face, she wasn't about to start asking questions now.

They were almost through the throng of people when the blade flashed in his hands. Blake's arm barely moved, and a set of severed tentacles fell at their feet. Rowen looked up to see swarms of the steel-tipped appendages piercing the necks of the sleepwalkers, their hoarse screams suddenly filling the night. Beside her, Blake tensed, his free hand holding her in a death grip. Rowen couldn't look away, a nauseous feeling in her belly as the throngs of people surrounding the old church all screamed in pain as the boy floated high above them, hundreds of writhing tentacles coiling around them like a python, the needlelike tips piercing their bodies. "What's he doing to them?"

Blake swore under his breath, his flashing blade making quick work of any appendage that came too close. "It's making copies of itself...lots of copies!"

As if something were suddenly triggered, the man in the striped pajamas at the back of the crowd suddenly spun around to face them, the tentacles snapping off him as he charged them, a wild look of madness on his face.

"We gotta go, kid. This is bad, really bad," he shouted, backing away, his blade a whirlwind of steel. "Run, kid. Run as fast as you can, and don't look back!"

Rowen did as she was told, ignoring the ear-piercing screams of the once silent crowd echoing into the night, running as fast as her legs would take her, praying it would be fast enough.

TWELVE

A NEW DAY

"It was mostly short flashes of places, people who seem familiar but are not. Not a lot of it makes sense."

"Please, Negry, Jonah," said Dr. Kolov, stumbling over his name. "Anton never mentioned any such thing happening to him, so even the smallest detail may help us find additional crystals."

Jonah crossed his arms over his chest, staring out at the cresting waves of the Atlantic. They stood on the bow of the drone carrier where they stored his regeneration crèche, so this was home as far as he was concerned. After he had placed the new crystal on his neck, he had returned here and spent the rest of the night in a daze as thousands of images flooded his mind. "It's like suddenly remembering something you'd forgotten," he said, eyeing the doctor, struggling to put his thoughts into words, still not comfortable speaking. "But they aren't my memories. It's like remembering a holovid I watched a long time ago. I can only put together bits and pieces."

Dr. Kolov shook his head, clearly frustrated, immediately regretting it as he clutched the bandages at his neck. "We need to find another source, before we run out of time."

"Then why do we sit here in Norfolk? We have the advantage, so why not press on?"

"Moscow has been disappointed with our progress. I had promised them a swift victory once we captured New York. It was an embarrassment when we were forced to withdraw. They have disavowed me, and the official stance of the Russian government is that I am some rogue scientist bent on proving his mad theories. Now, they refuse to resupply us."

"The drones are just fodder. I am all that is needed," said Jonah, sure that there was nothing that could stop him at this point. "I have never felt stronger, more capable. Nothing can stop me."

"I thought you said you didn't want to be a weapon, a monster."

Jonah raised his chin, a frown coming to his handsome face. "Time is short, so I will do what I have to do and be the weapon a little longer. Let's crush the Americans."

Dr. Kolov looked down at his feet, his brow furrowing. "I have been meaning to ask you for a long time now. Something that has confused me since you returned to us from that night when we lost New York, and we discovered your mind was intact, that you were yourself again."

Jonah looked down at the doctor with a small smile, having asked himself the same question many times over the last few months. "Why did I stay? Why didn't I just kill you all and be done with this?"

"Da...yes."

"The day you and the Russian forces invaded, my family was in the city for my mother's funeral. She had been killed during a covert mission a few weeks before," said Jonah, his mind casting back to that fateful day. He could still remember the hot sun on his back, the smell of the soil as he stood over his mother's grave. "My father tried to get some answers, but he was stonewalled—everything about her last mission was classified. The day of the funeral he was so messed up. I had spent my entire life worshiping my father; to me he was invincible...and to see him come apart, crying and broken over her grave. It made me question everything."

"I understand," said Dr. Kolov, nodding. "This is what I am feeling now. I have always been a loyal servant to the party and to the fatherland, never questioned the orders I was given, but now..."

"But now they have thrown you under the bus."

"Under the bus...what does this mean?" said Dr. Kolov.

"It means they are making you a patsy, someone to take the blame so they don't have to."

"Yes, this is it, but even now, I keep expecting a call from my superiors, telling me it's all sort of some elaborate plan to trick the Americans, that help is on the way."

Jonah placed a heavy hand on the doctor's shoulder, his deep voice dropping lower. "The most painful thing, when my memories came back, was that no one came for me. My sister looked so shocked when she saw me; they had just assumed I was dead. No one cared to look for me even if just to have something to bury. Then when I found out how America abandoned New York so quickly, all those people left to fend for themselves, I was angry, disgusted. Why would I want to go back to that? If they didn't care, why should I?"

Dr. Kolov blinked at him in surprise, his thick moustache turning up as he smiled. "Very well, Jonah. There is a quote from my favorite film *Conan the Barbarian*: "Let us crush our enemies; see them driven before us.""

"Never heard of it," said Jonah, his brows coming together. "But it sounds like something that was badly written."

"It sounds better in Russian. The film, it's almost a hundred years old. It was popular in Russia, long after it should have been. I guess it appeals to our nature as conquerors."

"Then let's do some conquering," said Jonah, raising a hand to his face, touching soft flesh to soft flesh, marveling at how human it made him feel. He hadn't felt that way for a long time even after his memories returned. It was impossible to see normal people as anything but targets. He felt nothing when he killed; they were only pieces on the board to be eliminated. Part of him, buried deep down, knew he should feel something when he took life, but it was far off, not real. Dr. Kolov was right: he was more than human; he was something new; he just had to figure out what that was.

A wailing Klackson forced him to banish his dark thoughts. He cocked his head, giving Dr. Kolov a confused look.

"We are under attack!" screamed the doctor, his voice taking on a frantic tone.

Jonah scanned the open water and sky, looking for any signs of a threat. The day was clear and bright with a light breeze rolling in off the ocean, but there was nothing he could see that would justify the doctor's mad panic. "Where?" he asked simply, his deep voice cutting through the wail of the Klackson.

"The base perimeter," said the doctor, just as the sound of heavy machine-gun fire in the distance filled the air. "Some sort of ground assault."

"Ground assault, you mean with mobile armor? Tanks?" asked Jonah, with a frown. Since the advent of modern drone technology, very little fighting was done on the ground. Predators, even as ancient as they were, were far deadlier than ground-based attack units. Tanks and mobile armor had become near useless in the last few decades, lacking the speed and mobility of drone aircraft, with most ground troops being used mostly on cleanup, after the aircraft had done the heavy lifting.

Dr. Kolov shook his head, pulling a small tablet from his coat and keying into the base's security grid. There was a brief hum, and then a medium-sized hologram of the security perimeter appeared in front of them. "On foot."

Jonah narrowed his eyes at the hologram, his jaw falling open as he watched while the men at the perimeter opened fire at a surging crowd of men and women, civilians. More than he could count pressed against the makeshift barrier they had erected when they had arrived a few days ago: twelve-foot-collapsible wire mesh container and heavy-duty fabric liner filled with earth. "Are they that desperate?" asked Jonah.

Dr. Kolov never looked away from the hologram, his face going pale as the civilians trampled over fallen bodies, using them as stepping stones to climb up and over the barrier then ignoring the hail of machine-gun fire, leaping from the top toward a line of military vehicles queued up to greet them "They have already overwhelmed the men outside the barrier, and look: those weapon mounts are fifty cal, enough to cut an elephant in half. Some of those people are taking a dozen shots or more before they fall."

"Have they been Ascended? Like the people who were with my sister?" asked Jonah, already knowing the answer. He could see they were civilians, dressed like normal people, going about their day, not some sort of paramilitary superhuman.

"I don't think so; this is something else."

Jonah closed his eyes, staggering for a moment as his mind was flooded with images, flashes of somewhere else, remembering crowds of people gone mad, killing, maiming, tearing soldiers apart with their bare hands. "I've seen this before," he said suddenly, a sense of deja vu washing over him. "The control crystal...something that happened a long time ago."

"Do you know how to stop them?" asked Dr. Kolov.

He nodded, his voice cold. "We have to kill them all. Stop this here and now, or it will spread."

"Then go; do what must be done. I will order our remaining troops to the perimeter to support you."

"No!" said Jonah, surprised at the harshness in his voice. "Get out of port now with the men on board: those who are on base have been compromised already."

"Have you gone mad! Those are hundreds of men."

"Doctor, they're already dead; they just don't know it yet," said Jonah, pressing his lips together. "What's happened to these people—it's ancient, like the crystals, and any contact the men have with this means they are as good as dead."

Dr. Kolov stared hard at the nightmare images from the perimeter, his eyes never blinking. Jonah could see him calculating the
losses, doing the math in his head for the bare minimum he needed to
complete his mission. "Very well," he said at last, his shoulders slumping, "We will head north along the coast. Do what you must, and
then come and find us."

Jonah nodded, turning to leave, when Dr. Kolov shouted after
him, "Crush our enemies, but save those you can!"

Taking to the air, a grim smile spread across his face, knowing he
had to do just that if they hoped to survive and complete their
mission.

———

Jonah flew from the deck of the drone carrier to the base perimeter in
the span of a single breath, arriving just as the makeshift line of
armored personnel carriers were about to be overrun. Even knowing
what to expect, he was shocked at the mindless ferocity of the crazed
men and women who charged the barricade without fear. Clambering over the fallen into a hail machine gun fire from panicked
soldiers, who fired wildly from mounted .50 calibers and Kalashnikov
assault rifles.

"They are out of time," Jonah muttered to himself, plummeting
directly into the heart of the chaos and smashing into the ground with
enough force to create a shockwave that shattered pavement and
blasted back swarms of attackers about to break through.Then using
his body like a jagged missile, he flew up and down the line, cutting
through the soft bodies in his path like a scythe. Stopping to pivot, he
waded into the densest throng of attackers who were attempting to
climb the armored personnel carriers that formed the barricade.

Wanting to clear off the crazed men and women attacking the
vehicle line, he waded into them with his razor-sharp fists and armor,
cleaving through flesh and bone, neatly slicing bodies in half with the
barest of efforts, then tearing off a pair of bulky men who were a

hairsbreadth from reaching the top of an armored personnel carrier, throwing them off bodily in the distance. The soldiers, seeing him pushing back against the insanity, rallied, using the room he gave them to fire grenades into the teeming mass, the concussive force doing its job and blasting everyone back. Leaping onto one of the armored vehicles, he pulled aside an officer, a round-faced man with large blue eyes that made him look like he was too young for the captain's epaulettes on his shoulders. "We are finished here," he said, his deep voice cutting through the din, "Withdraw your men. I will hold the line while you retreat."

The officer swallowed, finding his courage as he craned his neck to meet Jonah's glare. "Our commander ordered us to hold," he said in a thick Russian accent, licking his lips.

"Consider that order overruled," said Jonah. "The carrier group is withdrawing; take your men and head up the coast. Shoot anything that gets in your way. Don't stop, understood?"

The young captain looked out over the chaos surrounding them, the blood draining from his face. "It is not natural. They don't bleed, no matter how many times we shoot them," he said in a low voice full of worry.

"Just go," said Jonah, readying himself to plunge back into the teeming mass of flesh. "They are just machines with human faces now, and unless you want to be the same..."

"You have my thanks," said the captain with a nod and then screaming the order to retreat.

Wasting no time, Jonah waded back into the fray. Memories that were not his flooded his his mind from the control crystal on his neck. He knew this thing spread like a virus, infecting the minds of those it touched before converting flesh and bone to living metal. So, while on the outside they looked human, they were anything but.

He didn't know how long he fought, but his armored form was in constant motion like a living weapon, his great speed allowing him to be everywhere at once like a dervish, holding the line so not a single creature broke through.

The sun was low on the horizon as he realized the last creature had fallen, and the world was suddenly deafeningly silent, his breath rasping in his ear the only sound. As far as he could see, the terrain was littered with bodies torn asunder by his hand, many of them still twitching with their metallic guts spilled onto the pavement, a blood-less slaughter that no carrion bird would touch. Leaping on top of an abandoned personnel carrier, he kneeled down to inspect one of the bodies and slake his curiosity. Plunging his hands into the chest cavity of one, he pulled open its rib cage with a deep cracking noise. On the outside, the creatures looked like normal people, locals from town he would expect to see going about their day, and he was sure at some point they were. But from the inside, their basic anatomy had been replaced by ultra-thin strands of some tightly woven material he couldn't identify, many of the components that made up their organs so alien he couldn't see their purpose.

Jonah reached up to crack the skull open, to see what drove them, when a harsh burst of static in his ear almost deafened him. "Jonah, please. We are...attack...fleet...one—"

His pulse quickened when he tried to respond, recognizing Dr. Kolov's voice. "Doctor, doctor, are you there?" he shouted, a hand pressed against his ear as he stood to his full height. Jonah waited a moment, hoping beyond all odds that something else would come through, but there was only the hiss of static.

Bursting into action, he took to the air, a sonic boom exploding behind him as he accelerated past the speed of sound to reach the fleet. Thundering past the bay where they had been moored, Jonah came upon the burning ships moments later, the clear blue of the Atlantic stained by a vast armada leaking black billowing smoke that blocked out the sun. Scanning the empty horizon, he floated in stunned shock, unable to fathom how anything could have done this much damage so quickly. From a distance he spotted the drone carrier that was Dr. Kolov's flagship, and a spark of hope ran through him. When he saw it was still intact, and swarm of drones launching from its deck on cones of white-blue flame, he thought there might be a chance they would survive this unforeseen attack. Without a thought, he bolted, flying after the lead ship as fast as he could, desperate to ensure it didn't suffer the same fate as the others.

Jonah touched down just outside the bridge, grateful to have made it when the world went white, a massive concussive force reverberating through him as the entire vessel exploded beneath his feet, blasting him end over end far out to sea before he finally smashed into the ocean with enough force to knock him senseless, his world going black.

The shock of icy cold water all around him dragged him back to his senses, and he found himself in near darkness, his heavy armor having dragged him so deep he could only see vague glimmers of sunlight filtering in from far above, his lungs burning as he swallowed a mouthful of vile saltwater. In a panic he tried to propel himself upward, to fly through the water as he had so easily only a few days ago, only to flounder and sink deeper, like his entire body was made of lead.

Jonah could feel his limbs trembling, he was exhausted after his fight at the barricade, and now after the explosion on the flagship, his body was rebelling. He had asked too much of himself, and now he had nothing left to give. He would die down here with the rest of the fleet, alone and forgotten, just like the last time when his family and country had abandoned him in New York. His future, along with Dr. Kolov's, was dead and gone at the bottom of the Atlantic, any chance of him surviving past the next few months would have been slim at best. He had no clue how to find another command crystal like the one on his neck, and even if he did, he lacked the skill and understanding to make it work.

He was just about to give up when the image of a young man, with the bluest eyes he had ever seen, came to his mind. Jonah was shocked back to full wakefulness when he realized the man was talking to his sister, words spilling from his lips faster than Jonah could understand. What's more, he could feel the blue-eyed man was connected to him through the crystal somehow. A spark of hope blossomed. He had a chance, if he could find him. Digging deep, he found a flicker of strength, fanning it, growing it.

Focusing his energies, he fought his way to the surface, barely having the strength to propel himself upward, with only the hope in his belly to keep him going.

Exploding out of the water, Jonah sucked in a deep lungful of ocean air and then banked toward what was left of the flagship, only to halt suddenly in midair, his eyes locking onto a blazing halo of amber and gold floating over the smoking wreckage. Squinting, he realized it was a man, dark skinned and thick through the middle, with tightly curled black hair that was pure white at the temples. He wore a long leather red coat trimmed with gold, along with black pants and leather boots.

He stared at Jonah with a hungry look of a predator. It took him a moment to understand that the glow was coming from a flaming sword in the man's hand that looked like it was made of pure light, along with a massive pair of wings of the same material that held him aloft. Jonah flew out of the water to charge forward, hell-bent on beating the man down with his fists when he sputtered once again, crashing into the water, whatever strength he had managed to summon, spent.

Flailing in the water, he managed to grab on to a piece of wreckage before he sank again. Breathing hard, he rolled onto the wide piece of flotsam. Finally, after steadying himself, he scanned the roiling ocean, half expecting an attack at any moment, but there was nothing. The other man was gone, along with any hope of finding the source of the attack. Jonah squeezed his eyes shut to kill the pain, knowing that like the creatures he fought not long ago, he was already dead: he just happened to still be walking, unless he could find the man with the brilliant blue eyes, and that meant, finding his sister.

THIRTEEN

RUN LIKE HELL

"Blast it, Gibbs, where the hell are you?" shouted Rowen into her comm as she ran down the ancient highway, her breath rasping in her ear, pumping her legs as fast as they would take her.

Route 66 had been by-passed decades ago by the National Highway System and was no longer a major thoroughfare of the United States national highway system. Without access to federal funds, the old road was left to rot and had seen better days. The asphalt was marred with deep cracks filled with fast-growing weeds and more potholes than she could count, making Rowen question whether it was more dangerous racing down the road in the dark, or turning and fighting the people chasing them.

"If he ain't dead...I'm gonna kill him," said Blake, running just behind her, still holding the katana that Rowen had so many questions about, the thin silver blade flashing in the moonlight. When the crowd had turned on them, he had proven the weapon was not simply for show, wielding it with deadly skill and making quick work of their closest attackers. First hacking away the strange tentacles that burst from the boy's torso, then removing a few of the reaching limbs of the townsfolk who had turned on them. Luckily, they ran faster, pulling far enough ahead that the crowd chasing them was visible only at the edge of the night vision her goggles provided.

As if thinking of them brought them closer, she heard Blake grunt, crashing to the pavement with a bone-crunching thud. Turning quickly to help, she cringed when she saw he was being dragged back across the broken concrete by a disjointed metallic tentacle wrapped around his ankle, the boy they had come to get appearing out of nowhere, drawing him in with the strange appendages, somehow having raced far ahead of the rest of the towns-folk. "Stop moving!" she shouted at him, her SIG II coming to her hand faster than the speed of thought.

Blake looked back at her, raising a hand in protest, his eyes wide with fear. "No, no wait! Don't—" he shouted just as she pulled the trigger, her bullet ripping through the disjointed steel wrapped around his ankle. Without pausing, Rowen took aim at the other vile limbs snaking toward them, blowing them apart with her shots, each squeeze of the trigger making the gun kick in her hands, the muzzle spitting out flame that turned day to night. Then adjusting her aim, she added another three shots, two to the boy's chest, and another slamming dead center to his forehead, snapping his head back. The boy reeled when the bullets pounded into him, staggering back and falling over.

"Let's move," she said, eyeing the townsfolk who were closing the distance.

"Nice shooting," said Blake, struggling to his feet and breaking into a shambling run with a pronounced limp, favoring his right side. "I knew you were good, but that was some damn good shooting," he said in his deep rasping tone, glancing back, his face suddenly going pale.

"What?" said Rowen, following his gaze as she ran after him, not daring to holster her weapon, knowing that every second counted. The boy, who had just taken shots to the chest and head, who should be dead, was on his feet, his eyes locked onto them as the crowd brushed past him. "That's impossible," she whispered, pushing herself harder, faster.

"This thing...is the impossible," shouted Blake, running beside her, breathing hard, his limp more pronounced with each stride. Rowen had a million questions for him as they continued on in silence but forced herself to bite her tongue. She could see he wasn't doing well and didn't want to press him while rivers of sweat were pouring off his temples, a pang of worry creasing her forehead each time he stumbled over a crack in the road or a pothole.

"We have to stop," said Rowen finally when Blake slowed to a snail's pace, barely faster than a quick walk. "Find a place where they can't dogpile us, fight on our terms."

Blake stopped and bent over, breathing hard. "Just go, kid. I can't. I'm too old, too tired."

Rowen balked, frowning at him. "Are you nuts? You're my dad's age, and he can run a four-minute mile. You may not be Special Forces, but you're not some fat slob."

"I'm not what you think, kid," he said, wiping sweat from his brow. "I'll hold them for as long as I can. Find that idiot Gibbs, and get back, so you can report this."

"I don't think so. We don't leave anyone behind," said Rowen, looking around for something, anything, they could use to get a tactical advantage. "There!" Grabbing Blake by the arm, she pulled him off the road into the high grass, racing toward a small copse of trees.

"Kid, Rowen!" he sputtered behind her. "We aren't Special Forces; we aren't anything. Don't get yourself killed for my sorry ass; I don't deserve it."

"Shut up! We have tons of ammo, and your fancy sword. We can hold out."

"God Damn! I can't swing a freaking sword in the middle of a bunch of trees!" He swore after her when he saw where they were headed.

Rowen ignored him as she pulled him deeper into the small

grove, settling for a spot where their backs could be protected by a cluster of trees, and there was enough of a maze in front of them that no one could pile in all at once. "Don't just shoot wildly; breathe; take the time to aim; make every shot count," she said, scratching at her scar.

"Son of a bitch. I know that, kid," said Blake, thumbing off the safety on his Beretta with an odd frown on his face. He stared at her for a moment before shaking his head. "Thanks, kid."

Rowen gave him a shrug. "Don't worry. If it gets really bad, I'll shoot you in the knee and run. At least that way you can keep 'em busy while I get away!"

"Damn, that's cold," he said, taking aim as the first of the townsfolk entered the copse, an old man stumbling along without any pants on.

Wanting to have a better tactical view, Rowen pulled out one of the many smart devices she carried, quickly activating its flight mode, and set it to patrol above them, sending the feed to a small corner of her goggles. She immediately regretted it, questioning her plan, when she saw the size of the crowd walking down the highway, all moving in some odd unified gait that made them look like a crazy marching band. A chill ran through her when she realized there were far more than she could count, more than they could stop even with all the ammo they had. The roar of Blake's Beretta pulled her attention back from the view up above, and Rowen, seeing that the townsfolk were trickling in, followed his lead, aiming carefully and quickly at the incoming, doing as she had always done, breathing in and out with each shot, counting down her ammo with each pull of the trigger, the world slowing down, and a sense of calm washing over her.

"Holy shit, that's a wicked gun," said Blake, reloading after one of her shots removed a man's head clean off his body. Nodding in agreement, Rowen could only smile despite the dire situation, her SIG Mark II was a unique weapon, combining a chemical propellant of a standard 9mm with a micro railgun system that was powered by a sliver of the strange crystal Gibbs had found in New York. Gibbs, who had designed and built the weapon, claimed it had a muzzle velocity of over six thousand feet per second, despite only being a handgun. For Rowen that meant she had the stopping power of a state of the art sniper rifle in a compact weapon with manageable recoil, making her deadly at any range.

The weapon had proven itself during the battle of New York. First against Arthur, its deadly shots piercing his toughened skin, knocking the Ascended off his high horse and then fighting her brother, she was able to blow massive chunks off his armor when no one else could even scratch him. Now, it was proving itself again as her shots tore through their attackers, each pull of the trigger like a crack of a whip, driving the frenzied attackers back, making them pay for every inch gained.

The sound of steel whistling through the air drew her attention to Blake. She watched in awe, her jaw hanging open as he sidestepped a beefy man with a thick beard, who had gotten in too close, removing his reaching forearms with a blinding downward strike and then removing his head with a single neat stroke across the man's throat. He continued on, despite his injured ankle, flowing like water in motion, the brilliant silver of his blade never slowing as it cleaved through flesh and bone.

"Kid, look out!" shouted Blake as a heavy weight bore down on her, dragging her to the ground. Rowen cringed inside when her SIG fell from her hand, landing just out of her reach. She had been so mesmerized by Blake that she had missed a heavyset man, more than twice her size, who snuck in from her left flank. Luckily, Rowen's hours of training with her father instinctively kicked in. She didn't fight against the fall, instead rolling with it, so the air wasn't blasted from her lungs. The man on top of her began slashing and clawing at her, his face twisted in an angry grimace. From this close he looked almost alien, his eyes were a pale gray like all the color had been washed out, with only just the hint of an iris, and his rough, unshaven skin was covered in what looked like printed micro circuitry. Even his breath smelled like a foundry as if metal was being forged in his belly.

Dodging and blocking his attacks with her forearms, protecting her face as best she could, she was grateful that her duster was armored enough to take the blows. Thinking quickly, she used one of the first lessons her father had taught her in Brazillian jujitsu, using her attackers unbalanced aggression against him. While he was on top of her trying to choke her, she skillfully locked his left leg with hers in a leg trap, while gripping one of his forearms with her free hand in a monkey grip. Then lifting her hips, she rolled to her left, throwing him off balance and suddenly finding herself with the situation reversed, with her sitting on him.

Not wasting any time, she scrambled off him to get her gun and hastily fired two shots into his skull, recoiling in disgust when instead of blood, ultra-thin filaments that looked like wiring, exploded from his head, wriggling about and snaking toward her like they were alive. Feeling a presence behind her, she spun backward away from the deadman, firing from her knees as she came out of the roll, her bullet tearing open the chest of a blond woman who had gotten too close, and another man who looked like he had just rolled out of bed. Scanning the copse for Blake, she saw him using a pair of trees to keep the converted men and women away from him, unable to swing fully, he was using short, blindingly fast chops to cleave their skulls in half, resulting in a pileup of neatly cut bodies at his feet forming a makeshift barricade. Reloading, Rowen dodged another pair that had gotten too close, firing left and then right from the hip while she raced toward him, jumping up and then swinging off a low-hanging branch one handed while squeezing the trigger on her weapon as fast as she could to clear a path, an idea coming to her as she ran.

"We need to climb!" she shouted, getting close enough that she could be heard, pointing at a sturdy-looking branch above them.

"Are you nuts, kid?" he grunted, his eyes flickering upward. "I ain't no monkey. No way I'm gettin' up there."

"It's easy, my brother, and I used to do it all the time," she said, reloading again, speaking quickly. "You boost me up; I grab the branch. Once I'm up, I'll hang upside down, and you can take my hands. It's easy."

"Easy for you, maybe," he said, switching back to his Beretta now that she was in close quarters, "and what happens if these things know how to climb?"

Rowen took a quick glance at the drone feed in the corner of her tactical goggles, her stomach falling when she saw how many there were surrounding their small wood. "Not much of a choice: climb or die. It's up to you."

"Son of a bitch," said Blake, shaking his head. "We gotta be fast: we won't have more than a few seconds."

"That's all we need!" she said, taking a deep breath through her nostrils to steady her nerves, firing, and reloading as fast as she could, Blake doing the same in an attempt to give themselves enough breathing room to execute her plan. Then when they had a moment, Rowen took a single step back while Blake weaved his fingers together, bending his knees slightly.

"Hurry! Go!" he shouted, his eyes flicking behind her, a look of worry coming to his face.

Rowen didn't waste any time, stepping into his hands and leaping up as he catapulted her, easily catching the lowest branch and scurrying onto the rough wooden limb. Taking a moment to make sure it could support both their weights, she locked her knees and swung down, extending her arms. "Move it, and make it quick," she shouted, her face turning red like her hair from the blood rushing to her head.

Blake didn't waste a second, unloading the remainder of his clip before holstering the weapon and leaping up to grip Rowen's forearms, bracing his legs against the trunk of the tree, so she wasn't bearing all his weight with her small frame, then scampering over her.

"Move it!" she grunted, her arms straining. "You're heavier than you look."

With a groan, Blake slid onto the branch beside her, helping her sit up. "We should go higher," he said, standing up on the branch with an easy grace, using his height to grab another limb high above them, pulling her higher with him. "C'mon!"

"I think this is about it," said Rowen when they were a little past halfway to the top of the tree, the branches starting to bend with their weights. Down below, the townsfolk stood like they had at the church, stock still, eyes up. But instead of the boy being the focus of their attention, it was her and Blake. When she spoke at last, it was in a small voice, not much more than a whisper, "What the hell has gotten into these idiots?"

Blake scratched his beard, a faraway look on his face while he settled in beside her. "It's like a virus, airborne, spreading from person to person when they're in close proximity; that's why they keep coming, the more people they can infect, the faster it'll spread."

Rowen suddenly felt like she was about to fall out of the tree, her head spinning. "One of them was on top of me," she said suddenly cold despite the heat. "I could smell his breath…it smelled funny."

Blake looked at her at last, his lips pressing into a thin line. "Sorry, kid, I was afraid of that. I don't know what to say."

She ground her teeth together, wanting to shoot something, anything. "Am I gonna end up like them? I mean, they look human on the outside, but inside, they're like machines—and how the hell do you know about this anyway?"

"I don't— It happened to one of my friends a long time ago," he said hesitating, his shoulders slumping when he continued. "Happened to me too."

Rowen blinked in confusion, letting herself feel a flicker of hope. "So, we can fix this, right? Make it go away. I mean if you're here—"

Before Blake could answer, Rowen let out a yelp, nearly slipping from her perch when the entire tree shook violently, forcing her to hug the center trunk. She held on for dear life, pressing her face against the rough bark while a storm of green falling leaves cascaded all around her.

"Son of a bitch," said Blake, surprisingly nimble as he held on to the tree branch with his thighs, his Beretta in hand. "Kid's back; he's tryin' to shake us out!"

Rowen glanced down to see a mass of silver tentacles coiled around the thick tree trunk, the boy staring up at them with a blank look on his face, an ugly black smudge on his forehead from where she had shot him not long ago. "What do we do!" she shouted over the snapping and cracking of tree limbs.

"I would tell you to shoot the bastard, but it's almost impossible to get a clear shot from here," he said, shooting wildly, his shots ricocheting uselessly.

Following his example, Rowen drew and fired, her shots falling wide, or worse, blocked by the limbs of the tree. Seeing the trunk begin to splinter, Rowen prepared for the worst. "I'm sorry. This is my fault. We should have kept running."

To her surprise, Blake said nothing, ignoring the bending tree and shimmying closer to her. "I don't know if I got the juice for this. It hasn't worked in a long time, but we got nothing to lose," he said, offering his hand. Without thinking, she placed her smaller hand in his, watching him ride the shaking tree branch like it was a wild stallion, his face a mask of calm despite the chaos all around him.

Rowen heard a massive snap, and her stomach was suddenly in her throat when the tree began to fall like it was in slow motion. Her entire world was suddenly a blur of green and brown, panic taking over when she saw the ground quickly approaching. A heartbeat later, they landed with a horrible crash of snapping tree limbs, luckily bouncing off a series of springy branches that tore at her skin and clothes, pulled at her hair, but strangely none of which managed to pierce her skin, the tree limbs taking the brunt of their fall. Scrambling to her feet, Rowen was sick to her stomach when she saw that they were entirely surrounded by the townspeople, the only barrier between them a few branches that they were all haphazardly walking through, not caring that the sharpened and freshly splintered wood tore at their flesh, in some cases piercing their bodies. "All right, I'll take you all on, make you pay!" she said, readying her SIG, not willing to go out without a fight. She was about to take out the closest of the townspeople when Blake grabbed her by the forearm, pulling her close.

"What the—"

Rowen gasped in shock when he began to glow, a web of crackling amber light spreading out from his chest, like flames consuming burning paper. She flinched in shock when his entire body vanished before her eyes. In a panic, she tried to pull away, her heart racing, but he held her tight. When the arcing streams of what looked like electricity cascaded over her skin, she felt like she'd been dumped in a pool of effervescent water, her brows shooting up when her entire body began to tingle. Moments later, she raised a hand to her face and watched fascinated while her limbs faded from view.

"Stay close," he said, his deep voice tense and strained. "I can barely do this for one, much less two."

Narrowing her eyes in confusion, she spun about, eyeing the townsfolk who suddenly began to wander off, including the boy with the strange tentacles, trudging back down Route 66 toward the old church where they found him. "This is insane. How is this—"

Blake pulled at her again. "My powers haven't worked this much in years. Let's move away from these things before my head explodes," he said.

"Powers? Have you lost it? What the heck are you talking about?" said Rowen, her mind reeling. How could any of this be. Blake was just some crazy old prepper she recruited in New York. How the hell could he have powers? "You can walk and talk; it won't kill you, but I might shoot you if you don't."

They started walking, and she felt him wrapping an arm around her for support. "You shoot me, you die too, kid," he said, his voice full of amusement.

"That'll make two of us. Talk!" He was silent for a moment, and Rowen realized how little she knew about him. She accepted at face value what he had told her when they met. That he had assumed that New York would be attacked and had prepared accordingly by hoarding food, weapons, and ammunition. But he had never shown them where he lived, where his supply was. She had never thought to ask questions because he had defined himself to her, and she had accepted it completely.

"Okay, you win...anyone ever tell you you're a bit of an asshole," he said.

Rowen shook her head, still amazed that they were being ignored, that she might live just long enough to shoot Gibbs if he was still alive. "Yeah, all the time. I take it as a compliment."

"Okay, well, my real name is Finn O'Regan, and fifteen years ago I was one of the first humans to be successfully Ascended, and became part of Divinity Corps."

FOURTEEN

BELLEVUE

Arthur locked his arms behind his back, standing at a parade rest while he reached out with his power, changing the polarity of the smart wall in front of him with a thought. "Good morning, Dr. Fillipo. How are you today?" He'd asked the same question to the doctor every day for the last two weeks, and for the last week, the dark-skinned physician, trapped behind the thick glass wall, wasn't able to answer.

When he had first met him a few weeks ago at Bellevue Hospital, Arthur had liked him immediately. He was composed caring, and hardworking, if a little irritated most of the time, but that was part of the job for an attending physician.

In response to his greeting, the doctor surged at him, slamming his body against the glass wall with a loud thump, his handsome face twisting in a rage, his hands clawing at the barrier. Arthur had brought him to his lab at The Rockefeller University, hoping he could fix him, or at the very least understand what the hell was going on with him and the others. They had been lucky this time. Arthur had been at Bellevue picking up Gwen when the number of influenza patients had spiked, and he had, by happenstance, noticed the infection, the strange virus that defied explanation.

"I'm not sure why the fuck you keep that thing here. This is a nice lab you got here. If it gets you, it's gonna make a freaking mess," said Gwen. "You should put him with the rest we got locked up at Bellevue."

Arthur stifled a small smile as he turned to face Gwen. She sat with her feet up on his workstation, her fingers linked behind her head, bobbing to whatever song she was listening to on the ancient iPod that was balanced on her small breasts. He found it strange and amazing that she had actually stuck around after he had rebuilt her lungs. He had expected that she would have told him to *fuck off* and be on her way. But for some reason she had found it in her heart to forgive him, and he couldn't help but stifle a smile every time he looked at her. "He, not it. He's a real person, not a thing. His first name is George, named after his grandfather. He had friends, parents, a girlfriend named Nancy who calls every day."

"Yeah, and he'd rip your face off if you let him outta his cage," she said, bounding to her feet, bouncing on her heels, playing air guitar now. "And it's not like you can fix him or any of the others."

Part of him worried that she was right. When they caught the infection early enough, the people showing symptoms seemed normal enough, and because of that Arthur had ordered them quarantined at Bellevue Hospital, which had been a blessing and a curse. They had managed to isolate the infected from the rest of the population, but without fail, everyone of them degenerated into something similar to Dr. Fillipo: mindless, savage. Because he was able to detect them, they had rounded up every last one of them they could find, but now they had an entire hospital packed to the rafters, a powder keg just waiting for a fuse.

Arthur returned his attention to the doctor, looking him up and down, watching for a change—any change. From a distance, he still looked like the man he had met in the hospital weeks ago. But up close, his dark skin looked like an ancient circuit board, and his eyes, once dark brown, were now pale and silver and had their own inner glow. But to Arthur, it was what he could see when he shifted his vision to the quantum spectrum that was the most interesting. Unlike the dark shadow and muted blue spark of life that normal people displayed, or the blazing gold halo of an Ascended like himself or Gwen, Dr. Fillipo looked like nothing he had ever seen. He glowed with the spark of the bright blue electrical current of a machine, but overlain with a sheen of silver that coursed through him like it was blood. Arthur knew from experience that if someone got too close, this substance would emerge from his orifices in a fine mist, almost invisible. Aggressively attacking new subjects, seeking to infect them to begin the conversion process once more.

"I can fix this," muttered Arthur, not sure if he was talking to himself or to Gwen. With his ability to control machines, computers, and anything mechanical, it should have been easy enough for him to control the virus, which seemed to be a nanite of some kind, but it wasn't like any version of the technology he'd seen before. But so far he had managed only to contain it, slow it down from converting biomatter into the strange filament that replaced the internal organs of the subject, including the brain.

"That's your problem, dude. You think it's your responsibility to fix everything!" shouted Gwen from across the lab. "When are you gonna learn you don't have to do it all; the world isn't on your shoulders; you're still just a dumb kid."

"I fixed you, didn't I?" he said over his shoulder, keeping one eye on the doctor, "and I'll fix this city too if Cardinal Washington would realize he can't beat me."

"Yeah, but he did bone ya! So, I get that's why he thinks you're his bitch." Gwen laughed, throwing him a wink and a brilliant smile.

"He never touched me; he's not like that. It was his people, the ones he lets get away with those horrible things," grumbled Arthur under his breath, turning his attention back to the doctor, grinding his teeth. He had forgotten how cruel Gwen could be with her little jabs and insults. She always seemed to know where and when to hit him for maximum effect. Ignoring her laughter, he squared his shoulders, switching his vision to the quantum realm once more. He needed to understand what was happening to these people, if there was anything human left in them after they had been consumed by this virus, and that meant taking a risk, doing the dangerous thing. He reached out with his power, delving into the machine that was once a man careening down the infinite pathways of the strange filament that made up his internal organs before reaching what served as his mind.

The reality of the lab fell away, and Arthur found himself in a strange landscape of rolling desert hills, a city in the distance reflecting glimmering shafts of sunlight. He had seen this before, when they had destroyed the tower in New York. Arthur could tell that this was constructed landscape, something that existed in his mind while his body remained in place. Not knowing what else to do, he headed for the city, undoing his high collar, the hot sun beating down on him while he trudged along on the burning sand. The walk was surprisingly quick, yet seemed to take forever, time always worked differently in these constructs. The instant he crossed into the outskirts of the city he felt himself shifting, stretching, and squeezing all at once, moving without any sense of motion.

Arthur suddenly found himself deep in the heart of the city standing on an elevated walkway, surrounded by impossible towers of glass so high they looked like they touched the sky, buildings connected by bridges of thin delicate crystal that should have collapsed under their own weight. The place was eerily silent, so his every breath, every step, echoed like thunder. Even the beating of his heart sounded like a drum.

Locking his arms behind his back, Arthur began to wander up and down the walkways, crossing bridge after bridge, walking through vast open squares and parks full of lush greenery, searching for something, anything, to explain what was going on in the doctor's mind. Part of him wanted to enter the buildings, see what was inside, but oddly there were no doors, simply windows high above him. He was about to give up, pull his mind from the construct when he saw Dr. Fillipo sitting on a park bench not so far away, dressed in the same light-blue scrubs he had on the day they met, his balding pate glistening with sweat in the bright sunlight.

"Dr. Fillipo—George—are you there?" he asked, reaching out to touch his shoulder and then pulling back, thinking it better if he didn't touch the man.

The doctor looked at him with a blank stare, his lips opening and closing in silence. Blowing out his cheeks. Arthur smoothed the top of his uniform before sitting next to him, keeping his back straight. "Your girlfriend, Nancy, she's worried. Calls for you every day. I don't know how to tell you this, but she seems really clingy," he said, staring out at the glittering metropolis. "She says you guys were supposed to get married; she says you would do anything to avoid your commitments. If I were you, I'd want to get away from her too, but I gotta say, there are easier ways of getting out of a relationship."

"I should have married her a long time ago, but I just kept waiting; I'm not sure why," said Dr. Fillipo suddenly, his voice strained, far away.

Arthur shot up from the bench, blinking down at the doctor, who's blank expression hadn't changed. "George? Are you okay? Can you tell me what's going on?"

"I don't know," he said, speaking in a halting tone, his eyes narrowing in confusion. "How is Nanc? I miss her, but what I'm doing here is important."

"Important? What's important here?" asked Arthur, his words coming out in a rush.

"Changing the world requires doing the hard thing, giving up the things you love so that everyone can live a better life, be a part of something greater than themselves. Don't worry, you'll see. It'll all make sense to you soon."

Arthur took a step back as the doctor got to his feet, looking off in the distance. "I'll see what? George, please, I can help you if you let me."

"One voice, one purpose for all of humanity," said Dr. Fillipo, a tight-lipped smile coming to his face, his eyes taking on a dreamy look. "Can you imagine? No more war, just togetherness, unity."

Arthur continued to walk backward as the doctor came forward, reaching for him. "I'm not sure I like the sound of that," he said, fighting the urge to turn and run. "I like my voice just fine." he said, assuming a defensive stance, expecting an attack.

The doctor took another step toward him and then stopped, his outstretched hand starting to shake and then squeezing shut, his face contorting suddenly like someone was twisting a knife in his belly. "Arthur—go. Run while there's still time. He's coming."

"Who? Who's coming?"

"The voice," whispered the doctor, a single tear rolling down his face. "He's always there, in my head, in everyone's head. All the voices, one voice."

"Take my hand," said Arthur. "I can help you come back to the man you were. I can save you."

"No," he whispered. "I need you to go now. I don't know how much longer I can hold on."

"But—"

"GO!" he screamed, flailing his arms against Arthur's chest. "Get out! Get out! Get out!"

Arthur felt the world shift around him, like he was suddenly racing down a dark tunnel with streaks of light stretching out all around him, his mind pulling and pushing against a force he couldn't see. Then just like it began, it stopped, and he found himself on the cold floor of his lab, staring up at Gwen who gave him a half smile.

"What's the matter? You fell over laughing from my joke. It wasn't that funny."

"What? How long was I out for?"

"Out? You just fell over a second ago," she said, helping him up, dusting off his back. "Cute butt, by the way." With a laugh, she gave him a small tap on his backside, humming to herself while she returned to his workstation.

He was about to say something when he remembered the doctor. Turning his attention back to the doctor, he gasped, his stomach turning. Inside the glass cell, there was almost nothing left of the man, his entire body having liquified into a pool of a strange silver-green mess. Even his clothes were gone, nothing more than a stain on his floor.

"Well, you don't see that every day," said Gwen from across the lab. Arthur glanced back at her, irritated that she didn't take any of this seriously. He was about to scold her for sounding so cruel when every alarm in the lab went off.

Forgetting the doctor, he delved into one of the command consoles he had specially made for himself. He still regretted that Rowen and the others had destroyed the tower last year. Only at the end did they understand its use, its potential. With it, he would have been able to control almost any machine, any computer in the country, stop any threat. Since then he had tried to replicate what it did with the technology he had at hand, but nothing had come close to what he needed in terms of power and broadcast capability. Instead, he built and designed an interface using current technology to replicate the towers functions, even in a limited function. This console worked with his thoughts, his powers. So while he couldn't control everything, it allowed him access to much of the city.

In a heartbeat, he found himself observing through one of the many defensive drones he had circling the city, looking down with a bird's-eye view of the greatest city in the world. Not seeing anything, he expanded his consciousness, peering through every drone, every camera, anything with a lens.

He cursed, adjusting the high collar on his plain black uniform when he saw what caused the alarms to sound.

"What's the deal?" said Gwen, slipping the buds from her ears, her brow coming together in worry when she saw the look on his face.

Arthur fought to keep his tone calm even while his insides raged with worry. "We have thousands like Dr. Fillipo quarantined at Bellevue, and now it looks like we missed some," he said, swallowing hard, "and they're trying to free the others. If that happens, we lose the city."

"Well, then," said Gwen, stretching like a cat. "It looks like it's time to earn the big bucks you're paying me."

"What?"

"Listen, you can lie down and take it like a bitch, or you can fight back, kick 'em in the teeth like I know you can—you choose. If you're not up to it, I have no problem flying off to a beach somewhere and having a party."

A slow smile crept to his face despite the fear bubbling in his stomach. Somehow, as much as she could be mean and say the cruelest thing, she also said what he needed to hear most. Squaring his shoulders, he gave her a nod. "All right, let's go kick some ass!"

FIFTEEN

MUSIC AND LIGHT

Gwen rocketed through the Manhattan skyline with her arms locked at her side, the wind rippling the long, white leather coat Arthur had given her, like a cape. She relished in the rush of wind whipping through her hair while she dodged towers of glass and steel. The rush of flying was better than sex or booze, better than any of the drugs she'd ever taken. With her earbuds in place and music in her soul, she could go on like this forever, playing in the sunlight, dancing among the clouds. If she had the chance, she would forget everyone and everything in this life and live only in moments of pure joy like this for the rest of her life.

Banking hard to avoid the ancient Chrysler building, reality came creeping into her dream. Arthur followed close behind using a short-range VTOL transport called a peregrine, apparently named after a bird called the peregrine falcon, supposedly one of the fastest birds in the world—before it went extinct, anyway. Despite being squat and ugly, the small craft was fast as hell, and maneuverable too, but it looked like a minivan her mother would drive, and Gwen couldn't help but hate it.

The small transport was followed by a dozen or so Apex drones that the Russians had left behind during their hasty exit, and Arthur had converted them for his own use. Gwen thought they looked cool with their sleek A-wing design, topped off by a single rotary cannon sticking out the front, which she was sure could do some serious damage.

Seeing the hospital in the distance, she raced ahead to circle the old building and get an idea of what the hell they were facing. Bellevue was the oldest hospital in the city, and the idiots who ran New York for the last few hundred years had haphazardly expanded it time and time again to accommodate the growing city. You could see it in the jumbled style of architecture that made up each wing. Parts of the massive complex were made from rough red brick, weather stained brown and blackened by time, while other parts were made of high-tech polarized glass and steel, with sweeping majestic curves that looked like flowing water, all mishmashed together like some crazy two-year-old's Lego set.

Gwen pursed her lips when she saw that each entrance was crowded by small armies of crazed people like Dr. Fillipo, banging on the doors, some of them climbing up the sides, throwing their bodies without a care against the massive glass panels that made up some of the more modern parts of the hospital. "Arthur, do you see this shit?" she said, activating the private comm channel he had set up for her.

"It doesn't look good," he said, his voice crackling in her ear, interrupting the wailing guitar solo she loved so much.

· · ·

"So what? Do you have some sort of master plan here?"

"I don't want to hurt anyone, but we have to stop them from breaching the hospital. There are thousands of them already in there, so if they break out, we won't be able to stop them all," said Arthur through a burst of static. "We're going to have to eliminate them."

Gwen slowed, turning off her iPod, struggling to hover in midair, feeling for the subtle vibrations running through her. It happened every time she flew without music for some reason; she had a hard time controlling her power. At first, she thought it was because she wasn't high on anything, but it turned out, it was music, not drugs that helped her stay up in the air. "All right, I get it," said Gwen, biting the inside of her cheek when a worrying thought ran through her mind. "I don't want to rain on your murder parade here, but won't we get infected fighting these things?"

"Negative," said Arthur, bringing the Peri to a halt not far from her. "I included a polarity dispersion field in the lining of your coat. Anything that comes too close is given an electrical charge that—"

"You can just say no, dude!" she interrupted, irritation in her voice. "I don't need the college-level lecture. I get it; you're smart."

"Okay, sorry," said Arthur. "You'll be safe. Anyway, I'll take the north side of the hospital where the brick can take a beating from the cannons on the drones. You take the main entrance with all the glass. I've ordered the police to set up a perimeter, and Rodrigo will be on the ground hunting down any stragglers."

. . .

"Let's do this," said Gwen, punching up "Welcome to the Jungle" on her music player and sliding the volume up to maximum, her pulse quickening. "You know where you are, baby! You're in the jungle; You gonna die!" she sang, spreading her arms wide as if she were on a cross and letting her body fall, plunging headfirst toward the ground, loving the rush of the wind through her hair.

She was almost to the ground, ready to sow some mayhem when a flash of amber light caught her eye. Turning and banking, her breath caught in her throat when she saw Arthur's VTOL cleaved in half, exploding in a ball of white-hot flame, bits and pieces of metal drifting to the ground like burnt paper.

"What the fuck," she whispered in disbelief, racing to the explosion with a churning stomach full of worry. It would be just like Arthur to die when he finally became a decent human being. Before she could get close enough, she came to a sudden halt in midair, her jaw falling open. Emerging from the remains of the fireball was a dark-skinned man dressed in red, flaming wings of glowing energy spreading wide across his back, flames still licking the edges of his long leather coat trimmed in gold. He pointed at her with a blade made from the same translucent material as his wings, a frown on his face. With a single thrust of his powerful wings he was beside her, a hand raised to stall her attack. When she found her voice it was hardly a whisper: shaking with fear, she whispered a name she never thought would pass her lips again. "Cardinal Washington?"

"Here you are once again spending time with the lower classes, Gwen, with trash. I thought you had decided to serve your country, become someone with honor and decency," he said, looking down his nose at her.

"No, you had decided that part," she said with a sneer, the wind whipping around them. "And the way I remember it, the last time we saw each other, you called me a whore! So, I'm just living up to your expectations, aren't I?"

"I guess you don't ever really leave places like Eight Mile. The ghetto's always in you no matter how far you get from it," he said, smiling at the creatures throwing themselves at the hospital doors, looking pleased that they had almost broken through. "Not that it matters anymore. This city full of traitors will be razed to the ground by the end of the day, its people converted to my drones. But I'm not a man to waste resources. Arthur is dead, and so it's time for you to come over to the winning side, Gwen."

Following his gaze, a chill ran through her. "You did this, all those people. You changed them into those monsters."

"Of course, I told Arthur that I had a gift for him. How do—"

Gwen flinched, raising a defensive hand to protect her face when a shadow passed over them, the low whine of an engine turbine drowning out their conversation. She dodged to her left to avoid a hail of gunfire that suddenly rained down on the cardinal, slamming into his back and shoulders with enough force to wipe the smirk from his face and drive the older man toward the ground, the thunder of multiple rotary cannons filling the air. A smile came to her face when she looked up to see Arthur laying facedown on the back of an Apex drone with a dozen more behind him, their heavy-caliber machine guns spinning faster than the eye could see while spitting out fire and flame at Cardinal Washington.

"Cover me," screamed Arthur, rocketing past her with a grim look on his cut and bruised face, gripping the edges of the drone like he was holding on for dear life.

Plunging after him, she watched Cardinal Washington raise what looked like a medieval shield made of blazing transparent amber, above his head, the heavy-caliber bullets leaving small cracks in the construct.

With a roar, Cardinal Washington lashed out, counterattacking with the flaming sword in his hand, enlarging it to gigantic proportions and cutting a wide swath across the sky. She winced when the tail end of his strike carved through one of the walls of the hospital, sending a shower of jagged glass to the street below. Arthur had managed to turn away just in time, ducking his head low to avoid having it removed from his neck. Gwen wasn't so lucky, the broad side of the glowing weapon slamming into her and knocked the wind out of her, sending her tumbling to the ground.

She crashed into the sidewalk, plunging straight through without slowing, only stopping when she impacted on the subway tunnel down below, with a heavy thud, a rain of dust and grit tumbling onto her head. She clutched at her chest, rasping to catch her breath, wanting nothing more than to lay there for the rest of the day or at least until the pain went away. The sound of minigun fire and shattering glass made her roll over onto her back despite the pain. Groaning, she patted down her chest and was amazed that everything was still in place, Arthur's fancy coat and her invulnerable skin working together to absorb the cardinal's titanic blow. Looking up through the hole she'd made, she watched the strange dance of Arthur and Cardinal Washington circling one another in midair, an odd mix of parry and attack. Arthur and his Apex drones strafed past him every few seconds, spitting fire and lead at the old man, while the cardinal fended off his attacks with shield constructs made of pure energy, his blazing sword cutting swaths of machines from the air with every pass.

"All right, enough of this shit," she said, dusting herself off and getting to her feet, her voice echoing off the moldy subway walls. "I've had enough of this old fucker." Closing her eyes, she fell into the steady rhythm of the vibrations that ran through her, holding back and letting it build up until it thrummed faster and faster in her heart and soul, so much so that the pavement beneath her feet began to spider and crack with the energy she was holding back. Releasing it all with a yell, she exploded from the subway like a bolt of lightning, the shockwave of her wake tearing apart Cardinal Washington's human drones clustered around the hole in the street she had made.

In an instant she was under him, blowing past the cardinal's glowing shield as if it were cardboard, her fists smashing into his chest with a bone-shattering crunch that sent him careening out over the East River. Not slowing, she gave chase, pummeling him again with a haymaker that clapped like thunder, the air around them imploding.

· · ·

"Enough!" shouted the cardinal, recovering his wits enough to hurl a massive yellow hammer tumbling end over end toward her, the heavy weapon clipping her on the side of her head and sending her reeling toward the water. He followed up by materializing a wide slab of amber concrete beneath her, so dense that when she slammed into it, the wind was knocked from her lungs, her head bouncing hard enough to make her see stars.

Gwen blacked out for a heartbeat, her vision blurring like a spinning kaleidoscope of shifting colors. She opened her eyes just in time to find Cardinal Washington falling toward her, the old man's blazing amber wings spread wide as though he were an avenging angel, his brilliant flaming sword aimed at her breast. Using every last shred of her wits, she rolled to the side, her stomach heaving violently from the dizziness in her head.

She flinched when the cardinal's weapon sunk deep into the glowing slab a hairsbreadth from her face, the weapon then vanishing and reappearing in his hand a second later. Cardinal Washington gave her no quarter, not a second to catch her breath, coming at her with wide sweeps of the blade that forced her to scramble back until she ran out of room, and he was suddenly towering above her with the weapon raised above his head. She raised her hands defensively to protect her head and face when he gave a start, his sword suddenly vanishing and replaced once more by a heavy shield.

Behind her, the heavy whine of an Apex drone's rotary cannon thundered, and the cardinal's eyes shot open wide as he staggered back from an onslaught of burning metal. Gwen glanced back to see the sky filled with drones, weapons blazing in unison, Arthur at the forefront standing upright on one of them. With a growl the cardinal fell back, his translucent wings spreading wide, and with a powerful sweep he took to the air, giving them a look of pure hate as the slab under her pivoted midair to protect him.

"Son of a bitch," she swore, flailing midair while Arthur blazed past her on a drone, chasing after him. Blowing out her cheeks, she steadied herself, drifting over the river to catch her breath. She watched Cardinal Washington throw up a series of wide barriers to slow Arthur's pursuit and protect himself against the onslaught, using the defensive walls to force the Apex drones wide while the old man made his way back to the hospital. Gwen was sure he was still intent on cracking open the old building like an egg and releasing the thousands of infected they had locked up in there.

Shaking off her dizziness, Gwen bolted after him like an arrow, her arms extended in front of her, intent on cutting him off. Pushing herself to the limit, she managed to close the distance to only a few feet when he looked back, his eyes going wide. Twisting in midair his entire body began to glow with the same incandescent amber light that made up everything he created, and he gave her a grim smile. "You cannot stop me. I have already won; you just don't know it yet."

Gwen blinked, and suddenly there were three of him, all glowing like they were constructs, each one with the same hateful look in their eyes. Before she could react, they all split off flying toward different wings of the hospital. She hesitated, frozen in place while the copies raced off. "Fuck!" she screamed, chasing after the version heading to the newest section of the hospital, praying she picked the right one. She was almost on top of him when he looked up at her and winked out of existence, fading to nothing but tiny motes of swirling light, the only sound coming from the infected below, slamming their bodies against the glass doors.

. . .

Gwen had a sinking feeling in her stomach when the entire building shook, a deep rumble filling the street like an avalanche coming down a mountain. She was about to fly to the western portion of the building where the sound was coming from when the cardinal exploded in a shower of glass and steel from the building beneath her, a glowing amber wedge the size of a locomotive projected in front of him leaving a gaping hole. She blanched in horror when thousands of infected poured out of the hole in his wake, moving blindingly fast, scattering in all directions.

Cardinal Washington raised his flaming sword in a salute before turning away and flying off with powerful sweeps of his amber wings. Gwen was about to go after him when Arthur appeared beside her standing upright on an Apex drone, a dark look on his bruised face. When he spoke, his voice was cracked and rasping. "Leave him. We have to contain this," he said, staring hard after him. "He wants us to chase after him while the infected raze the city; we can't afford that."

"So what do we do when we catch them? Do we lock them up somewhere else?"

In response, the rotary cannons on the Apex drones circling the hospital, began to spin upward, the dozens of sleek aircraft scattering in all directions. "You were right. I can't save everyone, so no more. We eliminate anyone infected—no exceptions."

Gwen said nothing, only nodding when his drones opened fire. In the distance she could already hear the sirens, knowing there would be screams to follow. Watching the infected stream out of the hospital, part of her felt that Cardinal Washington was right. They had already lost the city; they just didn't know it yet.

SIXTEEN

BLAKE

"I was recruited into the Ascension program back in '63, and not by choice," said Blake, his deep voice grinding like gravel.

"What, they just dragged you in off the street?" said Rowen, adjusting his weight on her shoulders to better support him as he limped along, not that it helped much given how much taller he was than her.

Blake gave her a pained look, his face gray and ashen from having hidden them, cloaked them as he called it. He had held on long enough with his powers that they had managed to avoid the attention of anyone else, most of the converted townspeople having headed back in the direction of the old church. And now they were close enough to town that they could make out a few faint lights in the distance, but no matter how hard they tried to raise him on the comms, there was still no word from Gibbs, and they feared the worst.

"No, I was recruited by the church," he said, shaking his head. "I had lost my family the year before in a terrorist attack, and I became a ward of the state, too old to be adopted, too young to be on my own."

"So, they just put you in a secret government program for super-heroes," Rowen teased, using her tactical goggles to take a quick look at the feed from her drone circling above, making sure there were no more surprises headed their way. Route 66 was clear, with not a soul to be seen on the ancient highway, which was fine with her: she didn't think they could handle another fight at this point.

"It wasn't like that. Back in Boston, there were a ton of homeless kids, and the state had an agreement with the church. If no one was around to take you in, they put you in a religious studies program meant to guide you to become a priest or a nun, or at the very least an upstanding member of the community. The truth was it wasn't much more than the church getting cheap labor, making kids do shit no one else wanted to do."

Listening to his story, Rowen felt her face getting red, her blood running hot. "Why the hell is it people think kids don't have rights, that we don't get a say?"

"I hear ya. Kids get the short end of the stick. Only people you can legally hit, only people who don't get a say in a divorce, or like me, if their parents die."

Rowen nodded along with him, tamping down her temper. She wouldn't do anyone any good being pissed for nothing. "So, how did you end up...you know, being able to do the things you do?"

"Back in '62, a big part of Downtown Boston was destroyed. They said it was terrorists, but I knew different. I was close enough to see the bastard who did it, but for some reason I survived when the rest of my family didn't. Anyway, I was doing day labor, helping rebuild what we could in the area around what used to be Boston Common. One of the priests, Father Gary, a real winner who didn't think too much of me, sent in a sample of my blood to the Ascension program, hoping to cash in on the recruitment money."

"You're kidding, right?"

"Nope, and my blood tested positive," he said, getting a faraway look in his eyes. "It wasn't so bad. I found out there really was a God, and he'd answered my prayers. They sent someone to come and get me, and lo and behold, I walked into Father Gary's office, and standing there, beating the father to a pulp is the guy who destroyed half the city, the guy responsible for killing my parents, my brothers, and sisters."

Rowen swallowed hard, thinking that the story was too crazy not to be true. "Did you kill him?" she whispered, knowing what she would have done if anyone hurt her parents, or her brother.

"Naw," said Blake, shaking his head. "He had powers, and he killed Father Gary with 'im right in front of me. Apparently, the priest had done the same thing to him a few years back, sending his blood off to get the recruitment money. Anyway, I could see the writing on the wall. I didn't have a choice, so I went along with it, did as I was told, and bid my time till I could make the bastard pay."

"And did you?" asked Rowen, her curiosity getting the best of her.

Blake gave her an icy smile that sent shivers up her spine, "Yeah, we were a mission. There were five of us including myself, Tamika, Daniel. Good people, and the guy who caused all the trouble, Bobby, was a real prick. Daniel, he was infected by the same virus these folks seem to have, and he ended up infecting the rest of us. It's a long story, but we ended up in this ancient facility in the middle of the Amazon, a place out of this world with tech I've never seen before or since. There's an AI in this place with a machine that can cure us before the infection goes too far, before we turn into walking tin cans. So me and Tamika, we go first, get the shit out of our system, then Bobby goes in last. Well, knowing I might not ever have another chance, I took my shot, burying my sword real deep in the control panel of the machine, making sure the prick never woke up."

"I don't understand," said Rowen, a frown coming to her face, pulling at her scar. "My father can't fart on a mission without having to give an after-action report. Didn't the government want explanations as to what happened? Didn't they order you back to base?"

"I'm sure as hell they did," said Blake with a shrug, "and we would have gone too, me and Tamika. You see, when they changed us, they implanted explosives in our heads. We don't listen to orders and pop! You're done. But when the machine removed the virus, it took the explosive out too, so we were free."

"And you went to New York?"

Blake nodded once more, pointing with his chin at the low buildings in the distance. "Almost back where we started," he said, exhaustion in his voice. "I thought New York was safer than going home; no one knew who I was there, and with our powers, it would be hard for anyone to find us. We would lay low, live our lives and take anything we needed to get by, and no one would be the wiser."

"Really, and of all the names you could choose, you chose Blake?" teased Rowen with a wry grin.

"It was my dad's name," he said, bowing his head.

"And how is it that you're still alive?" asked Rowen. "Mary Beth and her brothers told me that the Ascension process kills you after a while, wears you out until you just break down like an old car."

"Yeah, that sounds about right, the broken-down-old-car part, anyway. Tamika passed early, but me, well it's complicated. I'm not thirty yet, but I got a wicked case of arthritis; on most days everything just hurts. My sight was going until I got corneal implants, lost most of my teeth too," he said, showing her his gums. "The powers started fading pretty bad in my early twenties, but I worked out like a dog, ate well. No garbage. I survived, not sure how though."

They had just made it back to the town proper when Blake finished his story for the most part, with promises to fill in more details later. Rowen drew her SIG II and nodded for Blake to do the same as they walked down Main Street with its empty storefronts. She cursed when she came to the entrance of the bar where they had left Gibbs. The entryway was blocked by a number of corpses, all looking very similar to the ones they fought earlier.

"Poor bastard probably got overrun," said Blake limping up behind her, toeing one of the bodies and rolling it over, pointing at a bullet hole in its forehead. "Looks like he got a few licks in though."

"Transport is untouched," said Rowen. "You should probably check it out; get it up and running, just in case."

"You don't want me in there with you?" said Blake, raising an eyebrow.

"I'm not an idiot. If more of those things are in there, I'm running like hell. I just wanna make sure we can move when we have to."

"Okay, got it," said Blake, heading off.

Rowen stood at the door holding her breath. She should have let Blake handle this. Part of her wanted to charge in, guns blazing, but she was terrified of what she would find. Gibbs was a pain in the ass, but he was a good friend, and she couldn't imagine life without him. They had been through so much together in New York, and her father loved him, and in some ways she did too. Finding her courage, she slowly pushed open the door to the bar, stepping gingerly over the corpses into the smelly place. It was as they had seen it a few hours ago, grime-covered walls and sticky floors so filthy she couldn't tell what color the wood was, the lights flickering with a dull glow.

"Well, it looks like he put up a good fight," she mumbled to herself, squatting to inspect another corpse, this one within strands of filament spilling out from the open skull. Moving deeper behind the bar she gasped, finding the tablet Gibbs used bent in half, the screen black and shattered. Rowen flinched suddenly when she heard a noise in the kitchen. Not wasting a moment, she peeked through the round window in the door, catching a glimpse of movement. Slipping through the door to the kitchen, she drew in a sharp breath when she found a waitress standing motionless in front of what looked like the walk-in freezer. It turned to face her, giving her a dull stare before lurching toward her.

Staying calm, Rowen drew in a breath, putting two bullets in its chest, and another one in its head, the last one snapping its neck back and sending it tumbling into a tiled wall. Cringing at the racket, she moved toward the fridge, putting another shot into the creature's head for good measure, her eyes moving everywhere with her SIG following.

Sure that the area was clear, she cupped a hand to listen at the freezer. Hearing nothing, she swung open the door leveling her weapon. She sighed in relief when she found Gibbs tucked away at the back of the freezer, shivering like a newborn foal. Holstering her gun, Rowen tapped the comm on her ear. "Blake, I got him. He's okay. We'll be okay in a sec."

"Good. Everything's quiet out here, so let's not risk it by staying longer than we have to."

"Rowen!" said Gibbs through chattering teeth, trying to stand and falling back down. "Sorry. Too cold."

She was at his side in a heartbeat, shrugging off her coat and wrapping it around his shoulders. "Are you okay?" she asked, helping him up. She flinched when his icy hand touched her shoulder, hating the cold.

He could only nod as they shuffled to the door, shuddering in relief once they were out in the warmth. "I felt them coming," he said, blowing into his hands. "The crystal was pulsing like crazy, and I was about to call you on the comms when those things burst in."

"How did you end up in the fridge?"

"I tried doing what you and your dad taught me, stay calm, aim, and squeeze the trigger. But that only worked for the first one," said Gibbs with a sheepish smile. "After that, I panicked. I was out of ammo by the time the third one came through the door. So I ran."

"Well, you did okay, not the best, but okay," said Rowen, rubbing his shoulder. "I'm just glad—"

"Kid, we got a problem. We need to get moving right now," said Blake in her ear.

Rowen swore under her breath, a million different worries running through her mind. "Do we have hostiles outside?"

"Negative," said Blake through a burst of static. "Your father sent an emergency message. Iron Mountain is under attack."

Hustling Gibbs along, Rowen rushed out into the night, hurrying to the Peri. "That's impossible. The reason the cardinal and his cronies evacuated to that hole in the ground is because it's impenetrable. It's designed to survive nukes for God's sake: have you tried raising them?"

"First thing I did," said Blake. "There's nothing but static, and your dad's message has been on a repeating loop."

Arriving at the small transport, she helped Gibbs settle in the back. "Let me see the message," she said, slipping into the front seat beside Blake, who was keying in the sequence to fire up the engines, the whine of the turbine forcing her to raise her voice.

Blake grunted, cycling through the holographic comm unit, pulling up an image of her father, her lips pressing into a thin line when she saw his flickering image ducking down behind a makeshift barrier, gunfire exploding all around him. "Rowen, if you're getting this, you need to stay the hell away from here. We're under attack. I don't know how they got on base, but some of them look like our own people, so it might be an inside job. Get somewhere safe, and keep your head down. I'll find some—"

The playback went white before he could finish, the hologram sputtering and stalling with data drops before finally vanishing in a burst of static. Rowen sat in silence, grinding her teeth, caressing the grip of her SIG, wanting to shoot something.

"My family has a place in Vermont where we can lie low," squeaked Gibbs from the back seat, his teeth chattering. "Cardinal Washington suspended congress so my dad will be home; he can help us figure out what to do next."

"Screw that!" she said, shrugging off his hand. She turned back to see a hurt look on his face and immediately regretted her outburst. "Sorry. I really am, but there's no way I'm going to Vermont and hide. We can't just abandon them."

Blake scoffed at her. "Just the three of us, kid. Are you nuts?"

"Are you afraid, a coward?" she shot back.

Blake's face went a deep shade of red, like she had slapped him. "I'm not a co—"

"What about you, Gibbs? You wanna run home to Daddy? You know how much he thinks of you. Neither one of you would be here without my father. He kept us all alive when everyone else had abandoned us. We have to at least try: we owe him that much."

Gibbs swallowed, regaining some of his color before giving her a short nod.

"Okay, kid," said Blake with a shrug. "I shoulda been dead years ago, so why the hell not!"

SEVENTEEN
FAMILY

Rowen buried her hands in her uncontrolled bird's nest she called hair, wanting to rip it out in frustration. "Can't this piece of crap fly any faster?"

"We're still an hour out, kid. No sense in getting riled up; it won't do you any good," said Blake over his shoulder from the front seat. Beside her, Gibbs gave her a nervous look, his eyes darting back and forth between her and Blake before he slid away towards the window.

"Don't worry, I'm not going to hit you," she said, knowing why he was shying away from her. "But you're probably better off out of my reach." The back seat of the small transport was far too small for her right now, and Rowen felt like a caged animal. She had spent the better part of an hour trying to raise someone, anyone, back at the base. She gave up a few minutes ago, and her fist still hurt from slamming it against the control panel in frustration.

Supreme Cardinal Washington had bragged often enough that the place was impenetrable; hence, why, after the destruction of DC had he relocated anyone he thought was important to the secure bunker in Western Pennsylvania. He and his cronies spent all their time safe and sound with their bellies full while the rest of the country struggled to get by. Rowen and the rest of the folks from New York were only there because they had provided intel, not to mention that, at first, the cardinal had them on the holo-net every day, touting their escape as a victory, and that they were pushing out the Russian invaders. But after a few news cycles, they were quickly forgotten and left in limbo.

"So, exactly how are we supposed to get back into this place?" said Gibbs, speaking slowly for once. "I mean, if the Russians have taken the base, we can't—"

"You're going to hack into the computer systems," said Rowen, pointing at him. "Didn't you tell me that with the little crystal on your neck that the system was really easy to get into?"

Gibbs scrunched up his face, confusion in his clear blue eyes. "Me? No way, I can't—"

"Yes we can," said Rowen. "The main door has tons of security so it's a no go, but there are launch bays for drones and not to mention the missile silos. Blake and me can cover you while you bypass the security."

"You want to go in through a missile silo! Are you insane?" he said, looking like he wanted to throw up.

"That does sound a little crazy kid," said Blake from the front. "Besides, there ain't much to hack. It's pretty much just a metal cover that opens from the inside. Not to mention they got cameras. They'll see you if you get close to the damn thing."

"Not if you cloak us," she said leaning forward. "I spent months bored out of my mind wandering around the place, there's a network signal, it showed up, even from outside."

Blake pressed his lips together, a frown coming to his handsome face, "Kid, what happened back on the highway was a weird mix of panic and shit luck. My powers, they're pretty much gone. I can't just turn 'em on and off anymore."

"Well, your other option is just to run back and hide," said

Rowen, her freckled face flushing red with anger. "That's what you're good at, aren't you...Finn."

Blake sneered back at her, his nostrils flaring. "You lookin' for another scar on that face of yours, kid? 'Cause that's where you're heading. I got no problem in beatin' some sense into that hard skull of yours."

"I'm not afraid of you or anything else," Rowen shot back, "but there's nothing that's going to stop me from getting onto that base and getting my dad. And if you're not going to give me your all, we can land right now, and you can get out."

"Rowen...please be reasonable," started Gibbs, reaching out.

"No! If we were reasonable, we wouldn't have made it out of New York," she began pointing at Gibbs, then turning her ire to Blake while she continued, "and Blake, if I was reasonable and left you in Winslow, those things would have killed you. Being crazy saved both your asses, so I'm not about to stop now."

Blake gave her a hard look, his brows coming together. He opened his mouth to speak and then snapped it shut, turning his attention back to the controls with a growl. He was quiet for a moment before he continued in a low voice, "That was mean, kid. I'm not a goddamn coward, so don't talk to me like that again, okay?"

Rowen scratched the jagged scar running from the top of her head to her jaw line, trying to keep the guilt from her voice, knowing it would do them no good if she went soft on them now, "When we land I can send up a smart device to scout ahead, at least we'll know what kind of hell we're walking into."

"Can I say something?" said Gibbs, raising his hand like they were in a classroom.

She raised her eyebrows, giving him an expectant look, her mind already turning toward a plan once they were inside the base. The last thing they needed was to get bogged down in a useless firefight. Stealth would be their friend, and luckily for them the base wasn't fully—

"I don't have my tablet; I can't hack anything," said Gibbs in a rush. "The people back in the bar, when I ran out of ammo, I threw it at one of them. It didn't survive."

In the front, Blake let out a throaty laugh, shaking his head, "What kind of idiot throws a tablet, what the hell were you thinking."

Gibbs looked down at his hands sheepishly. "I'm not like you guys; I was scared. Fighting and shooting is not really my thing,"

"Son of a bitch," she muttered under her breath. "Can't you use another tablet? I mean, I have one in my pack."

"It's not like that. My tablet was configured to use the crystal. It had software on it that I designed myself. I can't just pull it out of my butt and make it all work."

Rowen gave him a half smile, blinking at him like he was an idiot, "really, butt. What are you, a nine-year-old?"

"What! I don't like to—"

"Hold on, we got incoming!" said Blake in the front, snapping to attention. The small transport was rocked when a pair of aircraft roared past them, a flash of white-blue thruster exhaust turning the night to day in the blink of an eye.

"Attention, you are entering restricted airspace. Please withdraw, or you will be fired upon," said a voice over the comm system.

"Whoa, whoa!" shouted Blake, his hands furiously tapping on the controls. "We are inbound to Iron Mountain. Check our transponder; that is our base of operations. We got an urgent message, and we're heading back to check it out. We are not hostile. Repeat. We are not hostile."

There was a long pause while a pair of what looked like a pair of narrow fighter jets came up alongside them.

"Oh God, we're gonna die," said Gibbs, pressing his palms and face against the transport window. "Those are FX-35 next generation fighters. My dad was on the committee that approved the budget. They are the air force's first new fighter in thirty years."

The disembodied voice came on the channel once more, "You will disengage and follow us," he ordered.

Rowen climbed over Blake's seat to fall in next to him, snapping her harness into place. Acting quickly she slipped on her tactical goggles and activated the magnification function, scanning for the call sign that was normally on the side of most combat aircraft. She had spent enough time as a military brat to know that every fighter pilot worth their salt had one, a name their buddies gave them. It was always something you didn't like. If you were lucky, it would be inspired by your last name, and if you were really unlucky, from something really stupid you did. "Highball," she called out over the comms, spotting the name on the fuselage just under the cockpit, "My name is Rowen, you don't know me, but my dad is Captain Joshua Macdonald, Special Forces. He led the resistance during the occupation in New York. Two hours ago we received a distress call out of Iron Mountain from him. We are responding."

The line was dead silent, the hollow roar of the fighter jets flying next to them filling the transport cabin. "You think that'll work?" asked Blake.

Rowen shook her head, eyeballing the fighter on their other flank, noting the other pilots call sign, tick-tak. "If it's taking this long, they're calling in to get orders. Normally they would just shoot us down if we didn't do as told. This part of western PA wasn't restricted airspace as of yesterday. Something serious must be going on for them to create a no-fly zone this far out."

The comm chirped as highball came back on. "Ma'am, we are sorry about your father, but Iron Mountain has been on lock down due to an incident, this is hostile airspace, it's not safe. Central Command has ordered that we escort you back to base with us, we'll sort this out when we land."

Rowen opened her mouth to answer when Tick-Tak's FX-35 exploded in a ball of white flame without warning, the shockwave rocking their small transport, forcing Blake to fight against the controls as they went into a flat spin, their world tumbling out of control.

"What the hell was that!" screamed Rowen, bracing with all her strength against the window and Blake's seat beside her to keep herself in place.

"No clue!" shouted Blake over the emergency alarms on the control panels screaming for attention, the muscles on his forearms straining like cords of steel.

"Deploying countermeasures! We've got incoming!" screamed highball over the comms.

The night sky suddenly filled with streaks of dazzling light trailing from the rear of his fighter. A series of short sharp shocks set Rowen's teeth on edge when a wave of hypersonic missiles were drawn off by the chaff, just barely missing them and exploding all around them like fireworks, blossoms of white and yellow filling the night sky.

Rowen cringed when the airframe of the transport groaned in protest when Blake managed to regain control of the small aircraft, sweat dripping from his temples, "We can't stay here kid, those fighters, they have countermeasures, we—Jesus!.." They all were momentarily blinded when another wave of missiles tore through Highball's FX- 35. Rowen swearing when the high-tech fighter disintegrated right before her eyes, bits and pieces of flaming metal falling like burning ash against the dark.

A screaming alarm on the control's pulled her away from the nightmare outside her window just in time to see the color drain from Blake's face. "We're done...they got a lock on one us," he whispered, swallowing.

She cringed, squeezing her eyes shut, waiting for the end, pissed at herself that she just got them all killed, that she could be so stupid to think they could take on this mission on their own. Then to her surprise, they were still alive, and in the distance, she heard the deep thrum of more explosions. Curious, she snuck in a peek, opening a single eye to find the night sky strangely quiet. "What just happened," she whispered, her eyes darting between Blake and Gibbs, both of whom shrugged. Rowen let out a shuddering breath, relief flooding through her when the alarms went off again, screaming in her ear.

"That's another lock," said Blake in a rush, cocking his head, making a confused face seconds later, "and now it's gone. What the hell's going on?" In the distance there were a few blossoms of color against the inky-black sky, and then everything went quiet. They watched and waited in silence for another attack, but when nothing came they all stared at one another in confusion, Rowen burying her face in her hands and scratching at her scalp.

Then out of nowhere, the entire transport lurched, and the engines suddenly protested with a harsh, high-pitched whine, fighting against something they couldn't see. Blake fought the controls for a minute, but when he saw nothing was working he shut them off, giving her a questioning look. In the back-seat Gibbs squealed like a caged animal, and Rowen looked back to see what was wrong with him. The poor man was curled into a ball, paler than normal.

"What?" she asked, hanging over the seat, annoyed with him. She knew him well enough to know he was afraid of his own shadow on most days, and given they had almost been shot down, she wasn't surprised he was like this. "Gibbs, let it go. Everything is going to be fine."

He shook his head when the transport landed with a jarring shock, his mouth opening and closing but nothing coming out while he stared past her.

"Kid, you better look at this," stammered Blake, his voice catching in his throat.

"What the hell is wrong with—," she began, her voice catching in her throat when she saw what Gibbs was pointing at. Rowen' stomach dropped and she was suddenly cold, towering in front of the transport with his arms crossed, still covered in the odd crystal armor was her brother.

EIGHTEEN
CONFESSION

Jonah couldn't help but stare when his sister stepped out of the transport, an odd-looking pistol of some sort leveled at him. He remembered the weapon. It had hurt him, but it had also been his salvation, destroying the crystal covering his face, and along with it, the one used to control his mind. She looked nothing like the girl he remembered. She still had her wild mess of red curls, but her once-freckled face was now a mess of scars big and small. She was dressed in some sort of dark tactical armor, covered by a long duster that ran down past her calves, the holster on her hip looking like it was a part of her.

He could see himself reflected in the mirrored goggles she wore, tall and menacing covered in jagged crystal, and he could only imagine what she thought, given his appearance. He had been just in time to save her and her friends from the missile strike, but he could see that she considered him a threat in how she held the weapon, in how she moved. This wasn't the girl he knew; she was dangerous, and he had to find some way to convince her that he was still himself.

"So, are you gonna say something, or do I have to shoot you again," she said, breaking the silence, a tiny red dot appearing on his chest.

He frowned, just realizing how long he had been staring without saying a word. Cocking his head, he was about to come out and say he was here for her friend, the one with the bright blue eyes, when a memory came to mind. "You still don't have breasts. I thought they would have come in by now," he said in a flat tone that still sounded alien to his ears.

Rowen looked like he'd slapped her, her green eyes going wide at first. Then just like he remembered, she bared her teeth, and she flushed a deep shade of pink. "You son of a bitch. I should've killed you in New York!" she screamed, storming up to him like she always had. She raised a small fist about to punch him in the chest, then just as quickly she stopped, her thin lips pressing together, when she spoke her voice was little more than a whisper. "Is it really you?" she asked, flipping up her tactical goggles, her green eyes the same as his.

He began to nod, to tell her that he was himself when he stopped, wanting to tell her the truth. "Parts of me," he said having a moment of clarity, "are a mix of the old and the new, altogether making someone different...but I still have this strange urge to make fun of you, so I guess that's something."

He watched her eyes narrow in suspicion, and then in a flash she was angry again before a small half smile came to her lips. She took the butt of her gun and used it to punch him in the chest. "You're still an asshole!" she said, turning to the people with her. "Just a much bigger one than I remember. Guys, this is my brother Jonah. Jonah, this is Blake, and the crybaby over there is Scotty Gibbs."

Jonah gave both men a polite nod, frowning when the one named Gibbs broke down and began sobbing.

"Don't worry about him," said Rowen. "He just thought you were gonna kill us all."

"Are you the one who destroyed the fighters?" asked Blake with heat in his voice, accusation on his face.

"No," said Jonah, not bothering to explain more. He didn't like the look the man was giving him. With his salt-and-pepper hair and square jawline, he reminded him of a commander he had had in the air cadets, a bitter man who felt Jonah got special treatment on account his father was a member of Special Forces.

"So, you just showed up by some miracle," said Blake. "Just as a couple of our jets go down."

"Yes. There were missiles. I stopped them," he said, uncrossing his arms and taking a step forward.

Rowen stepped between them, looking like a child, barely reaching his chest. "Let's not get ahead of ourselves," she said. "Jonah, I'm sorry, but you've got a lot to answer for, so don't be surprised that people react like this. And Blake is right: why are you showing up now and not months ago?"

Jonah wasn't sure what to say. He hadn't really planned out anything past finding Gibbs. How could he explain his situation, and even if he did, he was sure this Gibbs fellow wouldn't simply hand over the crystal to him. He had seen enough to know that taking off a crystal for most people meant death—a very painful death. "I am alone," he said at last, thinking he had time, not much, but enough that he could speak to his sister when they were alone, make her understand.

"What happened, the Russians throw you out?" said Blake with a sneer.

"No, the carrier group was destroyed. Every last boat now sits at the bottom of the Atlantic."

"How...did you do it, Jonah?" asked Rowen, caressing the butt of the pistol in her holster.

"No, there was a man—one man."

Blake rolled his eyes, a frown coming to his face. "Don't bullshit us; that's not really possible."

Gibbs stepped forward, touching the crystal on his neck and then pointing at Jonah's chest. "He did. Your brother there wiped out the entire Eleventh Fleet at Norfolk in a single afternoon. What did this man look like?"

"I only caught the last bit of the attack," said Jonah, focusing his attention on Rowen, not really caring for the other men, "and even then, I was hurt and only saw him in the distance. He was a tall man, dark skinned, dressed in crimson."

"How the hell did he manage to destroy an entire fleet?"

"I don't know. He had abilities, powers, like nothing I'd seen before."

"Was it one of the people from New York from that day in the park?" asked Rowen, Jonah wincing when she scratched at a jagged scar that ran from the top of her head to her chin.

"No, none of them. No, he had a yellow glow, with wings that looked like they were made of light, and he had a—"

"A sword? A flaming sword?" said Blake interrupting, his deep voice hitching up an octave.

"Yes," said Jonah. "How would you know this?"

Blake shook his head, starting to pace. "Because now we're really screwed. All those months at Iron Mountain, and he didn't recognize me. I thought his powers had faded just like mine," said Blake, mumbling to himself, "but no. If he's figured out a way—"

"Figured out what?" asked Rowen. "Who the hell are you talking about?"

"Michael!" said Blake. "He was one of the first test subjects that survived the Ascension program. He's very powerful and very dangerous."

"I don't understand. Who the hell is Michael, and why haven't we heard of him before?" asked Gibbs.

"Supreme Cardinal Washington, the man in charge of the goddamn country. He was once the team leader, in charge of the Ascension project, but I thought what happened to me happened to him, that his powers faded years ago. But if he's anything like he was in his prime, there's no way we can stop him."

Gibbs stood up finally coming back to himself. "What's so special about him? I've hacked into most of the reports from the early days."

Rowen suddenly punched Gibbs on the arm, giving him a half smile. "You hacked into government files? Really, why?"

"I was bored," said Gibbs, rubbing where she had punched him.

"They were interesting, but almost none of them mention Michael. But he can't be any worse than that Gwen chick from last year. I mean, she blew up a city."

"Michael's strength isn't brute force," said Blake. "It's his mind. He can make anything he can think of: the only limit is his imagination and his will."

Rowen was suddenly between all of them, waving them to silence. "None of this really matters right now. Jonah, I'm really glad you're okay, and Blake, we can deal with Cardinal Washington later. Right now we have to get to my dad, and that means finding away into Iron Mountain."

Jonah's breath caught in his throat. He hadn't thought about his father in a long time. He hadn't seen him since the first day of the attack in New York. The last time they were all together. In fact until this moment, he had no clue if he was still alive or dead. He only knew that no one had come looking for him. "What's going on with da—with, with him?" he asked, choking back the bitterness he felt.

"We received an emergency message from him a few hours ago," said Rowen. "The base was under attack. He was sure that some of the invaders were their own people. Since then, only silence."

"You could help us," said Gibbs. "I mean, with what you—"

"No way!" said Blake. "This isn't some cheesy holovid; this is real life, and this bastard destroyed two entire carrier groups, killed thousands of sailors. I watched that massacre a couple of times. He threw helpless men and women up in the air as a distraction! And now you want him to join us like nothing happened?"

"Blake, he was being controlled; it's not his—" started Rowen.

"Blake is right. I did all those things," began Jonah, "and I was in control of my mind when I did. It's war, and we're on different sides."

"You're a goddamn traitor," spat Blake, sticking out his chin.

Ignoring Blake, Jonah continued as if he hadn't spoken. "But right now, the Russian fleet that I was serving is gone, sitting at the bottom of the Atlantic, and I am in a position to help you, if you are willing to help me."

Rowen put out a hand to silence Blake before he could speak, walking right up to Jonah's chest and craning her neck to look him in the eye. "What is it you want?"

He stepped back from her, despite her small size somehow feeling pressured when she was in his personal space. He was conflicted by not wanting to show any sign of weakness and still needing some kind of help. "I'm having problems, and I need him to help me," Jonah said, pointing at Gibbs.

Gibbs paled, looking like someone had just pulled a chair out from under him. "Me! Why me? I don't know anything."

"You carry crystals, like mine...on your neck, on your chest. The doctor who took care of me is dead; you are my best hope."

"Best hope for what?" asked Rowen.

Jonah looked away, his face growing red when he realized he'd said too much. It would be too hard to explain it all.

Jonah smiled to himself when Rowen scrubbed a hand through her tangled mess of red hair. She always did that when she was annoyed or frustrated. And worse, Jonah knew how much she hated her hair; she hated lots of things about herself, and had, since she could recognize herself in a mirror, he never understood it, her insecurity. To him, despite being a brat of a sister, he always found she had the best of her parents. Their father's bold nose, their mother's beautiful red hair. She was cute in the way that mattered, or at least his friends had told him so. With a sigh, she tilted her head, giving him a stern look, "Jonah, if we can help each other here, we will, but like mom used to say, 'If you don't trust, you don't win.'"

"You're still annoying," he said, nodding agreement and then looking to the others. "I have a few weeks at best before my mind starts to degenerate again, and with no more Russian control, I won't be much more than a wild animal, a—"

"A powerful wild animal," said Rowen, finishing his line of thought. "You could do a lot of damage if you're not controlled."

"Yes," he grunted, not wanting to think too much about what would happen when he lost control.

His sister squeezed her eyes shut, her freckled face scrunching up in thought. After a minute, she shrugged. "You help me get Dad, Gibbs here will try and make sure you don't go nuts...but I need your word, understood?"

Blake put a hand on Rowen's shoulder, pressing his lips together. "Kid, please, this thing may look like your brother, but we have no way of knowing if he's not just some Russian dupe."

"Rowen, I have no clue how to help him. I'm no expert," said Gibbs in a rush at the same time.

"Gibbs, you're the smartest person I know, and don't think that I don't know that the crystal on your neck is making you smarter every day. But as far as my brother is concerned, I know who he is!" she said, stretching her arms out. "And if he can help us on the mission, I don't really care what he's done. Once we get my dad, I'll let him decide what to do with him. Right now, we're running out of time, so unless you have something to contribute to the mission, then shut the hell up!"

Jonah kept his face still, but part of him was impressed by how in control she was of the situation, amazed that they all deferred to her. "We have a deal, then?"

Rowen nodded, heading back toward the transport, "All right, let's go blow up this shithole. Jonah, you're on point, and God help anyone who gets in our way."

NINETEEN

ON THE BRINK

Arthur slumped down on the hard metal bench, his bones aching with exhaustion. Drawing in a deep breath, he tried to block out the wailing sirens, the shouts, the screams, if only for a minute. He had fled into the mobile command center for a brief respite, but with the holographic data streams buzzing all around him, the police over-watch speaking in hurried tones ordering officers from one nightmare to the next, the place was a harsh reminder of his failures.

"We can't keep this up," said Gwen, falling in beside him with a groan. She looked like he felt, worse for wear and downright filthy, her short bob of blond was streaked with gray soot, and the once-pristine white coat he had given her was stained black and gray with sprays of red. Blood from someone, hopefully not hers, and hopefully they survived.

"We have to," said Arthur, bowing his head. "I don't think we have a choice. It's this or lose the city."

Gwen took him by the shoulder, forcing him to look at her. "Listen, we're fucked! This city is fucked. I know it; Cardinal Washington knows it. The only person who doesn't know it is you. We lost the day he broke all of the infected out of the hospital; everything else is just...bullshit."

Arthur brushed her hand off his shoulder and stood, locking his arms behind his back. "I made a promise to those people out there," he said, pointing at the open door of the van with his chin. "I told them I would keep them safe if they came here. That I would do a better job than the country that abandoned them when the Russians invaded. I don't care what it costs me. I'm keeping my word, no matter what."

"Goddamn, you're stubborn," she said under her breath.

"Me! You're calling me stubborn!" he said, raising an eyebrow at her.

"You're damn right I am. At least I know when to throw in the towel. Look at you. You haven't slept for days, and you smell really bad! To make matters worse, every time we think we have this under control and create a safe zone, we miss one or two of the infected, and eventually the freaking cycle starts all over again. Even with emergency services working round the clock, we can't keep up."

Arthur balled his fists with all his strength, stifling a wince from the pain. The pain was good; it gave him focus. Because if he was honest with himself, he wanted to do exactly what she said, throw in the towel; call it a day, but he couldn't let that monster win. "Cardinal Washington will not take my city. I'd rather see it burn than give him the victory," he said through clenched teeth. "I guess I'm not going to get any rest, so let's get back to it." Stifling his anger, he turned his back on her, leaving the police van before he said something they both would regret.

The command vehicle had been noisy, but outside, the streets of the Upper West Side were pure chaos, a symphony of violence, weapons fire echoing in the distance as the police did their best to keep the infected population at bay. Emergency services had managed to isolate parts of the city, setting up safe zones that were relatively free of the infected while they did sweeps to eliminate anyone showing late-stage symptoms, lethargy, the strange eyes, not to mention, of course, the odd-printed circuit patterns on the skin that were easy to spot in the latter stages. Arthur had been forced to do triple duty, not only fighting at the barricades they had set up, but with his abilities, he could spot the early stages of the infection, and in some cases remove it. But it was taxing and given the rate the infection was spreading, he simply couldn't keep up.

Arthur approached the checkpoint commander, a young woman with curly blond hair and bright green eyes named Sarah. They had met a lifetime ago at the refugee camp on Long Island. He had promised her if she survived long enough, that she could go home, that New York would be a safe place free of all the bullshit. Not long after he had freed the city, she had found him and was grateful that he kept his word.

"They're massing for another push, not sure if they're refugees looking for a safe spot," said Sarah, eyeing a group of people farther down the avenue, "or infected about to charge the checkpoint."

Arthur grunted in agreement, too tired to talk. He had assigned her to police services because she was quick and didn't miss much, and she had proven herself almost immediately, moving up in the ranks quickly. Most of the young people who had come in the early days were. They were people who didn't quit, survivors who took whatever life threw at them and came out better for it. He took a moment to shift his vision, cursing under his breath when he saw that the people massing were too far gone for him to help, fully converted from flesh and blood to the strange metal filament that filled the infected bodies.

"Looks like it's gonna be a fight," said Sarah, seeing the look on his face. She unclipped the magazine barrel on the auto shotgun she carried and then signaled to everyone else at the checkpoint to be ready.

Arthur did the same. Reaching out with his power, he activated the supply of "hornet" drones that were in the mobile command center. He had found the little drones among the Russian supply caches, and they had proven themselves more than useful in the last few days. They were only about the size of his palm, but they packed a deadly punch, flying about like true hornets but with four tiny propellers that allowed them to do precision maneuvers and get in close to a target. At the heart of the little machines was a small amount of C4 plastique that would explode on contact, instantly killing the victim by tearing a hole in their skull. He had first seen them in action the day he met Rowen and her father. They had devastated the bunker set up in New York's ancient subway system, killing hundreds without mercy. He had promised he would never use such a weapon, but given how difficult it was to stop some of the infected, he made an exception. He was able to control a few dozen at time if he stayed close enough, so he used them defensively to protect the men and women working the barricades, not to mention himself.

Satisfied that the smaller drones were on standby, he shunted his consciousness through an augmented communication hub on his wrist, riding the signal wave to the amplifier he had in his lab at The Rockefeller University, making contact with a squadron of Apex drones that he had on automated patrol. With Arthur's mind embedded into the machines circuitry they became like an extension of his body. He could feel the wind riding over the ultralight carbon fiber of his wings, the pulse-pounding thrust of their turbine felt like the beating of his heart, and the minigun cannon at the tip, his rage. An instant later, he was adjusted to the new sensations, returning his attention to the threat at hand.

Scanning the size of the incoming wave of infected, Arthur put a hand to his ear, activating his comm. "Gwen, we got another group amassing. We probably won't need you, but be ready."

There was silence on the line, and he was about to repeat himself when his earpiece chirped. "Yeah, yeah, no biggie, I'm here," she said with annoyance in her voice.

Wanting this to be over quickly and efficiently, Arthur broke one of the Apex drones away from its patrol route, the narrow craft plummeting down to ground level at the speed of thought. Pushing his tired mind, he flew down the avenue, the turret spinning faster than the eye could see and unleashed a torrent of destruction on the wave of infected just as they began to run for the barrier, the .50 caliber ammo tearing deep chunks off of the infected, ripping off limbs, and removing heads from bodies.

"My God," whispered Sarah, crossing herself then quickly bowing her head. "Sorry, I don't think I'll ever get used to that."

Arthur rubbed the tiredness from his eyes, giving her a tight-lipped smile. "I know. These were our friends, our neighbors, but they were already long gone by the time the bullets stopped them from moving," said Arthur, sending the drone back up to patrol. "That's why it's important that we stop this infection here and now."

"I know," she said, nodding to herself. "I think we can handle it from here. Why don't you go back to resting? You look exhausted."

Raising his chin, Arthur gave the commander an awkward pat on the shoulder and turned to leave when a panicked voice screamed on the comm system. "Holy shit! On the GW, thousands of them!"

The panic in the nameless voice drove Arthur to hurry back into the mobile command center, sweeping past a startled Gwen in a rush. He ignored the frantic looks from the operators and tore into the computer systems, his mind plumbing the network's depths faster than any words could explain to find the source of the message. "Holy shit," he muttered, shifting immediately over to the holo images of the massive double-decked suspension bridge that was the George Washington. A chill went down his spine when he saw the thousands of infected streaming across the span from New Jersey, surging over cars, trampling anyone who was in their way without a shred of mercy. "Gwen, I need you; we gotta go!"

Gwen was on her feet, and they were out the back of the command center in a heartbeat, Arthur quickly reaching out to every Apex drone he could control, the effort pushing him past his already taxed limits.

"You don't look so good," said Gwen, when he grabbed her arm to stop himself from falling.

He held on to Gwen for dear life while the world around him

spun like a top, his stomach wanting to heave. "I'll be fine. Just get us to the bridge, please. I'll have a swarm of drones waiting for us there to stop this incursion."

"Ohh, incursion, fancy word," said Gwen with a half-smile, "Sometimes I think you just want to impress me with your vocabulary."

"Is it working?" said Arthur, putting an arm around her shoulder.

"Hold on tight, and just watch where you put your hands. I know how much you wanna cop a feel," she said, slipping in her earbuds, swaying to whatever crazy song helped her fly. Arthur did as he was told, enjoying her warmth, the smell of the rosewood perfume she always wore, even if it was mixed with days-old sweat. He blinked, and his world suddenly shifted. One moment he was on the ground with blaring sirens and gunfire in his ears, and the next he was high above the Manhattan skyline, cool air filling his nostrils. He had almost forgotten the sound of silence, a world quiet, with only the roar of the wind in his ears. They flew for less than a minute before he saw the George Washington Bridge in the distance, the double-decker roadway was packed with a stampede of human animals racing across its width, with thousands more clambering over another at the entrance from the Jersey side, hungry to spread the infection.

Gwen landed on top of the tower just before the New York side, letting out a low whistle. "Can you stop that many?" she asked, slipping off her earbuds and keeping a strong hand on him to keep him from flying away in the strong winds that buffeted them at this height.

"I don't know," he said, sending his mind to every Apex drone he had circling the city. "I don't think I have enough ammo to stop that many." Pushing through the tiredness behind his eyes, Arthur raised a hand to bring the deadly machines to him when the world went spinning out of control again, and the contents of his stomach, mostly bile and water coming, spilled onto the bridge tower platform.

"Easy," said Gwen in a soft voice, letting him down gently so he could sit. "If we were out partying, I would say it's time to call it a night, get in a cab, and head home, but you're the type of bitch who would keep going until you passed out in the gutter, aren't you?"

Arthur wiped a hand on his sleeve, blinking slowly. He fought the urge to lie down and press his cheek on the cold metal. "We can't let that many get in. We're done if we do. I have to stop them."

Gwen cursed at the infected surging past them down below, with a grim look on her face. Without a word, she gripped him by the collar and lifted him to his feet. "You, my little nutjob, aren't doing a fucking thing," she said with an air of finality. She took to the air, more like a jump than actually flying, dumping him like a sack of garbage on a low-rise rooftop near the exit to the bridge. "You just sit here and look pretty, and I'll take care of this shit."

"What the hell is she doing?" muttered Arthur, feeling powerless when she took to the air, part of him worried that she was about to fly off and leave him. He staggered to his feet to get a better look while she circled the superstructure, flying over and under and between both levels. Finally, just when the bulk of the infected reached the center, she landed to face them, spreading her arms wide. He watched in awe as she brought her hands together in a mighty clap, wincing when he heard the sharp implosion of air, his jaw falling open when a massive shockwave rippled through the bridge as if it were a mirage, expanding with enough speed and force to blast him onto his back even from this distance. He sat up to see the center of the superstructure disintegrating, massive chunks of steel and stone falling like an avalanche of hail into the Hudson River.

His shoulders slumped in relief when Gwen emerged from the chaos unharmed, her long white coat fluttering behind her as she flew out of the mess she had created before finally skidding to a rough landing beside him. "You can dock my pay for the bridge," she said, looking at him with a sheepish grin.

Shaking his head in disbelief at the destruction, he wanted to be mad at her, and he should have been. Rebuilding that bridge would be a monumental task, but he could only imagine what would have happened if all of those infected got through, there would be no city left to defend. She had just saved their asses, bought them time to rest and recover. He was about to make a terrible joke when a dark thought came to mind. "Do you think this has spread across the country?" he said, looking out at the bodies floating in the river. "I mean, would he be crazy enough to infect the entire country?"

"He would have to be insane," she whispered, her smile fading.

"Dr. Fillipo said the Unity was coming," said Arthur. "What if he meant this—all of those minds, working as one, enslaved. What if the voice in his head was Cardinal Washington?"

Gwen bit her bottom lip, following his gaze out over the Hudson. "If that's the case, it means he doesn't care what he has to do to win, and he is willing to sacrifice every man, woman, and child to get what he wants. So God help us, because now I know for sure...we're totally fucked!"

TWENTY

THE WALLS OF BABYLON

Iron Mountain was designed to be an impenetrable fortress, to remain a fully functional seat of government even during the event of an all-out nuclear attack. A full frontal assault would have been useless, so it had been Rowen's plan to sneak inside, be subtle and stealthy. But with Jonah on their side, none of that was needed, but even knowing what to expect, Rowen swore under her breath in amazement when her brother tore through its massive steel gates with the force of an exploding volcano, leaving a gaping maw in his wake.

"We head straight for Captain Young's lab," said Rowen, leaping from the transport, activating a half-dozen smart devices that transmitted back to her tactical goggles, and sent them racing ahead. "All of the equipment we need for Gibbs to get into their system is there, and hopefully we can find out what the hell is going on. Then we get my dad and we get out. Got it?"

Both Gibbs and Blake said nothing, only staring past her at the spectacle of Jonah tearing apart the soldiers who responded to his incursion. "Focus, guys!" she said, snapping her fingers. "He's doing his job, so we can do ours. Let everyone shoot at him, not us. Move!"

Gibbs gave her a nervous smile, bobbing his head while he and

Blake fell in behind her. Rowen moved past the gaping doors with her SIG II in hand, entering a rough-hewn corridor that branched out in multiple directions, stopping at the first intersection just past the entry checkpoint, scanning for threats with the feed sent to her goggles from the smart devices deeper in the complex. The corridor leading to the western part of the facility was filled with screams, smoke, and death as Jonah ripped through the converted soldiers who stood in his way, their silver-spun innards spilling from severed limbs and covering the floors.

"This way," she said, heading off in the other direction, seeing the way was clear. Rowen hated everything about this place, from the rough-hewn walls, the cold lighting that barely pressed back the darkness, to the polished tile that stood in stark contrast to the rest of the place. They raced through the empty maze of corridors in silence, stopping only to get their bearings every now and then.

The Iron Mountain complex was originally a limestone mine, filled with tunnels that circled back to one another or some that simply went nowhere. Decades later when it had been converted to be a government bunker for high-level members of state and their families, the designers had used the chaotic layout to their advantage, keeping the maze in place in hopes that if for some reason an enemy breached its gates, the confusing tunnels would slow them down.

Luckily, because of an awful combination of time and boredom, she knew her way around. Coming to a familiar corridor, she raised a hand suddenly, stopping just before the end of a corridor. Catching movement up ahead from one of her smart devices, she ordered it to stop and move out of sight, not wanting to lose the element of surprise. From the images, she could see this part of the base looked like it had been through hell, with portions of the rough limestone walls chipped way by gunfire, some of the bullets still embedded into the stone, and not far past the turn in the corridor, a number of the overhead lights had been shot out, leaving the area in darkness.

"Oh good, we get to go through the creepy base with the lights out," said Gibbs, leaning in behind her, so close she could feel his breath on her neck.

Shoving him back, she raised her goggles to give him a stern look. "You two stay here for a minute. Blake, take the rear, and make sure Gibbs here doesn't do anything stupid."

"Really, you want me on babysitting duty?" he rasped, his deep voice echoing off the walls.

"Yeah...you're not in any shape to fight with that ankle, anyway. I just want to make sure we're not walking into an ambush. I spotted some weird movement up ahead from one of my smart devices."

Leaving the two of them behind grumbling at one another, Rowen cycled through to the night-vision settings on her goggles, transforming the gloom of the corridor to a sickly shade of green. Making her way to Captain Young's lab, it was clear that there had been a hell of a firefight, and she had to step cautiously around pools of sticky blood while doing her best to avoid the shell casings that scattered across the tiles. Finally coming to one of the many intersections, she found what had caught her attention on the feed from her smart device: a single leg sticking out from around a corner, still twitching.

Coming closer, she plucked the smart device from the air and crouched in low beside the twitching foot, angling the device's camera from the floor to get a view down the corridor without being seen herself. The hall was a house of horrors, with blackened bodies lining soot-stained walls, twisted and broken into shapes that would give Rowen nightmares later. The leg that was still twitching belonged to one of the base's soldiers; part of him was still flesh and blood while the connection to his leg was made up of ultra-thin filament that glowed brightly in low light, like waves of energy were rolling off the strange material.

Tilting the camera, Rowen found the source of the buzzing and was forced to return her vision settings to normal or be blinded. Standing motionless in front of a blazing laser barrier was a small battalion of men simply waiting, for what she couldn't imagine.

Magnifying the feed to get a better look, Rowen felt suddenly cold. Each one of them had the odd circuitlike pattern on their faces that she had first seen back in Winslow, meaning that the virus was here in full force.

Rowen rested her forehead against the cool stone of the wall, pounding on the unyielding stone with her fists. If these men were here, like this, that meant her father was like them now, some mindless machine with dead eyes staring off into the void. And if what Blake said was true, she was probably infected, Gibbs too, and had at best anywhere from a few hours to a few days before symptoms started to show...not that it mattered much if the whole world was like this.

She was about to creep back to Blake and Gibbs, tell them that it was over, that they should find a quiet place to put a bullet in their heads when the humming suddenly stopped. Rowen peeked around the corner to see the laser barrier gone, the soldiers shuffling forward. She ducked back for cover when she heard the booming crack of gunfire from a heavy pistol of some kind. Realizing that someone was still holding out, her pulse quickened. In a single breath she drew her SIG II and reactivated the smart device she had turned off, tossing it around the corner to line up her shots. Rowen counted off, slipping around the corner when she heard the familiar hollow click of an empty magazine. Controlling her breath, Rowen's world seemed to move in slow motion as she leaned out from cover, an electric thrill coursing through her with every squeeze of the trigger. The men surging forward barely had time to register that they had been shot in the back of the head, falling forward like blades of grass in the wind, heads snapping forward with enough force that they bounced when they hit the polished tile.

Ducking back, she sent her smart device down the tunnel to make sure the way was clear, and if she was lucky, to see who was still holding out. She was just able to make out a large shadow when another booming shot echoed down the hall, the feed she was using fading to static. A smile creased Rowen's face when she thought for a minute that it might be her father, knowing that the converted didn't use weapons, and taking out a small flying device in the dark wasn't a shot that most could make. Her hopes were dashed when another boom almost deafened her, and the wall next to her exploded, dust and shrapnel stinging her face.

"That one was a warnin'," said a familiar voice. "I'm a goddamn surgeon with this thing, so don't think ya'll can get the jump on me."

"Captain Young! It's Rowen," she shouted, her breath catching in her throat. "I'm here with—"

"Rowen? You infected! Be honest. I'll know if your lyin', girl," he accused in his Kentucky twang.

"No!" she said automatically then knowing the captain, she took a deep breath to calm herself and answered more slowly, "Yes—but not that far along. I'm still me, I swear."

The corridor was dead silent for a few moments, and Rowen thought he had retreated back to where he'd come from when he shouted down the hall, "Well, these things ain't got shit for brains, can't use weapons, an' I reckon the way you shot 'em all in the head like you did, that you're still you, for the most part. So, why don't you come out nice and slow with your hands up."

Rowen was about to step out when she had a moment of doubt. "How do I know you're you!" she said, gripping her SIG tightly in both hands. "You're in a base full of these things; why aren't you converted, I mean infected, or whatever we're calling them."

"I guess the only way you'd know I'm me is 'cause of my charmin personality," he said with a sigh. "As to why I ain't one of these things, I got a couple of ideas on that, an' I'd love to share 'em with ya. But nothin's goin' on till you come out."

"What's life without risk?" Rowen muttered to herself as she put her hands up and stepped out from behind the wall. Down the darkened corridor she could make out the captain's familiar bulk and too tight uniform, but she was surprised to see how well he carried himself with a weapon in his hand, recognizing his sidearm. "That's a Desert Eagle, isn't it? Not an easy weapon to be that precise with, and here I was thinking that you didn't know how to shoot."

Captain Young cocked his head, giving her a hard look before sliding the weapon back into a holster that looked out of place on his hip. "Yup, that's the mouthy girl I know," he said with a half grin. "The gun belonged to my daddy, first weapon I ever fired. Anyhow, I'm glad you still got your wits about you; not sure why you came back here though; this place was one of the first places to start to go to hell."

"We got a distress call from my dad; we came back for him."

"We?"

"Yes sir. I have Gibbs and Blake here with me. We were on a mission to— It doesn't matter. Where's my dad?"

The captain looked down at his feet, waving for her to follow him. "Your father's back in the lab. I'll take you to him once we're done here," he began, pulling out a long, thin canister from the pack he was carrying before continuing in his slow drawl. "Gibbs might be useful if he don't run his mouth too much, but I don't really remember the other fella. In any case, you better get 'em down here. We gotta short window till more of 'em show up, and I still gotta swap out the battery pack for the gate."

Rowen put a hand to the comm in her ear, ordering the two men to get a move on, and at the same time she set her smart devices to patrol the area. "We have someone else with us too," she began in worried tones, not sure what the captain would think, "and from the feed I'm getting from a smart device following him, he's wreaking havoc with the infected, keeping them occupied."

"Hold up, right here," said Captain Young, pointing at the floor behind him. With a grunt, he bent down to open a panel on the laser gate, straining red faced to pull out a battery of some kind embedded in the guts of the wall. Finally getting at it, he swapped out an empty canister for a full one, with a piggish grunt. "There, that should do it, should keep those things off our backs for a few hours, at least. So, who is it that you got with you that's makin' a right mess? We don't got no more Ascended, aside from that Arthur kid, and from what you done told me, he ain't the friendliest."

"My brother, sir: Jonah."

Young looked up at her, unblinking, his face flushing to a deeper shade of red than normal. "Are you outta your goddamn mind?" he said, bracing himself against the wall to stand and breathing like he had just run a race. "That sumbitch is a traitor, responsible for God knows how many sailors never comin' home. You should be puttin' a bullet in his head if ya still got any sense left in that head of yours."

Rowen balled her hands, her nostrils flaring. "I didn't really have a wide range of allies to pick from; I worked with what I had. Not all of us can sit behind laser gates to keep us safe while the world falls apart."

"Ya'll think this has been a picnic for me here, sittin' and waitin' for—" he began before stopping suddenly, his eyes darting over her shoulder. "Evening, boys." Rowen followed his gaze to find Gibbs and Blake arriving with perfect timing as always.

"While what?"

"Nothin', don't matter, anyhow," said Captain Young, turning away. "Walk where I walk if you wanna keep your toes. I got micro explosives on some of the tiles."

Gibbs was about to speak when Rowen silenced him with a look, and Blake was wise enough to read the situation and stayed silent. "He has my dad; let's not piss him off too much, so we can get the hell out of here while we still have time."

Rowen held her tongue while they followed Captain Young through his maze of booby-trapped corridors, her palms sweating more and more as they got closer to the lab. Without thinking, she caressed the grip of her SIG, comforted by the weapon's weight on her hip. When they reached the familiar corridor, she knew well enough from her visits with Gibbs, she slowed and whispered over her shoulder, "Be ready; something's not right."

"Are you sure?" said Gibbs, his eyes widening with a worried look.

"Your call, kid," said Blake with a shrug. "Never liked the fat bastard, anyway."

Rowen tightened the grip on her pistol when Captain Young punched in his code on the key pad to open the lab door, her gut churning with worry as the metal panel slid open with a loud hiss. With the door opened, Rowen shouldered past the captain, her head on a swivel while she scanned for threats. Behind her, Blake smoothly extended his katana with a rasp, pressing the tip of the blade against the big man's throat. Gibbs fumbled in behind him with an apology on his lips, rushing to the tiny corner of the section of the lab that was his.

"What in Sam Hill do you think you're doin', girl?" said Captain Young, his jowls quivering.

Ignoring him, Rowen switched to night-vision mode, gasping at the condition of the normally tidy lab. The control panels and holographic projectors were a mess, like someone had taken a hammer to them. Even the desks and workstations that were normally clear were covered in clutter, not to mention that it looked like every secure drawer had been pilfered, standing wide open. "Dad," she called out, scanning behind each long counter she passed, worry creasing her face. Finding nothing, she holstered her SIG, storming back to the entry where Blake had his blade to the captain's throat.

"Where the hell is he?" she said through gritted teeth. "What did you do to him!"

Captain Young blew out his round cheeks, shaking his head. "Nothin', I kept him safe."

"Then where is he?" said Rowen, throwing up her hands while pacing in front of him. "I know you're up to something: I can feel it."

"You got good instincts, girl, I'll give you that, but your daddy shoulda put you over his knee more often. Ya got no respect for your elders."

Rowen's SIG found its way to her hand once more, and without missing a beat, she shoved the weapon in his face, fighting hard not to empty the clip into his head. "And my good instincts are telling me I should blow your head off!"

"Rowen...you should come see this," said Gibbs from the back of the lab, speaking slower than normal.

"You should do what the boy says, Rowen," said the captain. Bowing his head, he continued, his voice barely a whisper, his eyes bright with tears. "I tried to do right by him, I swear. But I couldn't. I just couldn't."

Shoving him back to the wall, Rowen put her back to him, hurrying to where Gibbs was standing at the back of the lab in a corner tucked away out of sight. When she came up beside him, her breath caught in her throat, and she had to fight to keep her stomach from spilling. There, behind some sort of restraining field was her father. His eyes were a dull silver, his skin covered in the telltale circuit board look she was beginning to know so well. They were too late, far too late, for him and probably for everyone else.

TWENTY-ONE

CRAZY TRAIN

"I'm goin' off the rails on a crazy train," shouted Gwen, doing her best to imitate Ozzy Osbourne's high-pitched nasal whine while bolting through the smoke-filled sky, relishing in the electric thrill running through her. Gwen knew that Ozzy, the prince of darkness himself, had made amazing music well into his late nineties, and had only passed on some time in the early twenty fifties, but something about his early songs made her feel more alive than any drug she had ever taken and was one of the few things that had kept her sane through the nightmare she was living in right now.

Flying through the burning haze, she thundered past an emergency checkpoint, aiming for a group of charging infected that threatened to overwhelm it.

"Pull your people back!" she screamed over the comms, seconds before slamming into the pavement at maximum speed, the concussive force of her impact creating a shockwave that slammed back the oncoming infected like they were bowling pins. For a normal human being, the blast would have been enough to stop them in their tracks, the physical shock killing them. But the infected were not human anymore, not even close. Bounding to her feet, Gwen waited while

they regrouped, her once white leather coat, now mostly gray, fluttering on the wind. She had hurt them; she was their target now. It
was easier this way to let them come to her. She had to conserve her
strength while Arthur and Rodrigo had time to rest and could relieve
her. They no longer had the luxury of fighting together, and it was
decided that she would be on her own simply because she could
travel faster.

They came at her now, with their dead silver eyes and strange
skin, hands extended to rend and tear at her flesh in an attempt to
spread the virus. Their strength was unnatural, much more than any
normal human, but then again, nothing about them was natural, or
human. She waited until the last possible second, wanting to get as
many of them as she could. When they were almost on top of her, she
slammed her palms together with enough force that the implosion lit
the air on fire, her shockwave shattering bone and metal with equal
efficiency, consuming everything in its path.

A split second later, she stood alone over a burned-out crater, bits
and pieces of the strange filament that made up the insides of the
infected floating on the air. The first time she had used this power,
she hadn't been in control, and an entire city had died. For a long
time she had been terrified to even attempt it again, not wanting to
hurt anyone ever again. But these were fucked-up days, and desperation was a good teacher. She had learned control. In the last few days
it had been their saving grace, giving them enough time and space to
clear out what seemed like infinite waves of the creatures that were
heading en masse to New York. A few days ago, in what had been a
stroke of luck that they had managed to stop the wave of infected
from coming across the George Washington Bridge, and since then
Arthur had ordered her to destroy every bridge and tunnel that led on
or off Manhattan Island. Now they only had to deal with the infected
that were already in the city.

The men and women manning the barricade she had just
protected, gave her a grateful wave, and Gwen took a moment with
the commander, a girl Arthur spoke highly of, Sarah.

"Has it slowed down any?" she asked, striding up to the barricade, coughing from all the smoke.

Sarah hefted a shotgun of some kind over her shoulder, rubbing her eyes. "A little," she said, eyeing Gwen up and down.

"That's a big-assed gun," said Gwen, rolling her shoulders, her fatigue making everything sore.

Sarah gave the weapon a smile, leaning her head against the circular magazine. "I didn't like guns before...back before the start of the war, before the country went to hell, and I was living in one of those camps," she said, biting her lip. "Now, I can't go to sleep unless it's in the same room."

"I get it," said Gwen, nodding along. "We've all had to live through some fucked-up shit in the last few years. You'd think we deserve a break, but no, now we got this nightmare."

Sarah rubbed her eyes again, blowing out a slow breath. "Yeah, I'm so tired of it all. I just wish I could close my eyes and sleep."

Gwen nodded feeling the same way. "In the old days, I would have just dropped a few hits of what I could grab, gotten high, and said fuck the world, but now...man, it sucks to give a shit."

"You should go," whispered Sarah, squeezing her eyes shut, scratching at her neck and swaying in place.

"Are you okay?" said Gwen, laying a hand on Sarah's shoulder to steady her.

"I don't know, I just—" Without warning, Sarah shoved her back, leveling the shotgun at her. "Just leave!"

Gwen blinked in confusion, not understanding what was going on until she saw something moving under Sarah's skin, like a worm boring through the flesh. "You're infected," she said, backing away, swearing under her breath.

"I know," said Sarah, her green eyes starting to fade. "I've known for a while. I could feel it, but I just didn't want it to be real."

"We can help you!" said Gwen quickly, stepping forward. "Arthur has a lab at The Rockefeller University: we can isolate you until we figure this shit out."

"I've seen enough to know there's no figuring this shit out," said Sarah, the strange lines that looked like circuitry creeping across her face, growing under her skin.

"We can! Arthur's a smart little bastard. He fixed my lungs when I couldn't breathe. I promise he can fix you."

"No! There's no fixing; it's deep in me now, and I've killed enough of them to know what happens." Without warning, Sarah pulled the trigger, the autoshot gun booming, cutting through the chaotic din of sirens and gunshots in the distance, the heavy impact from the weapon forcing Gwen back, the heavy shells stinging a little.

Staggering forward with her hand outstretched, the reality of the last few days hit home for Gwen at that moment. Sarah wasn't some faceless jerk she could make go away with a clap of her hands. They knew her, knew her mom lived in Queens and cleaned apartments for a living. They knew she was a good person who had been abused in the camps because she was pretty and had nice tits: she was real. "Please, let me—no!"

Gwen lunged forward a second too slow just as Sarah flipped the shotgun around, putting the muzzle just under her chin. She heard the click, and suddenly it was like she was outside her body, watching everything happen as if it were some sort of holovid. Sarah's head was there one second, and gone the next, her body falling in slow motion, hot blood splattering in Gwen's face and staining her already filthy clothes red.

She stood paralyzed with her jaw hanging open while the rest of the checkpoint team swarmed around the body, giving her accusing looks, like somehow Gwen had pulled the trigger. Wiping the blood from her face, she moved to kneel beside the body.

"You could have stopped her," said one of the officers standing up to face her, his face red. "What's the point of you people unless you can stop this shit?"

"This shit isn't my fault," said Gwen. "I tried to stop her."

"Yeah, we saw how useful you were right then and there," said the officer, pointing a finger to her chest.

Gwen ground her teeth, staring at the finger with a frown. "You know what. Fuck you!" With a flick of her wrist she backhanded the idiot, sending him tumbling end over end to land hard against a steel barricade. "Fuck all of you, you ungrateful pieces of shit."

Without another word, she turned her back on them and took to the air, pissed that she lost control and glad that no one would see her tears.

TWENTY-TWO

OLD FRIENDS

"Why the hell is he like this and you're not?" shouted Rowen, turning to face Captain Young, who stood stock still at the doorway to his lab with Blake's katana pointed at his throat.

The oversized officer let out a deep sigh. "I wish I could tell ya, girl. It don't make much sense to me either," he said, making a motion to move away from the blade. "You mind."

Rowen gave Blake a nod, and the bright steel vanished, a sigh of relief escaping the captain's lips. She looked back to her father, her face flushing red with anger. From what she could tell, he was held in place by a restraining field, his handsome features twisted into a rage-filled snarl that made him look like a wild animal. Fighting to calm herself, she took a step toward him, wanting to see if she could reach him.

"I wouldn't do that if I was you," said Captain Young in a nervous tone, picking his way through the mess toward her. "He's way stronger than normal folks. Almost took my head off last time I got close. I had to increase the power to the field twice already."

"How long has he been like this?" asked Rowen, feeling helpless.

Captain Young cleared his throat. "Not long after he sent out the emergency message. We had barricaded ourselves in here when we realized we couldn't get past the infected and make it to the launch bay. All of a sudden, he goes limp, falls over like he'd been drinkin' bourbon all day. I had just managed to get him up on the gurney when he came to and started growlin'. Then before I could blink, he came at me like a wild dog."

"How did you get him in the restraining field?" said Blake, crossing his arms. "I mean, look at him: look at you."

"Shit luck, mostly," said Captain Young, plopping down at a workstation filled with empty coffee cups and half-eaten ration bars. His fat fingers danced over the controls, and a holographic representation of her father's vitals appeared, most of the normal colors subdued by a bright red glow. "The virus has converted almost fifty-five percent of his organic material to some unknown metallic compound. I've tried to slow it down with everything I could think of, radiation treatments, nanogrowth inhibitors. Hell, I even tried using CRISPR to re-initialize his own DNA replication, nothin'. He's more machine than man now, and I'm outta tricks."

The room was silent for what felt like an eternity when Blake suddenly cleared his throat. "There's a cure," he said, rubbing a hand across his face.

Captain Young looked up at from his workstation, his brow furrowing. "Is that so, and just how in Sam Hill would you know that?"

"You don't recognize me, do you?" said Blake.

Captain Young blew out his cheeks, pushing out his lower lip. "Am I supposed to?" he asked, looking back and forth between Blake and Rowen.

Rowen put a hand on the captain's shoulder. "You're not going to believe this, but he claims his real name is Finn, and that he was part of the Ascension program back when it first started."

"Well, that's the biggest loada horseshit I heard this week!" began the heavyset captain, shaking his head in disbelief before continuing. "That boy died on mission before you were outta diapers, girl. No way he could have been at this base for the better part of a year without his biometric data settin' off all kinds of alarms."

Blake leaned in, giving Captain Young a sly smile. "I may not have my full range of powers, but for some reason, people overlook me; I fade into the background. And did you ever see a body? Did any of you assholes even come looking for us?"

"Don't matter," said the captain. "Even if by some miracle you did survive down in that jungle, without proper medical treatment, without Diomoxicin, you'd be deader than disco."

"What's Diomoxicin?" asked Rowen.

"The Ascension process puts a ton of stress on the body, and over time it gets worn out—"

"I know," said Rowen. "Mary Beth told us all this."

"I'm sure," he said. "From what I remember, you had a firsthand experience with the drug Diomoxicin, D for short. We use it to stabilize them, keep 'em going for a while longer. Without it, the kids burn out, die by the end of puberty." Rowen swallowed hard, remembering the morning that Mary Beth and her brother held her down and punctured her back to extract spinal fluid. The base material for the drug.

Blake grunted, shoving the fat man back in his chair. "Yeah, they don't tell you that part, how you're gonna die young. They only tell you the good stuff, how they're gonna make your life better, and how much the country needs you."

Captain Young stood up, using his girth to push Blake back a step. "Yeah, we bullshit the kids a little, but most of 'em come from shit-poor situations, and given how tough things are in most places nowadays, they'll be dead and gone before they hit middle age, anyhow. We give kids who didn't have a future some hope."

Blake leaned in, poking a finger in Captain Young's chest. "You don't give them a goddamn choice!" he said, his nostrils flaring.

"Enough!" shouted Rowen. "The past is the past, and none of this matters right now. We have to stop this virus before there's nothing left to save. Blake, you say there's a cure, well, how do we get our hands on it?"

Blake pressed his lips together, giving the captain a sidelong glance before he began. "On our last mission, the one we didn't come back from, we were attacked by an unidentified creature. Daniel, one of our team members, got infected, and he spread it to the rest of us. I don't remember much, but he was further along than the rest of us, and he wanted to destroy these ancient bases that were scattered across the globe, filled with aliens or something. We never really did find out. All I remember at one point was he hijacked our transport and took us to a structure deep in the Amazon."

"Is that where you got rid of the infection?" asked Rowen, looking back at her father then back to the captain, who hung off every word.

Blake nodded before continuing, scratching at his beard. "We were pretty much under the virus's control when we got there. The place was full of tech that looked like crystals on your brother's armor or like the one Scotty there has on his neck. I don't remember anything after we got there. I only remember waking up in some strange machine listening to Bobby telling Tamika about how he cured us."

"Well, we're runnin' outta time, so let's go to this damn base, and get the damn cure," said Captain Young, eyeing all of them. "If you ain't fulla shit, lead on, man."

"I agree," said Rowen. "I'll tell Jonah to meet us back at the entrance. We'll pack up my father and get to it."

"There's only one problem with all of that," said Blake sheepishly. "I only remember bits and pieces from when we arrived, and I disabled the transponder when we left."

"But even if you did that, we can still pull the records from the flight database," said Gibbs suddenly, looking down at the tablet in his hand. "Or there must be some sort of satellite record."

Blake turned away from them all, letting out a deep sigh. "I didn't want anyone tracking us. I cloaked the Odin for the entire flight back to the States. Back then I could make anything invisible, hide anything from sight and sound, even electronics, didn't matter how big it was."

"Jesus H. Christ!" said Captain Young, throwing his hands in the air. "You're as dumb as dirt, boy. If I'd a known it was you, I woulda—"

Rowen raised a hand, giving them all an angry look. "Where did you dump the transport when you arrived in New York? You couldn't cloak it forever...could you?"

"Once I cloaked something, it took almost no effort to maintain. I could even do it in my sleep, and I did for a long time because I was afraid they would come after me. But once my powers faded, it didn't matter. I had a new life, and I was sure everyone who knew me thought I was dead."

"So, where is the damn thing?" said Captain Young.

"I sunk it in the reservoir in Central Park."

Rowen swore, shaking her head. "Really!"

"I'm really sorry, kid. If we can get the damn thing working, the nav coordinates are in the computer, but that means—"

"That means if we want to end this, we're going to New York...again!"

TWENTY-THREE
EXPECT THE UNEXPECTED

Jonah flew down the corridors of Iron Mountain tearing through man and machine alike, leaving a trail of twisted metal and broken bodies behind him, doing what Rowen had instructed. Create enough of a diversion, so all eyes would be on him so that she could find their father and hopefully, get him out of this nightmare in one piece.

Skidding to a halt in an eerily empty corridor, he took a moment to catch his breath, to think. This was the second time he had fought these things, and the first time he really was able to observe them. He wondered why anyone would go through the trouble of making them. They were piss-poor soldiers who couldn't use a weapon or improvise, for that matter. Their only real strength being that they could take a ton of punishment.

Turning down another corridor, he found a group of them standing listlessly with their backs to him, and he held his attack, his face creased with worry. To Jonah they looked like normal soldiers all dressed in uniforms normally worn on base for day-to-day operations, but on closer inspection he could see the horrors that the virus had inflicted on them. They looked alien, inhuman. He couldn't help but wonder if that drone hadn't fallen on him, if Colonel Anton and Dr. Kolov hadn't chosen him for the experiments, what would have happened to him? Would he be one of these poor bastards? Mindless, their humanity lost. "Killing them is a mercy," he muttered under his breath.

He was about to charge forward when they all turned to him in lockstep, raising their voices, droning in unison like they were performing a gregorian chant. "That will be enough for today, Jonah."

He flinched back, looking over his shoulder and then back again at the converted soldiers, who felt like they were closer all of a sudden. "You can talk? You know me?"

"They speak with one voice, my voice," they said, again in their droning voices. "And we know you very well Jonah Macdonald. We know you are running out of time, and we know your sister and her friends cannot help you."

When the soldiers extended their hands all at once, Jonah for once was grateful for the emotional detachment his transformation had given him. He had killed hundreds, if not thousands, of these things. Nothing they could do would possibly hurt him, "I don't know what you're talking about," said Jonah, swallowing, the rough, uncut walls amplifying his deep voice.

"The command crystal you have is slowly running out of power; when it goes dim, so will your mind. You won't be much better than the mindless bodies you see standing before you...but I can help you, if you join me."

A pulse of deep crimson flashed through Jonah's armor, his forehead creasing with worry for a heartbeat before he shook it off, raising his chin. "You want me to trust a faceless coward who won't show themselves over my own flesh and blood? I don't think so."

"I am no coward; I am merciful. I could have killed you at Norfolk, but I chose to spare you, knowing that I had freed you, and that you would return to our great nation better for your experiences."

Jonah bared his teeth, a mix of fear, anger, and revulsion running through him all at once. "You were the one with the golden glow who destroyed the Russian fleet," said Jonah, understanding dawning. "You didn't free me. You distracted me with your mindless cannon fodder and then attacked the fleet when I wasn't there to protect it."

"Yes, and that just shows how unworthy of you they were, so weak that I could destroy them all in such a short time."

Jonah braced himself to strike out at the mindless infected. "If that were true, you would have destroyed them in New York or before they even attacked."

A chill ran through Jonah as the clutch of soldiers in front of him laughed in unison. "Dr. Kolov and his fleet came to this country by my invitation and departed when I no longer found them useful."

"Why would you do that to your own country, to the people you're supposed to protect?" whispered Jonah."

"It doesn't matter," said the voices. "It only matters that we can help one another."

Jonah opened his mouth to speak when a chirp from the comm in his ear interrupted. "Jonah, time to go; we got him," said Rowen in a hurried tone like she was running. "We found Captain Young too, and he's leading us to a hanger bay where we can grab an Odin-class transport. I'm sending you the location now."

He stood there, clenching and unclenching his fist, staring hard at the cluster of infected soldiers, mesmerized. They took another step toward him, their lips turning up into a frightful smile. "I am your only option to keep your mind intact, to not lose who you are. Come with—"

"Jonah, do you copy?" screamed Rowen in his ear, shocking him out of his stupor.

"Time's up," said Jonah, shaking his head, exploding into motion and slicing through the cluster of infected like a Reaper's blade, destroying them all in the time it took him to draw a single breath. "Rowen, I'm on my way," he said, walking away from the carnage of severed limbs, not bothering to look back.

He was walking past a severed head when it let out a final breath. "Remember my offer when the time comes, and your new friends fail you."

With a roar, Jonah crushed the head under his crystal-clad heel, doubt swirling in his mind.

TWENTY-FOUR
BLAKE

Arthur locked his arms behind his back, raising his chin and looking out the window of his offices at city hall, enjoying the brief respite of the warm midday sunlight caressing his face.

"We've lost everything above 110th Street, along with everything outside Manhattan," began Officer Newman, his bland tone making Arthur's shoulders tense. He stood with his back to the man, only half listening, sure that the officer couldn't tell him anything he didn't already know. According to everyone who knew him, the young man was competent and well organized, but for some reason Arthur had a hard time warming to him, but when his previous head of police services, Sarah, took her life, he had been forced to promote someone quickly, and he seemed like the best choice. "We've been printing copies of the new handheld virus detectors you developed, as fast as we can, and it's allowed us to be far more proactive in stopping the infection in the safe zone, but we're still losing ground."

Arthur nodded to himself. "We have to get regular people more involved, build a militia to replace the numbers we've lost. I want you and your team to start recruiting anyone physically capable, put a gun in the hands of anyone who wants to fight. It's the only way we're going to survive this."

"We'll do our best, but so far we've been using the volunteers to get the bodies off the streets. I'm not—

"What are you doing with the bodies?" asked Arthur, his stomach churning with disgust at what was happening out there.

"We're doing what you ordered, sir," said Officer Newman in a halting tone. "Using the incinerator system from waste management services. So far, there have been no incidents, and we're keeping it quiet, just as planned."

Glancing over his shoulder, Arthur sighed deeply while looking Newman in the eye. The young officer was slight of build with hollow cheeks and jet-black hair that made him look paler than he was. "It's Arthur—just Arthur. I don't have any official rank. I just happen to be the one in charge. Anyway, what's the count so far, and how many have you been forced to kill?"

Officer Newman coughed uncomfortably into his hand. "I thought we were using the term, *cleanse*."

"Semantics won't do us any good when we tell families we killed their loved ones to prevent the virus from spreading, so that all of us could have a chance. Soft words make for soft people. Let's call it what it is."

"Yes...Arthur," he said, shifting uncomfortably in place. "At last count, we've been forced to...kill, a little over eighty thousand. This doesn't count those we couldn't recover from the George Washington Bridge incident, and any of those trapped when Gwen collapsed the Holland Tunnel."

The very thought of trying to recover those bodies made his head spin. They didn't have the time, much less the personnel to give the dead the respect they deserved. They were barely holding on as it was. At best, he was hoping they could do some sort of memorial service at the water's edge sometime soon, give those families who lost someone some sort of closure. Talking about the bridge and the tunnel brought other problems to mind. "What about Gwen? Has she had any contact since the incident last week when we lost Sarah?"

"No sir...I mean, Arthur."

He blew out his cheeks, amazed at the stupidity of it all. This was probably one of the reasons he didn't like Newman that much. He had been there with Gwen the day Sarah took her life, and he still wore an ugly bruise on his face from where she had hit him. The officer had placed the blame squarely on her, claiming that with her powers, she should have been able to stop it all from happening. Gwen had flown off in a rage and hadn't been in contact with him or anyone else since.

Clearing his throat, Newman continued, "But she has made appearances, saved people. She just happens to threaten the lives of anyone who gets too close...and I can't repeat half the things she says to people."

A half smile came to Arthur's face. Gwen could have left at any time, found a safe spot to ride this out, but she stayed, proving him right then that being a hero was built into her DNA. "She has been known to leave an impression on people with the things that come out of her mouth. Just make sure that your people have standing orders that if she shows up anywhere, that she's given a wide berth and latitude to do what she needs to do. No one gets in her way, understood?"

Newman snorted, saying nothing, and Arthur got the impression that—

The communication hub on his wrist suddenly screamed for his attention, and he reacted quickly. Forgetting Officer Newman, Arthur shunted his mind through the device to the larger network amplifier at his lab at The Rockefeller University, spreading his consciousness to every sensor, every camera throughout the island of Manhattan.

He cursed under his breath when he found the warning was from one of Apex drones that patrolled the airspace around the city. Strangely, there were no visuals, just static. Thinking quickly, he jumped from source to source, finding the same in every drone he could connect with, like someone had hacked into its systems to cover their tracks and sneak into the city.

Before he could do more, a shadow appeared in a shaded corner of the room, rippling like waves on a still lake, pulling Arthur's attention back to his physical body at city hall. Emerging from the darkness was a tall, olive-skinned man with a large beak of a nose and a high forehead, his dark eyes wide with panic. "We are invaded again!" he said in a thick Italian accent that sounded more like he was singing than speaking.

Arthur rolled his shoulders, tightening the grip of his hands behind his back. "I know," he said, "and I thought we agreed that you would come and go like a normal person, using the doors."

Rodrigo raised his perfect eyebrows, tiny wrinkles appearing on his brow. "This was meant as a joke, no?"

"No not a joke," he said, glancing over at Newman's panic-stricken face. "You scare people when you do that, Rodrigo, so please—"

The tall Italian waved him off, making a face. "This does not matter for now; what matters is that the supreme cardinal has sent another wave of infection."

Arthur shook his head, stepping away from the window. "That shouldn't be possible. Where?"

"They've landed in Central Park!" blurted Rodrigo. I don't know how they bypassed your fancy system, but they are here, at the reservoir."

Reaching out once more, he scanned the cameras in the park, at last finding the invasion Rodrigo was talking about. There in Central Park near the reservoir was a single Odin-class transport, the cargo ramp at the back wide open, not a soul in sight. "Take me now!" shouted Arthur. "Newman, I want every warm body you can get to head to that reservoir."

Officer Newman paled and ran from the office, eyes wide with panic, while Rodrigo came closer. Arthur tensed when the tall Italian placed a hand on his shoulder, knowing what was coming. The office at city hall faded to shades of gray and then to inky darkness like the curtain of night had been pulled over it all. Arthur gasped for breath, suddenly cold, gripping tightly at the hand on his shoulder, his heart pounding in terror. They took a single step, and he almost fell over from the effort, his limbs suddenly numb. He always wondered what would happen if Rodrigo let him go in here, would he wander in this horrid place half-frozen, gasping for breath until he was lost forever? Then just as quickly as it had begun, he blinked and found himself once more in the warm light of midday, his tingling hands wrapped tightly around Rodrigo, who was smiling like nothing had happened. "I hate you," said Arthur, unwrapping his limbs from him, shaking slightly. They had traveled like this hundreds of times in the last few days, jumping from crisis to crisis. Each time he thought it would be easier, but it felt like it had gotten worse with each jump.

Rodrigo gave him a perfect white-toothed smile and a wink. "You say you hate me, but you hold on to me like a crazed lover."

Arthur pushed him away, his caramel-colored skin flushing dark. With a grunt, he straightened his simple service uniform. Rodrigo had transported into a copse of trees not far from the water's edge, sunlight flashing in the distance off towering apartment complexes of New York's Upper West Side. Not far away, the massive Odin transport stood with its cargo ramp wide open, the missilelike vehicle was half as long as a football field, built for speed and not much else. Using all his strength, he took control of every Apex drone circling the city. Wanting to end this invasion quickly he brought them in close, planning to raze the transport and anything else that threatened his city. "We kill anything that moves," he said to Rodrigo. "Not one of those things leave this park."

Rodrigo nodded, drawing out the crystal blade he concealed at his hip. "Understood," he said simply, his handsome face suddenly grim as he faded to shadow and vanished.

Bowing his head, Arthur reached out again through the network he had created, hesitating for a moment before making the call.

"Gwen, if you can hear me, I need you. Rodrigo and I are at the reservoir in the park. I know it's not your favorite place, and you probably don't want to see me right now, but I could really use your help. Cardinal Washington has sent another wave of infected on a transport. We're about to engage, so please..." He stopped, knowing how much she hated when he begged, hoping that by some miracle she would show up to help.

Returning his attention to the transport, Arthur shifted his vision to see the world in its quantum state, scanning the transport for signs of life. To his surprise some of the infected were still on board, he saw a pair with the telltale, sickly green of the early stages as well as one in the deeper stages glowing a bright silver, but strangest of all was that one of them had a washed-out amber glow, something Arthur hadn't seen before.

Wanting to find the rest, he delved into the control systems, following a thousand virtual paths and taking control of them all, shutting down the vital electronics and locking them all inside to deal with later, hoping to interrogate any that still had their senses. Next, he brought his attention back to the Apex drones he had circling the park, using them as his eyes to hunt those that had left the transport. After the tower was destroyed, Arthur had quarantined the park, and given the stories of the area, most people stayed away out of fear, so he wasn't worried about hurting anyone who wasn't infected.

Circling the reservoir, he found nothing—no people, no crowds of converted racing to leave the park. He only caught the occasional glimpse of Rodrigo, appearing and disappearing at random. He began to suspect that it was all a ruse of some sort, a way to draw off the drones he had defending the city. Then without warning, the surface of the reservoir began to bubble and churn, and Arthur shifted his vision back to normal, not sure of what he was seeing. Sure enough, the crystal-blue waters of the reservoir were heaving, tall waves suddenly rolling up on the shore. He was about to strafe the water with a drone when something massive emerged, water cascading down its sides that were covered in slimy-green vegetation that hung vinelike from its surface.

"It's another Odin," whispered Arthur, stepping out from the trees without thinking, striding down toward the water's edge as the missilelike vessel floated toward its twin on the shore.

He hardly noticed when Rodrigo rippled into his existence beside him, matching his stride, the man's high forehead creased in confusion. "Che diavolo è questo," he said, crossing himself, pointing at a humanoid figure.

Arthur stiffened, stopping in his tracks when he realized the Odin wasn't flying on its own. A figure, almost invisible beneath the bulk of the thing, was flying it out of the water and carrying it to shore. For one of the few times in his life he was left speechless, his mind racing to calculate the power required to perform such a feat.

The deep booming quake of the transport falling to the ground shook Arthur from his stupor. In the blink of an eye he brought in every weapon he had to bear, the tiny hornets that would blow a man's skull to bits, the Apex drones with their heavy .50-caliber machine guns, all ready to annihilate whatever nightmare that could fly while holding aloft half a football field of carbon and steel. "Be ready," he said to Rodrigo at his side.

Arthur narrowed his eyes at the figure that emerged from under the shadow of the Odin. It was a man, tall, almost seven feet, covered from head to toe in odd plates made of some sort of jagged crystal that reflected the afternoon sun, the only flesh visible were its hands and face. They locked eyes for a moment, and Arthur paused, seeing something vaguely familiar in its green eyes. He was about to call out to him when Rodrigo pounced from the shadows behind him, sliding his transparent blade up into his armpit with deadly precision. The blade had hardly pierced flesh when the crystal-clad monstrosity let out a deep scream, spinning so quickly Rodrigo's weapon snapped in half. Rodrigo managed to only to blink before he was hammered with a bone-shattering fist to his face that sent him reeling into the side of the transport, his limp body slumping to the ground in a broken heap.

Arthur wasting no time, unleashed hell. Thrusting out his hand to send in swarms of hornets, the drones screaming with a high-pitched whine as they circled him. Not caring for precision, Arthur closed his fist, and the hornets exploded like firecrackers all around his flailing arms and head, the smoke obscuring him momentarily. Not taking any chances, Arthur opened fire with the half a dozen Apex aircraft that flew just above them, raining down a torrent of fifty-caliber rounds that sent sod and dirt exploding in all directions.

Staring hard, he could just make out the shape of his target, its forearms upraised to protect his face. Arthur took another step forward with both fists outstretched. Pushing his abilities to their limits, he brought in another wave of hornets, unrelenting. A chill ran through him when he saw the figure drop both his arms at his side and take a step forward, ignoring his onslaught as though it were nothing more than a light drizzle on a rainy afternoon. Arthur flinched when the monster moved without seeming to move, one minute at the edge of the water beside the Odin, the next it had slammed into Arthur's chest, pounding the breath from his lungs with a blow that was too fast for him to register. He blinked, and he was suddenly tumbling and tearing through the tree line, crashing into the woods to land hard on his back. Clutching at the sharp pain in his chest, he rolled onto his side, tasting blood. Then by instinct he dragged himself behind a tree for cover while scanning for his attacker.

Shifting his vision into the quantum state, he caught a glimpse of the crystal-clad giant tearing at the cargo door to the Odin Arthur had locked down. Realizing the power of the thing he had just fought, Arthur wondered for a moment if this was all they had sent, some sort of superinfected that could match the strength of an Ascended, or in this case be far more powerful. But from what he could see of the thing, its energy signature didn't look like an infected. In fact, he realized why he seemed familiar. He could see subtle shifting of color in the crystal that covered his body, very similar to the tower that once stood in this park, the tower that Uriel had destroyed.

Ignoring the sharp stabbing pain in his chest, Arthur pushed himself to his feet and then shifted his focus back to the Apex drones he had in the area. Taking in a shaky breath, he straightened the simple service uniform he wore and sent one of the Apexes careening toward his opponent at maximum speed. The narrow aircraft slammed into his armored back with enough force to pound him to the ground, the drone exploding in a roaring fireball that was so large it licked the sides of the Odin and was so bright it forced Arthur to look away. For good measure, he sent in another one, the blazing torrent of flame was hot enough that even at a distance Arthur had to shield his face from the heat.

Nodding to himself, Arthur squared his shoulders and strode out of the trees toward the Odin, wanting to see if there was anything left when he suddenly felt cold despite the heat of the day. There, stretching to his full towering height, was the armor-covered man walking out of the flames, unharmed. Swearing under his breath, he was about to turn and run when he locked eyes with him, and in that instant, he understood that he was about to die. There was no getting away; the crystal man was too fast, and Arthur couldn't stop him. Locking his arms behind his back, he raised his chin and pushed out his chest, waiting for the end. He was proud that at least he would die on his feet, knowing he did his best. He wished for a moment he could see Gwen one last time to at least explain, to at least say goodbye.

Arthur tensed for a blow that never came, the crystal man was about to charge when falling from the heavens like a goddess, salvation arrived, and the world around them exploded in a wave of chaos.

TWENTY-FIVE

OLD FRIENDS, NEW FRIENDS

She fell from heaven like the wrath of God, her titanic blow bending nearby trees and burying Jonah up to his chest in the soft earth. The girl in white was one of the few things he remembered from the night Rowen had shot him in the face and freed his mind. Their battle in the skies above the park had been pulse pounding, exhilarating. It was one of the few times since the crystals were placed on his skin that he felt any emotion. It was the same emotion he felt now as she towered over him with her white coat billowing in the wind...fear.

"That's for blindsiding me last time!" she said through gritted teeth, drawing back to smash him again. "Let's see how much you like a cheap shot to the face."

Not waiting for the haymaker to land, Jonah exploded from the ground and aimed for the skies, catching her just under her chin with his fist and snapping her head back like an elastic band. Jonah didn't want to face off against this girl and the small boy in the black uniform. His attacks had been little more than a nuisance at first, but when the Apex drone slammed into him, it had knocked the wind from his lungs, and his face and hands still stung from the exploding fuel. Jonah knew he had hurt him badly, so he decided he would deal with the girl then come back to finish him off.

Glancing over his shoulder and seeing her closing in, he pushed himself faster, the wind screaming in his ears. Sure that he couldn't outfly her, Jonah flipped around in midair and stopped short, using her forward momentum against her, he struck out viper quick. She yelped when he grabbed her outstretched arm and swung her around as though she were a kettlebell, almost tearing his arms out of their sockets from the effort. He released her with a grunt, hurling her like a shooting star toward the ground. She tore through one of the hapless apartment complexes that lined the park, concrete and steel bursting apart in a cloud of debris as the building fell on top of her. Jonah floated on the edge of the park, half-blind from the dust, allowing himself a moment of hope that he had bested her. He was caught off guard when she slammed into him like a cannonball, pounding his midsection with enough force to send him reeling back out over the reservoir, tumbling end over end. He barely had a moment to catch his breath when she was on him again, her fists and feet everywhere at once, snapping his head back and forth in a fury of blows that echoed across the clear sky like peals of thunder.

The girl caught him just under the chin, and Jonah saw stars, the world spinning like a kaleidoscope as he lost all sense of self. Dazed and confused, he fought on pure instinct now, feebly blocking some blows while taking the brunt of others, his body punished and pushed to its limits. He blinked, and suddenly he found the brilliant blue of the reservoir waters quickly approaching, the massive Odin transports sitting idly on the shore. He blinked again, and the world was a bright blue that was rapidly fading to black, the curvature of the earth and stars appearing in the corner of his eye. Spinning over, he found the girl dragging him by the leg, whether she was trying to lift him into orbit and leave him there or drop him from this height. He had no clue, but he had no intention of letting her kill him. Using his remaining strength, he twisted out of her grip and raced for a smattering of clouds he saw in the distance, hoping to lose her there.

He had almost made it when he was blindsided, hearing the the hollow whine of a jet turbine just before the dark shadow slammed into his side with a bone-jarring crunch. Jonah was suddenly blinded by stinging white-hot flame of the fuel exploding, cooking what little flesh that wasn't protected by armor. With his strength spent, he fell from the sky, barely conscious of the wind ripping around him, tearing through the branches of a tree and landing with a bone-crushing scream, plumes of dirt scattering in all directions. Jonah drew in ragged short breaths, pain throbbing through his entire body, his mind reeling from pain as he tried to stand, only to stumble forward to his hands and knees with his head bowed. When he saw the girl's boots appear in his field of vision, his heart sank. He was too exhausted, too broken to fight anymore. Desperate, he squeezed his eyes shut and raised his hands over his head in surrender.

"Stop, please," he croaked, breathing hard. Closing his eyes, he waited for the blow. When nothing happened, he opened an eye a crack to find the blond girl looking at him with eyes as wide as saucers, her raised fist trembling.

"You can talk," she blurted out, giving him a sidelong glance and lowering her hand.

"That night, I never meant to attack you," he began, not sure why he was trying to explain, but each word out of his mouth gave him a second more of life. "The Russians, they made me. Programmed me to attack."

The girl tapped a small device strapped to her wrist and then crossed her arms over her small breasts. "Whatever. You're with them, not us. So take your ball, and go home. We got enough problems and don't need shitheads like you making it worse."

"I understand," he said, his shoulders slumping in relief. "We just came for the navicomputer in the transport. We'll take it and go. You won't see us again."

"We? You mean there's more than one of you assholes?"

Jonah pressed his lips together, forcing himself to not react. He had been raised in a strict military household. Both he and Rowen had been taught to be polite, and while he knew that most people didn't grow up like this, it irked him when people lacked respect. "No, I came here with my sister and a few others."

"In that transport?" asked the girl.

"Obviously," said Jonah, regretting his tone immediately when the girl raised an eyebrow.

Waving him off, she touched the device on her wrist once again, her eyes never leaving him. "Arthur, did you catch all that? What do I do with this asshole?"

She put a hand to her ear while nodding along to whatever was being said on the other end. When she was done, she gave him a tight-lipped smile and shrugged. "Sorry. He says I have to kill you."

Jonah tensed, falling back on his heels and raising his hands defensively once more.

Seeing his reaction, the girl put out her palms. "Whoa! Sorry, kidding," she said, pursing her lips. "Not good with the humor, are we? Anyway, Arthur wants to see you. Are you gonna behave yourself if I let you fly, or do I have to drag you along?"

"If we go slow, I can fly," said Jonah, looking at her from the corner of his eye as he rose slowly to his feet, wincing from a sharp pain in his chest. The girl stepped aside, waving him on like he should lead the way. With what little strength he had left, Jonah took to the air, flying like a bird with a broken wing, shaking all the while. It wasn't long before they returned to where it all started, on the banks of the reservoir in the shadow of the massive transports. Jonah half landed, half stumbled to the ground near the small boy who had attacked him with the drones, his breathing still shallow.

The small boy stood in front of him at a parade rest, arms behind his back with his chest out, giving him a calculating look. "Welcome to New York," he said in a calm voice. "My name is Arthur. What can I do for you?"

Jonah frowned at him realizing he wasn't a boy, more a teenager who had started puberty late, slight of frame with deep brown eyes that bored into him. Hesitating, he gave the girl a questioning look.

The girl gave him a knowing smile, eyeing them both before shrugging. "I know he doesn't look like much, but he's the man. I'm Gwen, by the way, the chick who just kicked your ass!"

Jonah gave the both of them an unblinking stare, crossing his arms over his massive chest. "Will you let us go once we get what we came for?"

"You mean the infected you brought with you in the transport?"

Jonah eyed the massive vehicle up and down, noting that the running lights along with everything else was off. "Yes, my sister Rowen and my—"

"Rowen!?" said Arthur, his eyes widening. "She's infected?"

Jonah nodded, pointing at the transport with his chin. "She's in the early stages still, but my father—"

Before he could finish, Arthur turned his back to him, and suddenly the engines on the transport fired up, the running lights coming to life and glowing brightly, even in the midday sun. Arthur waved his hand, and the cargo ramp started to descend with a loud clunk, the constant drone of its hydraulics forcing them to raise their voices. "You know my sister. Are you sure?" he said, following him to the base of the ramp to wait for it to touch down on the grass.

Arthur looked up at him, his young face smooth without a trace of emotion. "She shot me," he said. "More than once."

Something about the matter-of-fact way he announced that Rowen had shot him touched a nerve, and Jonah couldn't help but chuckle, a rare smile creasing his face. "That's her." They waited in silence, standing stock still, none of them speaking. When he saw Rowen emerge with Blake on one side Captain Young hobbling along on the other, and Gibbs trailing behind all of them, Jonah felt like a weight had been lifted off his shoulders. That meant he didn't have to say anymore; he could let them take the lead, and hopefully get them away from this place as soon as possible.

"Did Supreme Cardinal Washington send you back here to spread the infection, or are you just here to shoot me again," said Arthur, breaking the silence, watching them like a hawk.

Rowen scratched the jagged scar that ran the length of her face, her hand easily falling to her hip and the weapon holstered there. "No, but I should for that stunt you pulled, locking us in like that," she said, stopping in front of him. "You cost us time we don't have."

The officer in the uniform that was too tight stepped forward, putting a restraining hand on his sister's shoulder. "We don't wanna mess with you, son. We came for that great big hunk a junk over there," he said in his friendly twang, pointing at the Odin that he had dragged from the reservoir. "You just let us go on about our business, and we'll be outta your hair in no time."

"And what exactly are you?" began Arthur, ignoring the Southerner and eyeing the tall man with salt-and-pepper hair, that for some reason, Jonah could never remember his name, even though he'd been told a few times. "You look human on the outside, but I can tell you're something else," finished Arthur.

"My name is none of your goddamn business—" he began in a voice that sounded like rocks grinding together.

"Blake," said Rowen, speaking quickly, "just Blake, Arthur—"

"You know I can tell a lot about someone just by looking," interrupted Arthur in a quiet voice, "and when I look at your friend Blake, nothing makes sense. In fact, none of this makes sense. That transport has been at the bottom of the reservoir for a long time. Why come and get it now? What's so important about the Navi computer that you risk traveling with a fully converted infected with you? Why risk coming here at all?"

Rowen pressed her lips together, and Jonah could tell she was about to lose it and start shooting, so he stepped between them, towering over everyone. "Our father is in the final stages of the transformation. We're trying to save him, save everyone." he said in a flat tone.

"I was infected a long time ago," said Blake, glancing at the transport from the water. "The location of where I was cured is in that Navi computer."

"The whole country will end up like this if we don't do

anything," said Jonah. "We have a chance to stop it before it's too late, and what's on that transport is our best hope."

Arthur opened his mouth to speak when Gwen suddenly pulled him aside, giving them all a tight-lipped smile and waving them off. "Just give us a second."

Watching them walk away, Captain Young leaned in, lowering his voice to a loud whisper. "What's the deal with this kid? Why won't he just give us what we want and throw us out?"

Rowen crossed her arms over her bird's nest of hair, shaking it back and forth. "He doesn't trust us, and from what I know, he always angles things so that he can come out on top."

Jonah cocked his head, tuning out the rest of the conversation while he watched Arthur and the Gwen argue. He was reminded of his parents. His mother had always been the aggressor, arguing with her hands, while his father nodded along, spine straight and stiff. He wasn't sure what they were fighting about, but it was clear moments later that Arthur had won when she poked him in the chest and then shoved her middle finger in his face. They returned moments later, Gwen behind him, her face flushed a bright red.

"I can remove the virus from you and Gibbs," said Arthur in a low voice. "That way I'm sure it's you talking, and you're not being influenced. Then if everything you say is true...I'm coming with you."

"Why? You got your city under control," said Blake. "Why take the risk of things going to hell while you're gone?"

Arthur shook his head. "We're barely holding on. We had to start rounding up people who we're too far gone and...and kill them," he said, glancing over his shoulder at Gwen. "She'll be staying here, along with Rodrigo, to get me back here if things get bad again."

"Just as long as you understand you're not in charge; you follow my orders. If you try anything like last time, I'll put two in your chest, understand?" she said, pulling aside her duster to make sure he could see the deadly weapon on her hip. Jonah knew well what she could do with it, never for a second doubting she could carry out her threat.

To his surprise, Arthur paled, and when he spoke there was a subtle tremor in his voice. "We're all in the same boat, and I know we can only hold out here for so long. At some point we're gonna slip."

Rowen nodded, letting her hand drop to the side. "If you can fix me, fix him too!" she said, pointing her thumb at Gibbs behind her.

Arthur nodded and motioned for both of them to come closer while he put a hand on each of their shoulders, bowing his head in concentration. They stood there for a long time, beads of sweat forming on Arthur's forehead while the wind rustled through the trees. Every now and then he glanced over at the blond girl, Gwen, who sat cross-legged on the grass bobbing her head to music only she could hear. With a gasp, Rowen staggered away from him, falling down on her behind while breathing hard. Gibbs let out a deep breath, blinking in confusion like he had woken from a deep sleep.

Arthur did the same, falling down on his haunches. "Are you telling me the truth?" he asked, finally, after catching his breath.

His sister ran her hands through her tangled mess of hair, scratching at the scar. "Yes," she said at last. "Every word."

"All right," said Arthur. "Let's go fix this mess before it's too late."

Jonah crossed his arms, fascinated as Arthur gracefully returned to his feet and gave his sister a salute. At that moment, Jonah realized that the girl he teased all the time was gone, replaced by a fierce woman, one who he would be proud to follow into battle. For the first time in a long time, his feelings didn't feel like they we're behind a wall: they were strong, true. He loved his sister, and it felt good.

TWENTY-SIX
CONTROL

Arthur's body was strapped into the pilot's chair in the Odin's cockpit, with its smooth obsidian surfaces that projected holographic controls configured to his liking, but his mind raced down the virtual pathways of its computer systems, expanding to dominate every aspect of its electronics, navigation, propulsion, and even the environmental systems were completely subject to his will, so much so that he was forced to trap the transports AI in a useless subsystem, placing it in an infinite loop so that it wouldn't bother him. When he ignited the plasma rockets that gave them thrust, it was like his own heart was coming to life: the sensors were his eyes and ears, the carbon fiber of its body his skin.

When they had boarded, Blake had insisted that he fly, given that he had the most experience with this type of vessel, but after Arthur explained that with his powers he could increase the efficiency by almost 50 percent, getting them to their destination that much faster, he relented with a wordless grunt. Still, he insisted that he stay in the cockpit while the rest of the team retreated to the passenger area midship where they could keep an eye on Rowen's dad. Arthur had tried explaining to Blake how much easier it was for him to push the vehicle to its limits. Most pilots had only a vague sense of the limits of an aircraft, but because Arthur interacted with most machines like they were a part of him, he could directly feel just how far he could push things.

"That's impressive," said Blake from the copilot's seat, scanning the readout of the ship's systems. "You've bypassed all the safety protocols; systems are well beyond their tolerance limits, but we're still in one piece, so far."

"Thank you," said Arthur. "Its not everyone who can understand what I do."

"I'm surprised the government let you go...The girl too."

"We didn't really give them a choice," he said, adjusting the fusion reactor to a higher output and pumping additional coolant into the lines that were part of the thruster assembly. "For some reason they thought it was a good idea to try and stop me with an entire fleet of aircraft, tanks, and every drone they could scrounge up on short notice."

Blake barked a laugh, sounding more like a hyena than a man. "Someone wasn't thinking. I mean they know what you can do, right?"

"I spent a lot of time thinking about it," said Arthur, adjusting their course to take advantage of a tailwind he detected. "I thought the supreme cardinal was a smart man, but the more I've faced off against him, the more I see his mistakes. He's made too many bad choices."

"Like deploying the virus," said Blake. "Not sure why the hell anyone would want to control a world full of mindless drones."

"They're not mindless," said Arthur. "I've done a deep dive into one of them, a doctor we knew from the early days of the infection. He was in there, trapped in some strange virtual reality. He was terrified; he said that 'he' was coming. That we would all be part of the *unity*."

"That scares the piss outta me, being trapped in your own mind without control."

"You know interfacing and controlling machines aren't the only abilities I have," said Arthur, wanting to change the subject, shifting his sight to the quantum world of atoms and electrons to scan Blake once again. Looking at him, he was still confused by the washed-out amber aura that surrounded the man. "I can see the building blocks off things, electrons flowing in a wire, waves, and particles moving all around us."

"What's your point?"

"You don't look like anyone else I've ever seen."

"What the hell is that supposed to mean?" said Blake, scratching at the salt-and-pepper stubble on his jaw.

"Well, to me, most people look like a dark silhouette with slight blue currents of electricity running through them. When someone is in the early stages of infection, the blue turns to this ugly shade of green. And when you have someone like me or Gwen, someone who's been Ascended, there's this bright golden halo, but you, you have this faded amber—"

"Sounds like you think you folks are better than the rest of us," he snorted, reaching to unbuckle the four-point harness of the copilot's chair. "That's cute, but I think I'll see what everyone else is up to."

"You were like me once, weren't you?" guessed Arthur, banking the Odin a hair and sending Blake back into his seat. "You know, they have this data vault deep in Iron Mountain. It's isolated, no access, totally off the main grid. I went down there the day I escaped, looking for information on my parents. What I found was more than I bargained for. I found out what happens to kids like me, made me a little crazy for a while."

Blake gave him a tight-lipped smile, looking away. "Yeah, they keep the dying part top secret. When I first got away, there were two of us, me and Tamika. She had been recruited and gone through the process about the same time as me. We came to New York, and with my powers and hers we could get anything we wanted if we kept things under the radar. We thought we could have a life, you know."

"She died?" asked Arthur in a small voice, already knowing the answer.

Blake nodded, rubbing his eyes. "Tamika, she had this crazy ability to turn to stone, obsidian, the reverends had told her, made her super strong. She had just turned nineteen the first time things started going sideways. We were sitting watching a movie on the holonet, and all of a sudden she loses control, starts shifting back and forth for no reason. We had had a couple of drinks and thought it was a joke or something, a one off. Had a good laugh about it."

"But then it happened more and more," said Arthur, his mind going back to the day they lost Uriel. "We had a friend, same thing happened to him. He hid it for a long time, but in the end..."

Blake nodded again, continuing with a grim look. "It had started over the spring and got worse over the summer, shifting back and forth out of control. It got to the point we had to leave the city, so we found a place upstate in the Catskills to lay low, figure it out," he said, tears leaking down his face now. "By Christmas she was gone. I went out for some food one afternoon, and when I came back she was standing by the Christmas tree like a stone statue, frozen that way forever."

"I'm sorry," whispered Arthur.

"She was a good person, deserved better," he said with a snort, wiping his nose. "We all did. Got the short end of the goddamn stick for sure, didn't we?"

"And you? When...how?"

Blake met his eyes, clenching his jaw. "It was different with me, I started getting tired, sore like I'd been in a fight or something. With my powers I used to be able to hide whole city blocks if I needed to. But as time went on It got harder to cloak anything beyond a few feet around me, then over time, I couldn't even cover myself on most days. Worse, though, were the changes in my body. I was twenty years old, and my goddamn hair was going white. My eyesight was going, and my stomach was a mess. I sprained my foot just getting out of bed once."

"But that doesn't explain why—"

"I'm gettin' to that part, buddy. Hold your horses. At the time I was going through this nightmare, I saw a news report on aging, and how we mess up our bodies. So I changed everything: what I ate, started exercising more, no matter how tired I was, but most of all, I stopped using my powers, went cold turkey, it was rough, but I'm still here."

"So, they're gone and nothing left?" asked Arthur, leaning forward.

"I'm still stronger than most people and can take a beating, but unless I'm under a ton of stress, I couldn't use my abilities to cloak my own nose."

"So there's a chance, then...of surviving this?"

Blake shrugged, his lips turning down. "I don't know. I'm no expert. I can't tell you why I'm still here and Tamika's not, but it's no picnic. I'm in my early thirties, and I look and feel like I'm sixty. Everything hurts so bad on some days, I just wanna shove my katana in my gut and be done with it."

Arthur adjusted their course again, venting plasma to reduce pressure in the drive nozzles. "Then how do they do it?"

"Who does what?"

"The major bishop looked like an old man, but he could still use his powers, and when Gwen and I fought Cardinal Washington he was very powerful. He didn't seem like someone who was holding back, even a little."

"I don't know about this major bishop fellow, but Michael must have found a way. I mean, he has unlimited resources and a whole boatload of government toadies doing the science for him, so who knows."

Arthur gritted his teeth and increased the flow of fuel to the fusion reactor, making the entire transport shudder as it blew past Mach 4. "I want Cardinal Washington to pay for his crimes. He doesn't deserve to lead this country. Anyone who would do what he did to his own people needs to die."

"On that...we are in agreement," rumbled Blake, sticking out an age-spotted hand.

Arthur took the other man's hand, feeling for the first time in weeks like there was a chance to come back from this, that he could put the nightmare to bed and move the country forward for once without Cardinal Washington dragging them down, and for that he was grateful.

TWENTY-SEVEN

WELCOME TO THE JUNGLE

She sighed in relief when she stepped into the cool dry air of the dimly lit alien complex, the strange corridor with smooth floors were a welcome change from the last few hours of dense jungle underbrush and cloying heat. Rowen had spent most of her young life in Colorado Springs and had thought the muggy New York summers were the worst thing she could imagine, but after some time deep in the Amazon, she realized how wrong she was.

"I expected this to be more difficult," said Jonah, his heavy step echoing loudly behind her.

"It's the armor," piped up Gibbs in an excited tone, pulling aside the collar of the service uniform he wore to show that the crystal that snaked down from his neck was glowing a beautiful cobalt, steady and smooth, almost tranquil. "It's like this place recognizes you, all the crystals are reacting the same way." Rowen couldn't argue with the statement. Blake had led them to a tall door made from what looked like a delicate smoked glass, covered and overgrown by the jungle. They had expected to force their way in somehow, but the moment Jonah approached the door, it slid open with a quiet whisper, revealing a dark corridor illuminated by tiny crystals lining the floor on both sides.

"Blake, we need to hurry," said Arthur in a strained voice. "I'm holding him for now, but he's fighting me, and it's getting harder by the minute."

Rowen looked back to see Arthur with his eyes narrowed in concentration, sweat beading down his caramel-colored skin. Beside him was her father, unmoving but trembling like a coiled spring, his face twisted into a snarl. When the small Ascended had told her that he could control her father for the journey, she was suspicious, but so far Arthur had kept his word, despite the apparent difficulty.

"C'mon kid," said Blake. "If I remember, there should be a central hub up ahead that branches off to where we need to go, and if we're lucky, the AI that runs the joint will still be up and running."

Rowen shook her head at the ragtag group. They were an assorted group of oddballs at best, but she was grateful to have them at her back. The only person who hadn't made the trek was Captain Young. He had insisted that someone should stay with the transport, and given how difficult the journey through the jungle had been, she was glad he stayed behind. She wasn't sure he would have made it considering she barely did. Flipping down her tactical goggles she drew her SIG from its holster, hoping for the best and readying for the worst. "I've got point, Blake. You bring up the rear...the rest of you pay attention. Don't get distracted, and if you see something, say something," she said. Her small group nodded in acceptance, and they set down the strange corridor. Stepping cautiously, Rowen marveled at how this place was beyond anything she had ever imagined. Every piece of it felt alien, from the wide corridors that looked like smooth glass with tiny symbols she couldn't make out just below its surface to the odd little lights that lined each side of the hall. Even the sound of her boots sounded strange to her ear, muffled, like someone had lowered the volume of her footfalls.

"I wonder who built all this," said Gibbs in a small voice. "I mean, it doesn't look like any style from human history."

"That's not true," rumbled Blake from the back. "When we found the first set of ruins, we found symbols that looked like hieroglyphics, Egyptian writing."

Gibbs almost seemed to bounce on his heels, stopping to look closer at the symbols underneath the surface of the glass walls. "Did you see any images of the people or clothing or artwork?"

Rowen rolled her eyes at him, preferring the quiet to his babbling. "Keep it quiet. We don't know what the hell's in here." To her surprise Gibbs listened for once, returning to following the rest of the group down the dim corridor without her having to threaten his life. They walked in silence until they reached the hub that Blake had described, a circular room a little brighter than the corridor, with a high dome that vanished into the darkness. Dim corridors branched off in multiple directions, some leading deeper into the complex and others heading upward, almost at an angle. At the center of the room was a slim crystal spire about twice her height diffusing a soft, multicolored light.

"What now?" asked Rowen, giving Blake a questioning look.

Blake gave them all a shrug, coming forward to stand beside her. "I dunno. I was pretty far gone from the virus when I arrived, but I remember that the hologram of the AI was here. Maybe if we—"

"We need to make it quick," said Arthur with a shudder, wiping sweat from his brow. "The deeper we go into this place, the more he fights me."

Watching the contorted rage on her father's face, Rowen swallowed hard, her stomach churning with worry. If Arthur lost control of him, the contingency was that Jonah would hold him, and that she would have to make the call of what to do with him. And while she was sure that Jonah could hold him, she was also sure her father would fight him tooth and nail. Her brother's armor was jagged and razor sharp and would probably cut him to bits, no matter how much they tried to be gentle. The last thing she wanted was to have to shoot her own father. Not sure what else to do, Rowen did the brave or stupidest thing she could think of, placing her hand on the spire that stood in the center of the room.

The light level in the room suddenly surged from end of day twilight to the brightness of high noon, and Rowen was grateful for the polarization from her goggles. She was about to remove her hand when a diminutive hologram in sleeveless white robes flickered to life in front of her. At first glance she thought it was a small child but looking closer she realized the hologram was nothing like she had ever seen. Looking only vaguely human, it was covered in odd geometric patterns on its dark skin with eyes that never seemed blink. It had an oddly sloped forehead with hair that started in the middle of its skull, flowing down to its shoulders.

"Greetings, guardian," it said giving her, what she could only describe as a smile, its lips turning up larger than any person she had ever seen. "How may I be of service today?" it said in a machine monotone that was infinitely calm.

Rowen's SIG twitched in her hand. Her first reflex was to shoot, but she fought against every instinct and reluctantly holstered the weapon. "You know me?" she said slowly, her eyebrows drawing together.

The hologram gazed out to the rest of the team before returning its attention to Rowen. "Your genetic profile has diverged significantly; however, the baseline of yourself, your sibling, and father are recognized by this system," said the hologram, nodding to her father and brother respectively. "In fact, we have several of your genetic ancestors in hibernation."

"I don't understand," said Rowen. "My father, he's sick. We need—"

Before she could continue, Gibbs pushed forward past everyone, his clear-blue eyes wide like giant saucers. "You mean the people who created you are still here?" he said in a rush. "They're alive!"

The hologram suddenly fell to its knees, touching its head to the smooth glass floor. "Forgiveness, Katib," it said in an awed voice, not looking up. "My systems have been compromised, and power levels in the complex are very low. Most of our current energy is being used to maintain the population. It was difficult to detect who you were...but yes, I have fulfilled my basic programming and over ninety percent of the population in stasis is still intact. They may be revived if surface conditions meet the basic threshold."

To her surprise, Gibbs gave her a warm smile, standing tall with his back straight and looking more confident than he ever had in all the time she knew him. "I know what this is, Rowen," he said, speaking at a normal pace for once. "This place, it's an ark!"

She cocked her head, looking back and forth between Gibbs and her father, who was now twitching like a crazed junkie. "A what? You know what, it doesn't matter. We're running out of time, and we have to get my dad the cure for this virus."

"I understand," said Gibbs, placing his hand on the spire in front of them before Rowen could stop him. The crystal beneath his clothes changed to a brilliant green, so bright she could see the glow through his shirt. The surge spread from him into the spire like a wave, rolling through the slim shaft and then into the floor, spreading from there into the walls, pulsing down the myriad of corridors that led off from this room. As a group they gasped, Rowen turning in a circle when the walls faded from dark to light, the now transparent glass revealing hundreds, if not thousands, of tall cylinders lining the corridors, branching off in all directions as far as the eye could see, each one filled with small creatures similar to the hologram prostrated in front of them. Removing a shaking hand from the spire, Gibbs blinked at her, his voice hardly a whisper. "An ark."

"What the hell?" said Blake. "We didn't see anything like this last time we were here."

The hologram flickered back to its feet, appearing in front of Blake without moving. "Subject male. Name unknown. We removed the virus from you on your previous visit. You are responsible for the damage to our systems that left a guardian in cryo hibernation."

"What is it talking about? I thought you said he was dead?" asked Rowen.

Blake looked away, his face flushing a deep shade of pink. "I thought...I was sure."

"You mean you left someone here, trapped?" said Jonah, frowning at him. "What kind of coward does something like that?"

"I'm no goddamn coward," shouted Blake through gritted teeth. "That bastard killed my family, my brother who wasn't even ten, my sister who was still in her crib. He deserved worse. If I had the chance, I would do—"

At the back of the group Arthur suddenly groaned and fell over, his head bouncing on the glass floor. Swearing under her breath, Rowen was about to rush to his side when her father exploded into motion, coming at her with his face twisted in a rage. All the things he had taught came rushing back, and Rowen found herself using his momentum against him, deflecting his attacks as opposed to blocking them or trying to dodge them, using a hip throw on the big man and sending him tumbling to the floor.

The minute he landed on the smooth glass floor Jonah was there, pinning him with his massive armored frame. Seeing that he had it under control, Rowen raced to Arthur's side just as the small Ascended was sitting up, cradling his head, and heaving like he had just run a marathon. Helping him sit up, she could feel he was drenched in sweat, his eyes half closed from exhaustion. "Sorry, Rowen, I tried to keep him under control, I really did, but I think we're in trouble."

Rowen cringed when she looked back at her father to see Jonah's razor-sharp armor cutting deep slices into his arms and chest while her brother struggled to keep him in place. "It's okay, you warned us, besides I think Jonah can hold him for now. You get some rest while we figure this out."

Arthur shook his head, pressing his lips together. "You don't understand. It's not your dad that I'm worried about. I could feel something pressing against my will the whole time I was controlling him, fighting to get back in, to wrench control from me. That's what happens with the ones that are fully infected; they become part of a hive mind; what one sees they all see. What one knows they all know."

She shrugged, helping him stand on shaky legs. "It doesn't really matter. They're mindless; they can't really act on anything they see."

"Yes it does," said Arthur, pushing her away and smoothing his uniform. "Because I understand now."

"Understand what?" said Rowen, worrying for the first time when she saw how pale Arthur had become.

"Blake and I were talking on the way down. We wondered why the hell anyone would want to control a world full of mindless infected. But it's not like that; they're not mindless; they're of one mind. Every single one of them is an extension of his will: he can see, hear, and control. So when I lost control of your father—"

"Cardinal Washington saw where we are, that we're trying to stop the virus," said Rowen, scrubbing a hand through her curls

Arthur nodded, swallowing hard. "And he's coming, with everyone and everything. He has to stop us."

TWENTY-EIGHT
GHOSTS

"That was our mission all those years ago," said Blake. "It was one of the reasons we never went back. Bobby may have been an asshole, but he was right: putting any of this tech in Michael's hands would be destructive for the world."

Arthur leaned against the taller man for support as they made their way past what looked like a machine shop of some kind, his voice trembling with fatigue when he spoke. "How far to the medical bay?" he asked, knowing that they didn't have much time. When he had delved into Dr Fillipo's mind a few weeks ago, it hadn't been anything like trying to control Rowen's father, of course; he was just looking into the man's mind, not trying to stand up against thousands of consciousness fighting him all at once. But now it was different. Cardinal Washington was coming, and if he had his way, the cure for his virus would stay buried here in the ark forever.

"You can't just wake up a hundred thousand people," shouted Rowen to Gibbs, just up ahead, looking like she was about to punch him. The two had been fighting since they had begun their trek to the medical bay, the flickering hologram leading the way. Behind them,

Jonah was holding his thrashing father in a fireman's carry, his armor leaving violent, jagged cuts along the older man's dark skin and face.

Making his way down the now brightly lit corridor, Arthur's gaze was drawn to the faces of the diminutive creatures in the hibernation chambers that lined the walls. At first glance they looked very human. Their faces were a little thinner, but everything in the right place, eyes, nose and mouth. But the more he stared at their sloped foreheads and the strange patterns on their skin, the more alien they seemed, and he wondered just how close they were to his version of humanity. Slipping his vision into the quantum state to get a better understanding, Arthur staggered, blinded by the brightness that surrounded them. The power was flooding through the floors, the walls, but most of all, the hibernation chambers were off the scale, overwhelming him with ease. Squeezing his eyes shut, he switched back to normal, blinking away the afterimages flashing on his retina, clutching at Blake while breathing hard. "My God," he whispered.

"What?" asked Blake, looking around in confusion.

Arthur rubbed his eyes. "The energy, this place...it's ridiculous."

"What do you mean?"

"Like I told you before. I can see the world on a quantum level, atoms, electrons. The energy that makes up the world. The energy requirements to maintain this place, it was brighter than the sun, brighter than anything I've ever seen," said Arthur, dropping his voice to a whisper. "The amount of power running through these walls is dangerous. I think Rowen's right. We can't let these people, these things, wake up. It'll be worse than anything Cardinal Washington might do."

"I'm not sure I follow you."

Feeling a little stronger, he squared his shoulders and locked his arms behind his back, walking on his own, grateful he didn't have to rely on anyone. When he began, he took on a lecturing tone, trying to put his thoughts into words that made sense. "From what Gibbs said before, anyone with the gene to get powers descended from these people.The crystals, Ascension, I think we can pretty much guess it all comes from them."

"So?"

"Well, what happens when they wake up and want their world back?" asked Arthur. "We see it all the time in nature: there are predator and prey, master and servant. Given how powerful they are, which one do you think we're going to be?"

Blake looked down at the floor, scratching at his jaw. "So what? We just kill them all," he said with a nervous laugh.

"It's them or us," said Arthur, looking at him and not blinking.

"That's genocide," he said, stopping in his tracks. "We can't just kill thousands of people."

"They're not people," said Arthur. "They've been gone for thousands of years. Wiped from history. And now they are trying to cheat their way back into the world after having been gone for so long."

"We can't just make that call without knowing all the facts," whispered Blake, pushing Arthur forward. "Who knows what happened."

"We don't have time to find out. We have a madman coming down here to take this place...and I'm not sure we can stop him."

Blake was silent for a moment, his gaze lingering on the sleeping faces of the creatures as they walked by. They had just come to another circular intersection, and the hologram ordered them to stop. It waved its hand, and the floor they were standing on was suddenly highlighted by a circle of small light crystals and began to descend deeper into the ark.

"Hey, Hologram guy," called out Blake suddenly, speaking over Rowen and Gibbs who continued to argue, Rowen's face growing redder by the minute. When the hologram flickered in place in front of him, he crossed his arms across his chest and continued. "Why did all these people go to sleep, and why haven't they woken up yet?" he said, motioning haphazardly at the crystal cylinders all around them.

The hologram flickered slightly, waving like the images from an old TV. "War," it said in its monotone, electronic voice as if the word explained everything.

"War? War with who?" asked Rowen, forgetting her argument with Gibbs.

The hologram flickered in place, settling its attention on Rowen. "Multiple hominid species were involved in the great conflict, but by the end, the only factions with any real strength were our own and the Naledi. It was they who released the virus."

"And the virus forced you into the ark, to go into hibernation," said Gibbs, nodding along.

"Affirmative, Katib. They designed the virus to specifically attack our gnome," it said just as the platform came to a halt, the flickering hologram heading down another brightly lit corridor. "The virus is still present in the atmosphere, and we calculate that at current rates, the surface will be safe within the next thousand solar cycles."

Arthur narrowed his eyes, staring hard at the small creature. "But Cardinal Washington has flooded the atmosphere with additional copies of the virus; millions of people are infected now, are being converted."

"Restoration of surface conditions is the responsibility of the guardians," said the hologram, offering nothing more. They came to an opaque glass door and vanished, only to reappear on the other side when the door slid open, revealing a compact area with walls that glowed a soft blue. Evenly spaced throughout the area were a series of low surgical beds that looked like they were designed for children, and finally, standing in the back corner of the room were a series of cylinders that were different from the hibernation chambers they saw on their journey down, taller with a control console attached at the side, filled with a blue liquid of some kind: all were empty, except one. Arthur could barely make out the individual who was frozen in the liquid, still dressed in the long, red leather coat that Divinity Corps members had worn in the early days.

"This is the place," said Blake, his voice just above a whisper, leading the way into the room as if he were in a daze. He stopped in front of the only cylinder that looked like it was occupied, running a hand along its damaged control panel, his fingers tracing what looked like a deep cut in its surface. After a moment, he shook his head and turned to face them, crossing his arms over his chest. "Tamika and I were put in these chambers; the AI did the rest. I'm not really sure how we can use it to help everyone, but it should be able to at least help your father."

"Affirmative," said the hologram in its electronic monotone. "However, the subject will require an extended period to return its biomatter to a nominal state."

"An extended period?" asked Arthur, knowing that they were running out of time. "How long is that? Cardinal Washington is coming with everything he has. We need to be ready to fight him."

The hologram flickered toward the front of the tall cylinders, and the glass cover on one of them slid open with soft hiss. "Several hours. Please place the subject in the chamber, and we will begin the process."

Ignoring his father's flailing fists and thrashing legs, Jonah carried him bodily to the medical chamber and placed him inside the narrow space. While he held him in place, the chamber began spraying a fine blue mist that calmed him, his strange silver eyes slowly rolling up into his head while his body went limp a second later. "What about this one?" asked Jonah, pointing at the other chamber. "Is he still alive? Maybe he could help. He was an Ascended, right?"

"The infection has been removed from subject O'Connell," said the hologram. "However, subject O'Regan did extensive damage to the control systems, and repairs must be effected before the patient can be revived."

Arthur frowned, moving closer to peer at the man in the cylinder. "O'Connell? I thought you said his name was Bobby."

"Yeah, Bobby O'Connell," grumbled Blake. "Robert, actually, but he hated being called that."

Arthur was suddenly cold, numb. "I killed him," he whispered, stumbling backward and falling on his backside like a drunkard. He could hardly believe what he was seeing; it was like a nightmare.

"You okay, buddy?" said Blake, dropping to his knee and moving to help him up. "Try and take it easy; you—"

Arthur pushed him away, narrowing his eyes. "I've been down in the secret records room in Iron Mountain. I know all the dirty little things they've hidden over the years," he said, pouring his mind into the chamber's control systems, his breath catching in his throat when he felt the gigawatts of electrical energy coursing through the power grid of this place. "There was no record of Major Bishop O'Connell coming on the mission here, or any association with you or the others of your team. In fact, the only mention of the name Bobby was that the Major Bishop hated the name; it was an embarrassment to him."

Blake frowned in confusion. "Major Bishop O'Connell was Bobby? I don't think so. I saw that asshole on the holonet; he was an old man—shit." Blake looked down at his age-spotted hand, cocking his head as he pressed his lips together. "How?"

"Rodrigo," said Arthur, taking control. The systems in the cylinder were extensive, and the programming was like nothing Arthur had ever seen, but the basics of any system were the same to him, the rhythm and beats universal for his powers.

"What are we talking about, now?" said Gibbs, his bright blue eyes blinking in confusion.

Rowen crossed her arms over her small breasts, frowning at him. "Yeah, I think you've lost us. Isn't Rodrigo the guy with the big nose? What does he have to do with this?"

"When Uriel and I met Rodrigo at Iron Mountain a few years ago, we fought. He lost his head; it wasn't pretty."

Rowen made a face, doubt in her eyes. "Like Captain Young says...sounds like horseshit to me."

"No, it's true. The Rodrigo we know now is a copy, a clone," said Arthur, bypassing the damaged control panel and beginning the revival process, the tall cylinder humming to life. "And if this Bobby never came back, they must have made a copy."

Gibbs put his hand up to speak then blushed when Rowen rolled her eyes at him. "Well, why doesn't Cardinal Washington have a copy of everyone, every Ascended they ever made? Hell, an arm of Gwen's could level the planet: he would be unstoppable."

"I don't know," said Arthur, focusing on the man in the chamber. If everything was true, that O'Connell he knew was a copy, then he had never really met the man, only a modified version of him, with his memory and personality edited, but did it really matter. The core of who he was wouldn't be any different; he would still be a monster, an abuser. He would still be the man who drove Arthur over the edge, to the point where he almost killed Gwen.

"Bobby was really important to the program," said Blake. "He was the one who recruited me, Tamika and Daniel too. It was something to do with his power. He could detect the Ascension gene, so if he didn't come back, they would have been screwed."

"Hey, are you waking him up?" asked Rowen, snapping her fingers in front of Arthur's face when he didn't immediately respond.

"Yes," said Arthur in a flat tone, pushing her hand away. "Biometric data is coming online. Heart rate increasing; body temperature is coming up on nominal, and I'm seeing some limited brain activity."

Blake leaned in, his deep voice loud even while he tried to whisper. "You sure you wanna wake this guy up? There's a reason I shoved my sword into the control panel. Bobby's a worldclass asshole. He doesn't deserve to come back."

He nodded, finally breaking his gaze to look up at Blake. "Yes. If he's anything like the man I knew, he was a monster."

"Then why are you waking him up?" said Rowen.

Rowen placed a hand on the gun in her holster, the gun that had almost killed him, and Arthur's heart started beating out of his chest, his breaths coming in quick bursts. He had no doubt she would shoot him, and with her brother looking like a giant behind her, he was sure there would be nothing he could do to stop her. Looking at her, finally he relented, knowing it wouldn't be long now, a thrill running through him at the thought. "I'm waking him up, so that his evil will be gone from the world...so I can kill him!"

TWENTY-NINE

FIFTEEN YEARS

His first thoughts were of Elizabeth, of her dark eyes. When she was angry they were cold and distant like a winter moon, and at other times when she looked at him, they were warm as a summer's day. He remembered springtime walks in the Boston Common, hand in hand, with the sun on his face. He remembered being worried, being afraid. But after he met her, she showed him what it was to be a good person, to know what bravery was. She could always make him feel better, feel safe... But then he remembered what he did to her, all in the name of duty.

Bobby could still feel her turn to ash in his hands, with nothing left but dust that slipped through his fingers and vanished on the wind. He swore that on some days, even after she was long gone, he could still feel her lifeforce coursing through him, that a part of her was still with him. Not that it mattered anymore: she was and always would be with him as the voice in his head, guiding him to do the right thing.

Ice-cold air unexpectedly filling his lungs banished the memories, pleasant and unpleasant, and Bobby suddenly realized where he was, frozen, trapped, fifteen minutes or fifteen hours, he wasn't sure. A feeling of dread came over him, and his pulse quickened when he remembered clawing at the glass while the hologram AI counted down his time required to cleanse the virus from his body, trapped once more in a small space where he could hardly move. When blood began sluggishly pumping through his heart, his senses came to life, and the first thing he felt, before he could see, hear, or feel, was that unpleasant itch in his brain that he could never scratch, that tic just beneath his skull that would have driven him mad if he hadn't learned to control it. The itch that allowed him to feel life, and right now he could feel it all around him.

There must have been thousands of individuals, human but not human, strange creatures barely alive that filled the complex, their hearts beating ever so slowly, like they were trapped between life and death, every breath slow and steady. Closer, very close, were others like him...human. Bobby felt an electric shock of surprise run through him when he realized each one of them carried the Ascension gene, some of them stronger than he had ever felt before, and then his eyes shot open, his blood running faster, hotter. Anger bubbled just beneath the surface when he recognized one of them...Finn. Finn was there, with only a thin sheet of transparent material separating them.

"You can't just kill him," said a woman's voice, muted through the glass. Her tone was blunt and forceful. He could tell she wasn't Ascended, but there was a raw power to her, and that she would be very strong if she ever went through the process.

"You don't know what he did to me," said a voice Bobby had never heard before, so full of bitterness, he felt a swell of pity for whomever it belonged to. "He ruined me, killed a part of me that I can never get back."

"I think Arthur's got a point," said Finn, his voice sounding strange, tired. "Bobby ruined his life. Hell, he ruined my life too. The guy has a ton of blood on his hands, and he needs to pay the price."

Bobby couldn't believe what he was hearing, the ignorance and half truths, the lies. He knew he had taken lives, but every time he didn't have a choice. Elizabeth and Andrew would have killed millions in Boston and New York if he hadn't stopped them, and Cardinal Washington would have done the same if he didn't make the choice to hide the technology from this base and the others they had found. And now these ungrateful vultures wanted to kill him for it, strangers who had no idea of the things he'd sacrificed to keep people safe. For once, Bobby easily found his rage, embracing the burning torrent of anger at these people circling him like vultures. He would show them. He would kill them all; drain them dry, so there would be nothing left but ash.

He didn't bother letting the field of dark energy build slowly. Instead, he lashed out, brutally snapping the field in place and not only encompassing the people just outside his icy prison, but spreading it, so it touched the strange creatures in deep sleep. Bobby relished in the gusts of power running through him, the infinite torrent of energy flooding every inch of his whip-thin frame until he was near bursting. He shrugged off the last remnants of the cryo hibernation, and with a titanic roar he smashed through the transparent cover of the cylinder as though it were fragile glass, exploding into the compact med bay to find a small group writhing at his feet.

With a start, Bobby took stock of the strange band of would-be murderers, and he slowed the torrent of energy coming from them to a trickle, inflicting pain but not killing just yet. He was confused; he had expected to find Finn, but who the rest of them were was a mystery. Stranger still, while he could feel that the tall man on the floor was his old teammate, the salt-and-pepper hair and age-spotted skin made him question everything, and he wondered how long he had been trapped. The rest of the group were strangers. A small boy with a red collar, a redheaded girl whose face was a mask of scars, clutched tightly to a pale boy whose bright blue eyes were wide open with fear, and giant of a man covered from head to toe in jagged crystal armor lay next her.

Bobby was about to finish them off when the small boy with

caramel-colored skin fought his way to his feet, his handsome features twisted from the pain.

They locked eyes, and even without his strange sense, Bobby could feel waves of hatred coming off of him. "I made a promise that you would never hurt me or anyone else ever again," he said through gritted teeth, taking a step toward him even as his skin became hollow and gray. "Die!"

Bobby cocked his head, not understanding the threat until a heartbeat later when the cylinder he had just escaped from exploded in a wild surge of electrical energy that arced madly in all directions. Every muscle in his body spasmed when the jagged bolts of cobalt coursed through him, setting every nerve on fire and hurling him bodily across the room where he tumbled over a low medical bed, sliding on the smooth, polished floor until he hit the back wall. The torrent of dark energy coursing through him was cut off the moment he lost concentration, but he managed to use the last of it to heal the electrical burns, banish of the pain to memory as his skin healed from charred black to healthy pink, while he watched. Not wanting the boy to keep the initiative, he grabbed his monowhip from his hip, uncoiling the deadly weapon while vaulting to his feet.

Dark smoke poured out of the destroyed cylinder, covering the room in a choking haze of smoke, making it difficult to see, but for Bobby it didn't matter; he could still sense all of them. The redheaded girl was helping her pale friend to his feet; the titan in crystal armor and Finn were still shaking on the floor. Thinking he had a moment, Bobby found his concentration again, stoking the fires of rage to finish them off when the boy, the one Finn had called Arthur, leaped at him through the haze, his knee aimed at his head. Bobby ducked down instinctively, letting him fly over and slam into the softly glowing wall, spider-thin cracks appearing in the glass from his strike. From his low position Bobby wasted no time, sweeping out with a leg and taking Arthur's feet out from under him just before he touched down, sending him tumbling on his back. Then with brutal efficiency, he slammed his heel into his head, knocking him senseless.

Turning to face the rest of them, he was forced to dodge to his side to avoid being cut in half by Finn's katana. Taking advantage of him being off balance, Bobby unleashed a quick jab to his face, forcing him back so he could spin up his monowhip. Cutting a figure eight with the near invisible line, he advanced, forcing the taller man on the defensive. Sparks flew when their weapons connected, both of them striking and parrying in a frenzy of steel and near indestructible monofilament, neither man gaining nor giving advantage. Behind him, Bobby could sense Arthur was recovering, and somewhere through the haze the big man covered in crystal, had just gotten to his feet. Not wanting them to flank him, he surprised Finn by drawing the line back in and causing him to overreach. Then Bobby grabbed his forearm and spun him bodily, hurling him directly at the crystal-clad giant and knocking them both over before he could enter the fray.

Then Bobby ducked down to grab Arthur by the collar, and it saved his life. The wall in front of him exploded from a pair of booming gunshots that tore clean through the transparent material, leaving a pair of massive holes where his chest would have been. Bobby cursed under his breath, and recognizing the threat of the weapon, he changed tactics. Dragging Arthur to his feet, he spun on his heel, holding him up in front of him like a shield. Master Sergeant Cook had warned them so very long ago that a sufficiently powered high-caliber weapon could cut through his toughened flesh just as easily as a normal person's, so he would use the boy to protect himself. "Enough," he shouted, eyeing the redhead's strange gun that was leveled at him. "I swear I'll kill him if anyone even twitches."

"Still a goddamn murderer, aren't you, Bobby?" said Finn, pointing at him with his flashing blade, his angry sneer the same, even if he was so much older.

"You all were talking about killing me. I heard you talking," said Bobby, narrowing his eyes at Finn, still confused. "Why do you look like that...how long was I in there for?"

"Since I left your sorry ass in there," said Finn, showing his teeth.

"We have the drop on you," said the redhead, her weapon rock steady in her hand. "There are four us and one of you. How do you think this ends?"

Bobby hesitated, having a moment of doubt. The girl and her strange gun were dangerous. In fact, so was this Arthur kid he was using as a shield, and he could only imagine what the towering man in crystal could do. But the girl was only human, and he'd had them all at his mercy just a few seconds ago. "I don't think you understand, but Finn does. He knows...I'm not the one who should be afraid. You are!"

Bobby watched them spread out, stepping slowly to flank him, the boy in his hands starting to squirm. He began to gather his rage, his power, when one of them stepped forward. The one with the bright blue eyes full of fear. "Rowen, we can't afford to lose any of you. Cardinal Washington is coming, and if he takes the ark, we're done. The world is done."

"Finn, what does he mean!? What the hell is he talking about?" asked Bobby, his eyes narrowing. "Were you stupid enough to let Michael find this place? Did you let your idiot vendetta with me blind you to what he would do?"

To his surprise, Finn lowered his katana, swallowing hard. "I wouldn't...I didn't. You've been gone a long time; things have changed."

Arthur groaned, and Bobby, not wanting to lose his advantage, drew on his rage and raised a hand to the boy's throat, dark tendrils of dark energy writhing and circling around his fingers. "If you blink, you won't live to see your next breath," he said nodding to Finn and the girl. "You say things have changed, but we still have Michael wanting to take over the world, chasing after this technology, so he can remake it in his twisted image."

"He's already done that," said Arthur in a low whisper, flinching when Bobby brought his darkened hand closer to his face. "The virus, he spread it to most of the country...millions of people are infected. They're all part of him now; he controls them completely."

Bobby felt numb suddenly, shaking his head in disgust. "God-damnit, Finn, that's not possible. We stopped it!" said Bobby, his voice breaking. "We did our duty to keep this thing out of his hands, to keep everyone safe."

The frightened one with the bright blue eyes stepped forward. His hand out in front of him, he began speaking so fast it was almost impossible to follow what he was saying. "We came here to find a way to stop it—that and save Rowen's father. Blake...I mean Finn here...you know him as Finn; he said that your team was infected, that there—"

"Shut up, Gibbs," said the redhead. "Blake told us you murdered his family in cold blood, and Arthur, over there, says you abused him...physically. I'm a big believer in justice, so before I put a bullet in your head, what's your side of the story?"

Bobby debated for a moment to just unleash his field of dark energy and draining them all to husks, but then he would most likely have to face Michael on his own, without any clue as to what was going on. He was tired of being vilified, being made a monster by strangers even when he was doing the right thing. "Okay, I'll play along. I couldn't tell you if I killed Finn's family, I did kill thousands of people stopping an attack in Boston that would have killed millions if I didn't do what I did," he said, bowing his head. "But feel guilt and shame every time I think about it. And as for Arthur here, I have no clue who you are. Yes, I've fought against my demons my whole life, but I've never once done the things you're talking about."

Arthur looked back at him, his large eyes full of doubt. When he spoke, there was a tremble in his voice. "It's at the core of who you are...I know, I've, I—"

"Yes, but someone who believed in me, someone who loved me very much, taught me I can be more than what God made me. I don't have to give in to sin."

"Liar," said Arthur, his eyes bright with tears, his small body trembling.

Seeing the fear in him, Bobby let his rage fade away, the dark tendrils of energy circling his hand dissipating. Without another word, he pushed him away, watching the others from the corner of his eye. "I don't know what happened to you, Arthur, but I'm sorry it did. I can only tell you I would never be able to live with myself if I hurt anyone because I know what it's like to be betrayed, to be angry all the time. It can ruin you; make you do the worst things. And Finn, I know words can't bring them back, but I'm sorry about your family. I didn't know...how could I?"

Across the room, the redhead, Rowen, holstered her gun, motioning for the others to stand down. Without a word, she strode right up to him, flipping up a pair of mirrored goggles that she wore. "I'm Rowen," she said, sticking out a small hand. "You've met Arthur and Blake over there. The tall one there is my brother Jonah, and in the pod over there is my father. He's in the last stage of the infection, and we hope this place can fix him. I know this started off a little rough, and you've been out of the game for a long time now, but the world is in trouble. Michael is coming, and if he takes this place, gets rid of us, there'll be no one to stop him, so I'm asking for your help...if you're willing."

Bobby blinked in surprise at her. Up close she wasn't pretty. Her face was a mess of scars and too many freckles, her nose sharp and pointed, and her lips were too thin. She was the type of person who would never get a second look, who the world would ignore if it could. But despite not being Ascended, she wasn't afraid. She had guts, and he found himself nodding while she spoke. "Bobby O'Connell," he said, taking her small hand, an odd thought running through his mind, "you know no one's ever asked me before."

"Asked you what?"

"If I wanted to help. Pastor Warren, Michael, even Lieutenant Young. They forced me with threats, or with false promises, or whatever else they could come up with to make me do their dirty work," he said, feeling light all of a sudden. "So yes. I'll do it, let's stop this nightmare once and for all."

THIRTY

OVERRUN

"I've never seen so many at once," said Gwen, her voice filled with awe, "even on the bridge."

"We should leave this place, bellissima," said Rodrigo, still looking handsome despite his jet-black hair being out of place and his normally pristine robes covered in grime and soot. "Do as you say, find some clear skies."

Gwen didn't bother to correct him; it didn't matter anymore. Despite everything they'd done, hundreds of thousands of infected were pouring into the city, more than they could stop. "Arthur gave me one job, to watch his city, and I totally fucked it up!" They stood on top of one of the buildings on the Upper West Side, overlooking Central Park, watching the infected stream up the avenue, Gwen's heart sinking when she realized there was nothing she could do; there was no one left to save. She had ordered emergency services to broadcast the message that people should find some way to barricade themselves from the infected, preferably someplace up high. With that done, she told them to go home to their families if they had any, and do the same.

"How could you know they would come from the water? You are

no saint with an ear to God," said Rodrigo, "and we are well past the age of miracles."

She nodded, knowing he was right. They were all completely taken by surprise when an army of infected appeared out of nowhere in Lower Manhattan, overwhelming the barricades and security checkpoints. She had flown faster than she ever had to find the source of the new invasion, cursing at herself when she saw hordes of them emerging from the waters around Battery Park, more than she could safely kill without endangering the city with the blast wave she would generate to stop them.

"So, what do you think of my suggestion?" he said, leering at her, showing her his perfect teeth as if smiling at her would make her change her mind.

"I think it's a bad idea. I'm much stronger than you, and I might tear something off if I get too excited," she said, smiling to herself when she saw him pale beneath his olive skin.

"So what, we stay here and die?"

"No, we do what Arthur said we do. We hold until he comes back to fix this."

Rodrigo snorted, a deep frown coming to his face. "You think this little black will return to you. No, no, he is long gone, like we should be. This city is lost."

She raised a fist to his face, narrowing her eyes at him. "Arthur is an asshole sometimes, but he gives a shit, more than most people. If he says he's coming back, he'll be back. So, we do like he said: we hold what we can, and pray that there is something left for him to save when he gets here."

"You have more faith than I do," said Rodrigo, lowering his voice and staring out at the hordes of converted.

Gwen followed his gaze, muttering under her breath, praying that her faith in him was worth it, doubt nagging at her about what would happen if he didn't come back.

THIRTY-ONE

FAITH

Arthur couldn't stop staring. Bobby reminded him of the major bishop in so many ways, from his pale blue eyes to the small bend in his nose, even the way he brushed his hand through his hair. But the more he spoke, the more he could see the difference from the man who had caused him so much pain. They both had the same seething rage just beneath the surface, but the major bishop had been domineering, looking down his nose at everyone, and he never liked that an idea that wasn't his. But under that anger, Bobby had a kindness, a warmth, and to Arthur's surprise, a strange desire to protect others. "How is it that you're so different from him?" said Arthur, interrupting the intense debate of their planning session.

After Rowen and Bobby had decided to put aside their differences, and with Cardinal Washington just an hour away, they had all settled in around one of the low medical beds to make plans on how to stop him, but no matter how hard he tried to focus, Arthur couldn't move past it. He knew that when Cardinal Washington cloned someone, he edited their personality, changed things to make them more like he wanted, like he did with Rodrigo. But the tall Italian, despite his desire to be a better person, was still fundamentally an ass, even at the best of times.

Bobby looked at him, narrowing his eyes in thought before finally shrugging. "I don't know. I'm just me. Until a few minutes ago I had been on ice for almost as long as I've been alive, and I had no clue why Michael would clone me...or why. We were friends once; at least I thought so, but he hated me at the end."

"The other you, he was so angry. He hurt so many kids I...I just...if you're the same person, won't you just do the same as you get older?"

Bobby brushed a hand through his hair, pressing his lips together. "Part of me will always have that desire. I can't control that. But I have faith in God and my love for Elizabeth. I think maybe that's the difference, the thing Michael took away from the clone. I'm sure that without faith, without love, I would become a monster too."

"Okay, can we get back to our meeting now?" said Rowen, sitting right in front of them with a half-smile on her face. "I mean, unless you guys wanna hug it out."

Arthur put a hand up to forestall Rowen, still not satisfied with Bobby's answers. "But faith and religion, that's just a way for the church to control us. God doesn't exist: we all know that."

The moment the words left his mouth, Arthur felt the room go cold, and he saw a quiet rage smolder in Bobby's eyes as he answered. "Faith is real. It's the only thing that has kept me sane, kept me going after I lost my mother and when I was forced to work in the church. At my lowest, I turned to the Lord for comfort, for protection, and he sent me Elizabeth to help guide and protect me."

"Those things are just coincidence," said Arthur, standing up and locking his arms behind his back.

"The great thing about faith, Arthur, is it doesn't matter if you believe or not," said Bobby, touching his chest. "It only matters that I find what I need in my belief."

Arthur opened his mouth to speak, struggling to find the words before finally shaking his head. "Sorry, we're running out of time, so let's get to it," he said, realizing that everyone had kept silent and was waiting for him to say something, that they had watched with their jaws hanging open at his and Bobby's little exchange. Arthur sighed, feeling like a weight had been lifted off his shoulders.

"Good," said Rowen, eyeing all of them. "Our problem is twofold, one is Michael himself. From what Blake tells me, he's one of the most dangerous Ascended ever created. And two, we need to protect the thousands of creatures in hibernation here. If he gets enough infected in here, he'll destroy—"

"We can't still be talking about this," said Arthur, not believing what he was hearing. "We can't protect them and stop him, at the same time. Worse, what happens if we save them, and when they wake up, they end up being a greater threat than Michael ever was?"

The hologram flickered into place suddenly, piping up in its monotone voice. "The ancestors in hibernation are a kind and noble people, the best of their—"

"We only have your word on that," said Arthur. "History is written by the victors, isn't it?"

"They weren't winning," said Bobby suddenly. "They were on the verge of being wiped out. The people who created the virus, they had beat them back to only a few cities and then only to one. In the end, they evacuated to places like this."

"How would you know that?" said Gibbs, his eyes wide like he was drinking in every word.

"One of the first sets of ruins I found, I can't explain it, but I had these visions, connections to the past. And every time we found another, the visions got more intense."

"I remember those," rumbled Blake. "I thought it was all bullshit, but now...I don't know."

"It doesn't matter," said Rowen. "I'm not going to let thousands die, not while I can do something about it. If we're gonna make a plan to defend this place, I need to know what resources I'm working with. Myself, my brother, and Blake over here, I know what we're capable of. Arthur and Bobby, I know you guys are Ascended, so

you're tough and fast, but I need to know the rest of it—your capabilities."

Arthur shrugged, giving Rowen a wry smile. "I can control
machines, computers, and whatnot; they become like a part of me,
like an extra hand or eye. I can see what they see, feel what they feel.
I can also see the basic building blocks of reality, the motions of particles and whatnot: it all seems to go together with me controlling
things."

Rowen scratched at the jagged scar that covered a large part of
her face, and Arthur winced, still wondering how her face had
become such a mess. "Okay," she said, standing up and starting to
pace, "I can work with that. What about you, Bobby? What do you
have up your sleeve?"

"I'm like everyone else who's gone through the process, maybe a
little more agile from what I've seen. I have this weird ability where I
can feel people, know where they are, what they're feeling, but for
the rest...it's hard to explain."

"I know you've been out of the loop for a while," said Rowen,
spinning on her heel and casually dropping a hand on the butt of her
gun. "But we don't have time to coddle you, so spit it out."

Arthur cringed, expecting an explosion from Bobby, but to his
surprise, he leaned in close and whispered to him. "Is she always like
this? She knows we're the ones with godlike abilities and not her,
right?"

"Yes," said Arthur, giving her a sidelong glance. "But it doesn't
seem to matter to her. The last time I didn't listen to her she shot me,
more than once. Almost killed me."

"How?"

Before he could answer, Rowen suddenly stepped between them,
staring hard at him. "Seriously, are you ever going to let that go,
Arthur?"

"You shot me for disagreeing with you," said Arthur, taken aback
that she was so close.

"She beat me up!" said Gibbs, eyeing her sheepishly, "and then got mad at me when I wouldn't forgive her...and she punches me all the time for no reason."

Blake suddenly cleared his throat, coughing into his hand. "She's threatened to kill me at least three times in the last few days, had her gun in hand when she did it too."

Rowen spun around, face red, eyeing them all. "You've got to be kidding me! I swear—"

Before she could finish, her brother stretched to his full height, towering over them all "She shot me twice in the chest and then in the face," he said in his deep voice, making a face as if he were in pain, "but her temper has always gotten the better of her even when she was little."

"Okay, okay, I get it," said Bobby, putting his hands up, a smile coming easily. "Most of what I can do isn't in the official record anyway. It's best summed up by saying I take life or give it. Taking it is easier. I can create a form of dark energy that drains the life of everything around me: people, plants, animals. Either directly or like a giant explosion, it doesn't matter which way I do it because when I'm done, there's nothing left but husks that look years dead."

Arthur looked over at Blake and felt a wave of pity for him. The older man had bright eyes full of tears, looking haggard and broken. "And what happens to that energy from those lives you take?" said Blake, finding his voice and running a hand across his eyes.

"I can use it...to do different things," he said, his face going red. "Most of the time, I've healed myself...but I can give it back too! Heal other people."

"What about the infected, does it affect them?" asked Rowen.

"Yes," began Bobby, looking at Blake, who shook his head and crossed his arms. "Daniel, one of our teammates, was heavily affected by the virus. When he attacked, I had no choice but to put him down. There wasn't much left after that."

"That's it?" asked Rowen, raising an eyebrow.

"No, I can feel if someone has the right genetics for Ascension, and if I give back enough energy to someone like you Rowen...I can Ascended them, make them like me, like us,"

Arthur smoothed down his uniform, his high collar suddenly feeling uncomfortable. "Having another one of us would go a long way to giving us an advantage," he said, locking eyes with the redhead.

Rowen shook her head, her jagged scar turning an ugly shade of pink. "You know what happens to you guys, don't you?" she said, nodding at Blake. "If you're lucky, you end up like Blake over there, old before your time. At the worst, you're dead before you—"

"I know," said Arthur, interrupting, "but sometimes we need to make the hard call for the greater good."

"That's what you idiots keep telling me, and I keep telling you no!"

Arthur stepped up to her, putting a hand on her shoulder. "Rowen, you're asking all of us to put our lives on the line to do the impossible, and that's okay, we signed up for that. But I'm sorry, I've seen you in action. You're impressive, but you're still only human. One wrong move, and Michael, or some random infected, will cut you down in a heartbeat."

She went silent and walked over to the cylinder her father was in, placing a hand on the glass surface. At first Arthur thought that he had gone too far, and any minute she would turn around and shoot him, then to his surprise, she turned around and gave him a hard look. "Fine...do it...but if this doesn't work, I'll kill all of you."

THIRTY-TWO
PRELUDE TO MADNESS

Rowen felt like a new person, lighter than air, almost like she could fly. Her muscles pulsed with a newfound strength, and her skin was bright and clear, glowing. Her senses were the biggest change she had seen so far. Her eyes were sharper, and she found she could read the tiny hidden hieroglyphics on the glass walls even from across the room. She could make out the pores on Bobby's tired-looking face and hear Blake breathing ever so slowly. She had expected the transformation to be painful. Pain was easy; she could handle pain. But it wasn't anything like that. It felt amazing, beyond belief. With a start, she patted down her chest, thinking just maybe. Feeling nothing different, she sighed, cursing under her breath.

"Are you okay?" asked her brother, putting a hand on her shoulder. For a heartbeat he looked like their mother and had that same worried look that she often gave her, gave them both, after they had a fight.

"I've never felt better, but you'd think if I was gonna get super powers that would kill me eventually, that I would at least get boobs out of it...I just can't win, can I?" she said, putting a hand on his and giving him an awkward pat. She found it strange that they had spent so much time fighting, showing each other kindness was difficult at the best of times. "But everything else seems okay, so far, eyes and ears are a little sharper. I mean I can see little cracks in the crystal that make up your armor, and I can hear Blake's ragged heartbeat over there."

Jonah frowned at her. "It would be just like you to not be like everyone else, to be a troublemaker. You're supposed to be tougher too, right?" he said.

"Stronger too," she said. "I'll probably be back to kicking your ass soon.

"That's strange," said Bobby with a groan. "The others I did this to, they responded right away."

Rowen could tell that what he did to her had exhausted him. His skin was ashen, his eyes sunken. Even his voice was thinner, like he had aged decades in a few minutes. "Are you gonna be okay? I don't want to sound cold, but if you're not able to fight, it's just going to make things more difficult."

"I'll be fine, just need a few minutes."

Rowen nodded, turning to the rest of them. "Okay from the Ark's early warning system. We know Cardinal Washington constructed a massive transport with his abilities, bigger than anything we've ever seen before. And he's coming with thousands of late-stage infected, not to mention hundreds of soldiers that still have their wits about them, so there'll be shooting."

Gibbs put his hand up to speak, earning him a withering look from her. "What exactly does he want with this place anyway?" he said, spreading his hands. "I mean, it's just a few thousand people who'll be asleep for the next thousand years."

"Michael's always wanted the tech these people have," said Bobby, getting to his feet with a sigh. "At first, I think he was just following orders from Pastor Warren, but in the end he knew the real prize were the data bases full of ancient technology that would get him the edge he needed to expand his control. I mean, look at what he's done with just a sliver of it, gaining control of the entire country, using the virus to control the population, and worse, still having his abilities when he should have died years ago or at least ended up like Finn...sorry, I mean, Blake: no offense."

"None taken," said Blake from the corner. He had been strangely quiet the whole time, and Rowen was worried about how he was taking all of this.

Ignoring the interruptions, Rowen continued, "He will most likely be going for the data core of the caretaker hologram that has been helping us. With that, he can pretty much replicate anything it has access to."

"I can stop the infected," said Bobby. "My powers can cut them down, the soldiers too, but I'll kill anything else within the radius, so we need to do this outside of the Ark to prevent me hurting the population; you guys too. And the minute I start, Michael will come for me. If I'm going to do this, I need cover."

Rowen crossed her arms across her small breasts, nodding along. "That means we have to meet him in the field, cut him off before he gets here, Jonah. Can you intercept him by air, draw him off?"

"I'll get it done," said Jonah, stretching to his full height. "But he'll see me coming from a mile away."

"We also need to make sure he can't find this place," said Rowen, scratching the long scar running down her face. "It's too bad Blake is out of commission. He would be perfect."

"Keep dreamin', kid. I'm about as useless as tits on a bull here," he said, looking away. Rowen bit her tongue to stop herself from saying anything, understanding now why he looked so beaten down. No one wanted to feel useless.

"I have an idea about that," said Arthur, raising his chin, looking at her for permission to continue.

"Go for it; let's get everything on the table," said Rowen, nodding for him to continue.

"I've been looking at Blake on a quantum level, and I can see the nanites that give an Ascended their abilities are still in his system, but because he stopped using his abilities, they atrophied: sort of like if you don't use your muscles, they get small and weak. That's why he's still alive; they stopped destroying his cells to replicate because he wasn't activating them."

"So what? Can't you just turn them on?" asked Rowen, her brow wrinkling.

"Sort of," said Arthur, squaring his shoulders and looking over at Bobby. "I've only tried turning them off. It worked once, and it almost killed the person I did it to. But to turn them on, I would need something to work with—energy, and lots of it."

Rowen watched Blake's eyebrows perk up, a small smile coming to his face. "Is that even possible?" he said. "I mean, won't that pretty much kill me?"

"Not necessarily," said Arthur. "It would be like a shot of adrenaline that lasts a long time. "We'd have to be careful with you when you come down, but I think we can manage it. What do you think, Bobby?"

"I think you're insane," he said, looking impressed, "but I think we can do it...and I think it would be good to see Finn in action one more time."

"Okay, do it," said Rowen, a plan forming in her head. They could win this; she was sure they could.

"What about the virus?" asked Gibbs suddenly, his eyes darting in all directions. "Even if we stop the cardinal, what happens to all the people under his control? Do they just die, or do they go back to being normal? I mean the whole country is infected, right?"

Rowen's shoulders fell, and it was suddenly like the weight of the world was on them. She wished her dad was awake. He was the one she turned to when everything went to hell, but he was locked away, being healed up, so she had to deal with this on her own. "We'll deal with one thing at a time," she said finally. "There's a cure for the virus here, so it's a start, but I promise you, we'll find a way to save everyone."

THIRTY-THREE
KILLING SKIES

Bobby was amazed that it had worked and was still reeling from how little energy it took, but from the moment that he had finished, Blake vanished in an arc of crackling yellow energy, only to reappear a heartbeat later with a wide grin on his handsome face. Combining his abilities with Arthur's was a stroke of pure genius, and when it was done, he raised an eyebrow, the look of surprise on his face mirroring his own. For some strange reason, Arthur reminded him of himself, and the more time he spent with him, the more he liked him. They shared similar values, and when he learned how he had pissed off Michael by making New York its own city state, with him in charge, he couldn't help but laugh.

"Michael is only a few miles out. Are you ready?" asked Blake, sounding almost nice for the first time since they'd met.

"Yes, and you, Jonah?" said Bobby, eyeing the crystal-clad titan up and down. Rowen's plan was simple: meet him in the air and take him out before he arrived. It was insane, but it had potential.

Jonah nodded, offering his hand. Eyeing the hand, Bobby sighed. "You know, it really feels like everyone can fly but me, I gotta be carried around like some kid holding his father's hand."

"I can't fly," said Blake. "Neither could Tamika, and only this big brute here can. "Stop whining and man up."

"Well, that didn't last long," said Bobby, giving Blake a half smile.

"What?"

"You being nice to me."

Blake scratched at his graying beard, looking Bobby up and down. "Me cloaking you is me being nice. Now, sit still, and let me do my thing." Without another word, Bobby felt the familiar tingle, and his arm began to vanish in a wave of crackling energy, which crawled all over his body like a thousand tiny pinpricks. Within moments, he couldn't see any of himself. He waved his hand in front of his face but saw nothing. Luckily, he could still feel his body.

"I've made it so that you can both hear one another," said Blake, "but Michael shouldn't see or hear a thing till you're close enough to see the whiskers on his chin."

"We'll make quick work of them," said Jonah, tightening his grip on Bobby's hand. "You just make sure that you hide the entrance to the base. Who knows what else the

cardinal has in store for us."

Before Blake cloud answer, they took to the sky, and Bobby felt like Jonah was trying to rip his arm out of its socket.

"You could have warned me!" he shouted over the wind ripping past his ears, finding the humid jungle air hot and muggy even at high altitude.

"You spend too much time talking," said Jonah. "Cardinal Washington is close, and we need to crush him completely to make sure he can never rise up against us again."

Bobby agreed. Michael was a threat that needed to be stopped here and now, and nothing short of his death would do that. Pastor Warren may have been a monster, but he was right about Michael and his ambition, and his transformation from the friend he knew and the man who wanted nothing but power, had nothing to do with the crystal the pastor had put on his neck. He could still remember the day he walked into the recovery room, only the second one of them to survive Ascension. He had been charming, all smiles and hand-shakes, a politician born, if ever there was one. The moment he had been given even a small taste of power, that all changed for the worse.

"This is it," said Jonah, pulling Bobby from thoughts of the past and drawing his attention to a massive aircraft carrier flying in the distance.

"He was never this powerful," said Bobby, swallowing hard, not believing his eyes. The entire carrier was made of the glowing amber energy Michael used to craft the wings he used to fly, or the sword he favored in combat, but on a scale he never imagined possible. "How can he be doing this? If Arthur and Rowen are right, our power is supposed to fade over time."

"It doesn't matter," said Jonah, his deep voice grim. "He cannot stop me with tricks. I destroyed an entire fleet at Norfolk; this won't be any different." Bobby wished he could see Jonah's face so he could know if it was truth or bravado, or worse—insanity. As they got closer, he could make out thousands of infected on the deck of the carrier, all standing stock still like living mannequins...waiting.

"It's not a trick," said Bobby. "Michael can make anything he can imagine. If he made that carrier, it would be just the same as one made of titanium and carbon fiber."

"Then I can tear through that hull as if it were made of paper," said Jonah, his tone ending any discussion.

As they drew closer, Bobby let his thoughts drift to his former friend. The friend who had threatened him, forced him to murder Elizabeth, and had to control him at every turn. He let the rage inside him bubble and boil, like an inferno that needed to be fed, that would consume everything in its path and leave only ash.

"Drop me on the deck and then get clear," seethed Bobby, unclipping his monowhip from his hip, on the edge of unleashing his power, ready to kill. Jonah did as ordered, and when he strafed over the deck, Bobby leaped, flipping through the air and tumbling onto the glowing aircraft carrier with catlike grace. Finding himself surrounded by an army of infected that came to life the instant he landed, Bobby spun his monowhip around him defensively, the invincible line neatly cutting through flesh, bone, and metal with scalpel-like precision, giving him enough room to focus, if only for a heartbeat.

With a roar, darkness exploded from him, expanding in a field faster than the light it consumed. Bobby shivered despite the heat as he drained torrents of life energy from the thousands of infected filling the carrier, his breath catching in his throat from the rush of power burning through his soul. All around him the infected fell in silent screams, the essence that animated them ripped away, then suddenly they fell apart like they had never been real, bodies sublimating into pools of vile liquid that smelled of heated metal, like a foundry.

Not wanting to touch what was left of the creatures, Bobby leaped high, his strength amplified by the thin sheen of crystal armor covering his skin and the power coursing through his veins. Aiming for what looked like the command deck of the aircraft carrier, he easily made the distance, landing gingerly on the railing next to the bridge and then falling onto the main platform. Entering the bridge, he narrowed his eyes in suspicion when he found it empty, not a soul in sight. He was about to return outside when the comm system buzzed, a familiar voice filling the command deck. "Can you imagine my surprise when I saw a dead man come back to life," said Michael, amusement in his voice. "How did you manage to hide from me all these years?"

"Not dead, not hiding," he said, just as Jonah landed on the deck, giving him a salute while he surveyed Bobby's work. "I'm just here to clean up your mess. You have to stop hurting innocent people and do your own dirty work now. You can't hide behind an explosive in my head or your rank anymore, so come out and face me."

"Oh, so you're a saint now, Robert, defender of the innocent? It wasn't so long ago that you killed a stadium full of people and would have done the same a second time if Rodrigo hadn't stopped you."

"You ordered me to do that; you were just as guilty as I was," said Bobby, balling his fist.

"Not that it matters. You're a killer, Bobby. That's all you can do for the world, so just accept it," said Michael, laughing now. "You know, I find it ironic that today of all days you return, just in time to watch my greatest achievement happen."

"We killed your little invasion. You can try and take us all on, but we have a full team of Ascended. We'll break you in half if you even try," said Bobby, ignoring the laughter coming over the intercom. Without another word, Bobby left the bridge, bypassing the stairs, leaping the six stories, and comfortably landing on the glowing amber deck, his head on a swivel as he sprinted to Jonah. "He's not here."

Jonah crossed his arms over his massive chest, looking around. "How is that possible? Didn't you say he has to be close to maintain this construct?"

"I don't know, maybe. But if his powers have grown over the years, who knows."

There was a screech, like nails on a chalkboard, and Michael's voice came through a PA system of some kind. "You're right, my powers have grown; my little army has seen to that, but don't worry, I will still take care of both of you once I've taken the data core on the Ark."

"Something's wrong here," said Bobby, locking eyes with Jonah. "He's never this calm, especially when he doesn't get his way."

"Are you saying he planned for us to attack the aircraft carrier?"

Bobby shook his head, his breath coming in faster now. "No, he was surprised that I was alive; he couldn't have planned that far ahead."

"A feint, then," said Jonah, grabbing Bobby by his red coat just as the deck began to fade, "to draw out whatever defenses or defenders the base had, knowing—"

"Oh God, no!" said Bobby, suddenly floating in midair.

"What?"

Shaking his head, Bobby tapped the comm in his ear: "Rowen, are you there?!"

The line was silent for a moment, but when Bobby heard the hiss and crackle followed by her voice, the tension drained out of his shoulders. "Bobby, what is it? Did it work? Did you guys get him?"

"No, it was a ruse, a trick, to get us to show our strength."

"What was the point of that?" said Rowen, hesitation in her voice. "We've been speaking with the caretaker hologram. We've locked down the front doors. It'll be impossible for him to breach, not to mention, with the way Blake has this place cloaked, there's no—"

"No, the first time I was there, I got in through—oh no!" Bobby flinched, raising a hand to shield his eyes as the sky went white.

"What the hell was that?" said Jonah, scanning the horizon, unaffected by the brilliant flash filling the sky.

Bobby rubbed his eyes, trying to blink away the shadows dancing in the corners of his eyes, "Orbital laser platform," he said, squinting. "The first time I came here, there was an outpost hundreds of miles out near the coast, but it led right into the heart of the base."

"So, Rowen and the others..."

"We have to get to them because Michael and whatever army he brought with him are going to be in the Ark in the next few minutes!"

THIRTY-FOUR

JUST YOU AND ME

"Warning! Breach of security at Outpost Omega. All external communications are offline," said the hologram, flickering into existence, just as she lost contact with Bobby and her brother. The operations center was similar to the area where they had first encountered the hologram, circular with small crystals that glowed brightly for light around its circumference.

Rowen walked over to one of the many spires that reached from the floor to the ceiling of the space, placing a hand on one of them that was flashing a brilliant crimson. "Show me," she said, still trying to get the hang of how everything worked. When she had told the hologram she needed a space where she could run Overwatch of the area, it had led her here. The smooth glasslike walls suddenly vanished, and she saw what looked like a base underwater with its doors blown open, a steady stream of infected pouring in from a glowing amber path that led back to a massive submarine that looked the size of an ocean liner.

"How far away is that?" said Gibbs in a rush, tapping his foot nervously at her side. Rowen had assigned Blake to the front of the Ark to maintain his cloak, while Arthur had stayed in the medical lab to watch her father and hopefully figure out how to use the cure on a large scale, leaving her and Gibbs to run the operation from here.

"Close to twelve hundred miles," said the hologram, "but there is a rapid-tram system. Estimated time of transport from the outpost to here is less than six minutes."

"Well, there's only one subway car, so they can't all get in at once, right? Can they?" said Gibbs. "I mean, that gives us time to lock down that section, no?" As if to answer his question, MIchael appeared, looking regal in his billowing crimson robes and blazing amber wings on his back, a flaming sword in his hand that made him look like the angel that was his namesake. Rowen watched with a mix of awe and horror as he pointed with his sword, and out of nothing, thin lines of amber and gold appeared, looking like a rough drawing at first and then to her amazement coalescing into a carbon copy of the subway car that was already there.

The hologram vanished for a moment before reappearing. "Affirmative. However, that can only be done on location with a manual override."

"Well, we better get down there," said Rowen, fingering her SIG in its holster as Michael created a second, then a third, copy right before her eyes. "Where's the override?"

The image of the infected streaming onto base shrunk down in size to a lower section of the wall, replaced with an image of what looked like a subway platform. "Here," said the hologram, highlighting a panel at tunnel entrance in red."

"So, what is there, a lever or some sort of button?" asked Rowen, her hopes that it could be easily dashed when the hologram spoke up."

"Negative. The interface will require a reprogramming. Katib, here, should be capable of achieving such a task."

Rowen smirked at Gibbs, who had just turned white as a sheet. "Looks like you're coming with us. Let's hope you do better than the last time you were in the field," she said, her thoughts going to the diner back in Winslow and how GIbbs had panicked.

To her surprise, he nodded, swallowing hard. "We have to protect this place. God knows what will happen if we lose."

"Are there any weapons on the base or in the area?" asked Rowen, knowing they were running out of time.

"Negative. Energy for the base's defensive systems has been reassigned to primary life support."

"Then we go at it with what we have. We only have to hold out long enough to lock down the area," said Rowen. She had brought enough ammo to take down a small army but given how many infected were boarding the tram car, they would have to work fast...very fast.

"What about everyone else? Blake, your brother, and Bobby?" asked Gibbs, starting a weapons check on his sidearm, almost dropping the nickel-plated Beretta because of his shaking hands.

"I don't know. I don't dare take Blake off the front door, just in case Cardinal Washington has something else up his sleeve. I'll get Arthur to meet us there, but for my brother and Bobby. It doesn't look good." Seeing his eyes shoot open, Rowen put both hands around his. "Here, let me." Without a word, he let go of the weapon, exhaling slowly.

"I'm sorry I'm so useless," he said, his eyes downcast.

Rowen pointed the gun away from them and engaged the safety, ejecting the clip, and pulling back the slide to eject the bullet in the chamber, then quickly checking the barrel, "You're not useless; you're awesome, and I'm sorry I don't tell you that more often. You're the one who's gonna be locking down that door. I can't do it without you, so you get to be the hero here. Can you do it?"

Gibbs gave her an awkward smile, his large eyes suddenly bright. "Yeah...yes, I think I can. I know I can."

"Good," she said, turning the weapon around and handing it to him with a confidence she didn't feel.

"Warning! Four minutes to breach," said the hologram, its monotone voice drowning everything out.

"Arthur, meet us at the tramway if you can; the shit is about to hit the fan," said Rowen into the comm in her ear, patting herself down and checking her ammo, comforted by the feeling of her SIG bouncing off her hip. "C'mon, Gibbs, it looks like it's just you and me, and they're playing our song, so let's dance," said Rowen, racing out of the operations center with her long duster streaming behind her, praying that they had enough ammo to hold on long enough.

THIRTY-FIVE

WAKING THE DREAMER

Arthur blinked when Rowen's voice chimed in his ear. He was so close; all he needed was a bit of time and a miracle.

"Is that it?" said Captain Macdonald, Rowen's father, towering behind him.

"Yes," said Arthur, holding the long, glowing strand in a suspension field just above his hand. "There's still large amounts of it in your bloodstream too."

"What exactly is *it?*" he asked, looking timid, despite his large frame. Eyeing him over his shoulder, he could see where Jonah got his size: he was tall and muscular without an ounce of fat on him. He had only come out of the cylinder thirty minutes before, staggering out in confusion as to where he was and wondering what the hell Arthur was doing with him.

"Artificial RNA," said Arthur. "It's like a computer program that tells your body what to do with its raw materials: acids, proteins, fats...everything gets coded through RNA. This artificial version of it reprograms the virus, tricking it into converting the metallic material it creates back into normal flesh and blood; quite brilliant actually."

"Can you use this to make a cure?" asked Rowen's father, rubbing a finger along his square jaw.

"Yes, if I can replicate enough of it...but for now we are out of time, sir. We have to go help Rowen."

Hearing the name of his daughter, the big man stood up straight, his hand reflexively reaching for a sidearm on his hip that wasn't there. "Where? What have I missed?"

"Cardinal Washington has invaded the base with a full army of infected. From what I understand, she's going to meet him, to slow him down."

"Alone!?"

Arthur pressed his lips together, thinking back a moment to his own father, and how different both men were—polar opposites, in fact. His own father would have never reacted like this; he wouldn't have cared. "Yes, sir...but there's more."

"You're walking a thin line, son. Make it quick, and find me a goddamn weapon," he said, starting to pace the room, breathing hard.

"Rowen will be fine, sir. She's like us now...like me."

Captain MacDonald's brow wrinkled, his jaw clenching and unclenching. In that moment of rage, he almost looked like Rowen. "You have one minute to explain before I rip your head off and spit down your throat," said the big man, seething.

"It was her choice," said Arthur, raising his chin, "and despite our size difference, I would break every bone in your hand if you touched me."

"I bet you would, wouldn't you? It doesn't matter; we're done here. Point the way to my daughter."

"Yes, sir," said Arthur, with a nod of his head. Reaching out, he delved into the base's system, careful not to go too deep, not wanting to risk activating the Ark's defenses. A moment later, the flickering hologram of the base's AI appeared. "Take Captain Macdonald to the tram station to meet up with Rowen, and find him a sidearm," he ordered.

"Affirmative," it said, gesturing that the captain should follow, before flickering down the exit corridor. "There are sidearms that are still functional along the route we are going to take."

"You're not coming? I thought you said she needs us," he said, stopping at the entrance to the med lab.

Arthur looked up from the strand of RNA he was working on, shaking his head. "You need to go save her, so go! But I need to stay here, so I can save everyone else." Before Rowen's father could say more, Arthur shut the door with a wave, his mind racing to do as he just bragged. It would be useless to stop Michael, only to find themselves in a world full of mindless monsters. He had to stop this, and no sacrifice would be too great.

THIRTY-SIX

NOT ENOUGH

Rowen cursed through gritted teeth when another glowing tramcar arrived with hordes of infected pouring out. This was the third car of infected to show up, and she had fallen into an easy rhythm, squeezing the trigger on her SIG, holding tight against the smooth kick of the weapon's recoil, steadily breathing in and out with the explosive flare of the muzzle. Her Ascension had made her deadlier. She was faster, more precise, moving from target to target without a single shot wasted...yet she was still losing ground. There were too many of them, and they just kept coming. "How much longer, Gibbs?" she shouted behind her, smoothly releasing her empty clip and instantly sliding another in its place in a single, smooth motion.

Gibbs was pressed against the smooth glass wall, smack-dab in the middle of the tram station with a tablet in hand, while his fingers danced across a series of slim glass protrusions that emerged like glittering diamonds along its surface. "I don't know!" he screamed, his large eyes wide with panic. "This is way more complicated than anything I've ever tried."

Returning her attention to the nightmare in front of her, Rowen was forced back when a wave of infected were just inches from her, their reaching fingers and hands a hair's breadth from her face. Seeing so many so close, she stopped thinking, acting solely on intuition, pumping shot after shot into their heads, her powerful SIG tearing skulls to shreds, leaving quivering bodies with odd strands of tightly woven metal filaments spilling from gaping wounds to pile up in front of her.

"Rowen, up top!" screamed Gibbs from somewhere behind her. Rowen had only a heartbeat to dodge an infected who had leaped from the top of the tramcar and was falling toward her Without skipping a beat, she readjusted her next shot, firing from the hip and leaving a gaping hole in its chest, the bullet nearly tearing the thing in half when it tore straight through it.

Her eyes flickered back to the horde in front of her, and she found another half dozen of them so close. She could smell their acrid breath washing over her, stinking like a foundry. The coppery taste of fear filled Rowen's mouth, and suddenly, for a moment, everything moved as though it were underwater, slow and measured, almost frozen in place. Ducking by their reaching hands, Rowen found that she was moving and they were not, like she was sneaking through the seconds of a ticking clock, stealing time.

She unloaded clip after clip while moving through them in slow motion as they were inching along ever so slowly, watching in fascination as the bullets exploded from the muzzle of her SIG. Slowly creeping along their paths on trails of flame, the very air hissing like a snake as the metal cut through it. She released a breath that echoed in her ear, and everything returned to its normal speed, and the dozens of infected that were clawing and reaching for her fell in unison, their heads and hearts exploding all at once.

"What the hell was that?" shouted Gibbs, his voice loud in the now empty tram station.

"Hell if I know," muttered Rowen, looking down at her shaking hands and smoking gun, her brows coming together in amazement at the carnage she had inflicted, still not sure of what she had done or how she had done it. The high-pitched whine of another car coming down the tramway tore her attention away from the mess of bodies. Following the sound, she saw another glowing amber car racing toward them and readied herself, steeling her reserve and counting off at the ammo she had left, realizing she had gone through almost half of it. Watching the tram arrive, she held her fire. She had wasted ammunition on the first one, only to find that her shots did nothing, the glowing tram appearing to repair itself while she watched.

"Got it!" shouted a triumphant Gibbs just as a thick glass barrier slammed into place with a deep rumble, shaking the platform and blocking the tramline entirely. Rowen turned to see him with his arms raised in celebration, a geeky look of wonder plastered on his face. Her shoulders fell as the tension drained from them, and she ran to Gibbs, wrapping her arms around him as they smiled at one another.

"See, I told you, hero material!" she said, holding him at arm's length and poking him in the chest.

Gibbs shook his head, beaming with joy. "I didn't think I could do it, and you were amazing. What was that you did? I mean, for a second I blinked, and it looked like you were everywhere at once."

Rowen pushed him away reluctantly, knowing how she looked, and simply shrugged. It never was worth it getting too close, even in moments like this.

"What?" he asked, his smile fading.

"Nothing, it's just—" A loud boom reverberated through the entire complex, and Rowen flinched, cocking her head at the door Gibbs had just closed. They both staggered when another boom echoed through the door, sounding like a giant was pounding a hammer on iron.

"That shouldn't be possible," whispered Gibbs when a third boom caused cracks to appear, fine lines in the smooth surface.

"I think you should head back to the operations center," said Rowen, her smile fading, replaced with a look of determination. "I think Cardinal Washington is done playing with us now, and if I'm right about what is on the other side of the door, I won't be able to protect you."

"Rowen, we should both go. There's no—"

"If you don't want me to kill you before the cardinal breaks in here, then you better move!" shouted Rowen. "Now!"

With a start, Gibbs headed for the elevator just when another titanic blow shook the foundations of the place, forcing Rowen to fight to stay on her feet. She held her breath, waiting, and when the glass wall exploded, she found herself standing defiantly as shards of glass and crystal fell like hail all around her, bouncing off her newly hardened skin and armor. Seconds later, through the haze and the pall of dust, Cardinal Washington emerged at the vanguard of a vast host of infected, blazing amber wings on his back and flaming sword in hand. With her improved senses Rowen could see the look of printed circuits on his face, see the dull silver that made up his eyes. Part of her brain swore that she could even smell the acidic odor of metal on his breath.

He stopped, flying onto the platform and facing her. "You are a very impressive young lady...but then Bobby's creations always were; he always had an eye for the young."

Rowen smirked at him, tightening her grip on her SIG. "Really, you're gonna be dramatic like this is some cheesy holovid story? Let's not be ridiculous; this works one way. We fight. I kill you. The end. Got it?"

"That's the problem with youth these days: no manners, always rushed," said Cardinal Washington, eyeing her up and down, "but I am nothing if not kind, so if you want to die quickly, I will accommodate you."

Rowen said nothing, waiting for him to come. Both Arthur and Bobby had warned her about him, had told her about his ego and flare for the dramatic, and she knew the moment she had met him she could beat him, her boast was the stone-cold truth. She just prayed she wasn't lying to herself.

THIRTY-SEVEN

THE CURE

Arthur had rebuilt the matrix from scratch almost a thousand times in the last few minutes. The Ark's quantum computer along with his intuitive abilities with machines, made it possible for him to explore every avenue, every possibility within the blink of an eye. The virus, while potent, was not really built to attack humans; it was made to kill a species that had vanished from the planet long before the great pyramids of Giza were built, in an age where multiple species of humans and hominids lived and died in a war long forgotten.

With a start, he almost dropped the glowing strand that he was concentrating on, his mind burning down a new path of thought. Focusing hard, he extracted a portion of the nanites floating in his own blood, combining it with the strand of artificial RNA, using it to program new abilities into it, new possibilities. With a smile, he tapped on the comm in his ear. "Rowen, are you still alive?" he asked, hoping she was, his mind making plans if she wasn't. After all was said and done, Arthur liked her: she was nice, a capable leader, except for the temper.

. . .

A voice crackled over the comm. "I'm here," shouted Rowen, sounding strained. "Just a little busy trying to not get killed by the cardinal."

Arthur smiled to himself, looking down at the glowing construct in his hand. "Do me a favor, and keep him busy. I'm coming."

For a moment, Arthur thought he had asked too much, fearing that she was gone or too hurt to speak. He felt a wave of relief when her voice came back through the static. "That's a pretty big favor. You're gonna owe me big-time," she shouted through a series of explosions before cutting the line.

Gathering his things, Arthur raced from the lab. Shunting his mind through the communicator on his wrist and connecting to his main hub back at Rockefeller university, "Gwen, if you can hear me, I'm sending you a set of coordinates. I need you and Rodrigo to get down here on my signal," Without another word he hurried to get to Rowen before it was too late, hoping that the untested cure he carried would work, and that he could figure out a solution to its failings, before it was too late.

THIRTY-EIGHT

PATH OF DESTRUCTION

Jonah plunged like a torpedo into the roiling waves of the South Atlantic, the water bubbling and boiling in his wake as he descended into the cold abyss, leaving the world of light and warmth far behind them. He felt two taps on his hand, the signal that Bobby, who he was dragging along, was still with him, still alive, despite the lack of air and crushing weight of the water all around them. Bobby had given him vague directions to the Ark complex, and given the level of destruction Cardinal Washington had inflicted on the outpost, they were sure it would be easy to follow his trail.

He was about to turn away and return to the surface when he caught a glimmer of color through the murkiness, shades of red and orange just at the edge of his vision. He squeezed Bobby's hand twice as he pulled him along, their signal that he had found something. Pressing ahead, he accelerated, catching sight of a broken crystal spire rising up from the bedrock, looking like it had been cracked in half, a jet of flame pouring out of where its top would have been. Having no fear, Jonah flew through the flames as though they were air ignoring the heat and pressure until he emerged on the other side, tumbling end over end and landing in a heap with Bobby the moment the pressure changed.

"How do I keep getting caught up in these messes?" said Bobby, untangling himself and rolling onto his stomach, coughing up seawater.

Pushing the thinner man away, Jonah stretched to his full height. "This area looks like it took the brunt of the laser attack," he said, noting the blackened and melted crystal walls of the place.

"Not one for conversation, are you?" said Bobby, coming to his feet.

"No."

"Okay, then, that should lead into the main complex," said Bobby, cocking his head and pointing to a dark tunnel. "That's where I found the pod that took me in last time, but the tunnel should be good enough for you to fly us down."

Jonah followed his gaze, grunting in agreement. "Take my hand; I will get us there. If the cardinal is on-site, Rowen and the others will need our help," he said, taking to the air and jetting down the darkened tramway, flying near blind. They had flown in silence for a few minutes when Jonah saw the telltale glow of amber in the distance.

"There are infected farther down the tunnel; I can feel them," shouted Bobby from behind. "Thousands of them. That means Michael is in the base already."

Getting closer, he saw the infected were standing listlessly in tramcars that were gliding swiftly and silently toward the main Ark, the bright glow of Michael's constructs illuminating the way. "It doesn't matter," said Jonah, extending a jagged crystal fist in front of them. "We shall cut our way through them and crush him. I've had enough of his games."

Jonah looked back to see a smoldering rage reflected in Bobby's eyes. "Let's finish this, then." He pressed forward at that moment, flying faster than he ever had, hardly feeling it when his armored body cut the tramcars in half as he plowed through them. The infected had no time to react; they simply found themselves tumbling head over heels and being torn apart when the vehicles they were riding in vanished in a storm of destruction. Then he watched approvingly as thousands of thin, snakelike tendrils of dark energy poured out of Bobby's hands, stabbed and pierced through the bodies that were still standing, draining whatever force sustained the creatures, leaving behind little more than smoking pools of vile fluid.

Jonah held his breath when a loud boom reverberated through the tunnel from up ahead, pulling his attention away from the carnage. "I think we're out of time," he said, looking back at Bobby, "but I can't go any faster."

"I have an idea," screamed Bobby, a wide-eyed, desperate look coming to his face. "It may not work, but it's worth a shot."

"Do it!"

Bobby grimaced in pain, the hand clutching his shaking. Jonah wondered what the hell he was doing when his armor began to glow with a pure, blinding white light, his breath catching in his throat when a rush of energy poured into him, making his heart beat out of his chest as if he were holding a live electrical wire. Every nerve, every muscle tensed, and Jonah had never felt more alive, more powerful. With a roar he accelerated, feeling like nothing could stop him. He didn't slow when he tore through the remaining tramcars in their way like they were made of cardboard.

When they were past the main vanguard with a trail of destruction in their wake, Jonah looked back in amazement to find Bobby still grimacing in pain but wearing a look of satisfaction, nodding that he should go on. Jonah plunged ahead, drinking in every ounce of power he could give him. Relishing in the thought that he would have his revenge—and would kill the cardinal once and for all.

THIRTY-NINE

SLOWING TIME

Cardinal Washington came at her on blazing wings made of amber, his flaming sword cutting wide swaths and threatening to cleave her in half. Rowen moved on instinct, using every ounce of her newfound strength, moving with pantherlike dexterity to avoid the blazing weapon: at first leaping over it, and then running along the wall and floor as the glowing blade tore deep gashes in the crystal walls behind her. All the while blasting at the infected, along her path, with her SIG, firing blind from her hip and over the shoulder.

Having put some distance between them she spun, leveling her weapon and aiming for the cardinal's arrogant face, only to growl in frustration when her shot was blocked by the swarms of infected between her and her target.

"This has been entertaining—but enough!" shouted Cardinal Washington, hints of anger in his tone when he saw her SIG pointed at him. The path in front of Rowen was suddenly blocked by a wall of amber that at first looked like a child's drawing, rough and unfinished, and then solidifying into something that felt solid and real when she slammed into it. She pivoted to change direction, and another one appeared in its place in front of her, and then another behind her, and finally another finished her cage. She heard the cardinal laugh when the walls began closing in, and Rowen cursed at herself for being so stupid. "He was just playing me," she said under her breath, eyeing the glowing constructs as they closed in.

She sucked in a deep breath to calm herself, knowing she only had seconds, wishing she had more time to figure this out. Rowen had a sudden flash, if she could do what she had done only a few minutes ago, while fighting the infected, she would have all the time in the world. Thinking back, she realized she had been doing it well before Bobby had poured all this energy into her and made her into this new person. It had always felt like things slowed down when she was shooting. Even without powers she was still doing it, slowing everything down to make the impossible shots. "Breathe," she whispered, and her voice echoed in her ears, everything around her coming to a stop. Rowen smiled to herself when she looked at the wall when everything was slowed, realizing it wasn't really solid. It was pure energy of some kind, and she could see the individual strands of matter that made it up, connections in a web of power. And like any web, she just had to pull at the seams to tear it apart. Bracing her back to one of the walls, she leveled her SIG, then in the blink of an eye, squeezing the trigger a dozen times, her bullets neatly slicing apart the connections that made up the construct all at once. A moment later, the barrier in front of her fell apart, and Rowen sprang from the tiny space, time returning to normal.

"That's not possible!" shouted Cardinal Washington, clutching his head, the confident smirk he wore replaced by a wide-eyed look of shock, the infected all around them halting in their tracks.

"I told you I was going to kill you," said Rowen, calmly ejecting an empty clip, and sliding another one in its place, striding along the wall in hopes of getting a clear shot.

Cardinal Washington shook his head and squared his shoulders, his silver gaze full of hate. "Impressive, but you don't have enough bullets to stop all of my little tools here, no matter what tricks you have up your sleeve."

Rowen smiled to herself, knowing she had him. She had spent the last few minutes trying to get a clear shot, racing to avoid his horde, but then she had been fighting on his terms, his way. No more. "I think we're done playing your games."

"I don't think so. This is my world now, so my terms, but if you think you can take me, come get me" he said simply, just as an amber glow surrounded him. Rowen blinked in surprise when he blurred and shifted, and then he was no longer just one man, but three, each an identical copy, with the same smug grin and blazing sword.

Rowen fell back on her heels when they all came at her, like a machine working in perfect unison, forcing her on the defensive. She ducked and dodged multiple versions of the cardinal's flaming sword, leaping back to avoid having her belly opened by a horizontal cleave, and then sucking in a breath, she slowed down the world for a moment to shift on her heels and twist out of the way to avoid being cut in half down the middle, only to run straight into his third copy blocking her way. In desperation, she leapt high, flipping over and tucking into a ball to avoid having parts of her sliced off, only to yelp in pain when the flaming weapon clipped her thigh, leaving a deep, cauterized cut that burned like acid.

Landing clumsily, Rowen staggered and fell then quickly scrambled to her feet, hopping on one leg trying desperately to avoid the scores of infected that now surrounded her. Desperate, she squeezed her eyes shut, calling on her new ability one more time, slowing the world around her to a snail's pace. Snapping her eyes open, she spun in place, firing again and again, her SIG spitting fire and flame, leaving a garish circle of headless corpses standing around her, falling ever so slowly.

She pivoted on her good leg to hop away when time returned to normal unexpectedly, throwing her off-balance, and sending her tumbling face-first onto the hard floor. Blinking in surprise, she rolled onto her back just in time to avoid a flaming sword cutting a deep gash in the floor where she just had been and finding all three glowing versions of Cardinal Washington towering above her. She stuck her hand out defensively, sucking in a deep breath to slow things down once more, only to gasp in shock when nothing happened, pain exploding in her skull like someone had pounded a nail into it. "Shit!"

A wide smile creeped across all three of Cardinal Washington's faces as they raised their swords above their heads. "All out of tricks, are we?" they shouted, bringing down the flaming weapon.

"Screw you!" shouted Rowen, watching the blade fall, facing her death with courage. Before her skull was cracked open, she was blinded for a moment by a flash of blinding white light, her ears filled with a bone-crushing scream followed by a loud series of crashes that moved progressively farther away. Rubbing her eyes and blinking away the spots in her vision, she sat up to find Cardinal Washington along with his copies gone, the air around her filled with hundreds of thin smoky tendrils, black and red like an ugly bruise. They snaked their way through the entire area, coiling around the infected, plunging into their bodies like hungry parasites. And whenever they touched, moments later the hapless creatures collapsed into pools of some vile liquid whose odor made her want to vomit.

Following the dark energy back to its source, she saw Bobby standing in front of the sundered tunnel door with his arms extended and his face twisted in pain. One hand was masked in shadow, controlling the hundreds of tendrils attacking the infected. His other hand was brighter than the sun, projecting a thick beam of pure white light. Rowen smiled with glee when she saw that the brilliant torrent of power was washing over her brother, his normally dull gray armor, pulsing a bright white while he fought with the cardinal, driving the three copies of the man backward with powerful haymakers that blasted through any construct he tried to make.

Stumbling to her feet, she winced when she tried to put weight on her leg. She was about to fall when someone caught her. "I got you, kiddo," said a familiar, deep voice, holding her up.

She turned to see her father, standing tall, and giving her a toothy white grin. "Dad, you're okay," she said, looking him up and down for hints of circuit-printed skin or strange eyes before hugging him, drinking in his musky smell that reminded her of home, of not so long ago when she used to climb into his arms to feel safe.

"Is that your brother?" he asked, unable to look away while Jonah picked up one of the cardinal's copies by the throat and slammed his jagged fist through its chest, the amber construct coming apart like a shattered mirror.

"Yes," said Rowen, unable to hide her smile, an odd sense of pride filling her heart when he bolted like a torpedo into another copy, slamming them both into wall, the impact shaking the tram station and leaving a deep fissure when the construct disappeared. Before Jonah could attack him, the remaining version of the cardinal, spread his glowing wings wide, plunging his flaming sword into the floor in front of him with his head bowed. An ultra-thin web of amber spread out in front of him, growing exponentially with every passing moment, thousands upon thousands of layers spreading across the entire area with each passing second.

"What the hell is this?" said Rowen when the web covered her, trapping her and her father in the sticky substance. She couldn't see Bobby, but from what she could see of Jonah, he was trapped too, thrashing like a caged beast, the webbing growing tighter the more he struggled. Turning her attention back to the cardinal, she raised an eyebrow when she saw his flaming wings and sword were gone, tiny beads of sweat rolling down his temples.

"Your defiance is admirable," said Cardinal Washington, getting to his feet. She could tell he was trying to hide the strain of what he was doing, but Rowen could see him shaking, "But you cannot stop me. I will have the technology on this base, and I will use it to make the world a utopia."

Rowen snorted, wanting nothing more than to spit in his face. "You mean you want to enslave everyone!"

"Of course not," said the cardinal, shaking his head. "But freedom is dangerous. Freedom creates war, violence, hate. Imagine a world where those things exist only in the past, long forgotten."

"All under your brilliant leadership," shouted Bobby from some-where behind her. "I've lived with your bullshit for a long time: I don't think so."

"He can't maintain this," shouted Rowen. "He's had to make thousands of layers of this web to hold Jonah in place, us too. He's at his limit."

"Don't be stupid, girl," said Cardinal Washington, his nostrils flaring.

A thin tendril of dark energy slipped past her, slowly crawling its way through the layers of webbing, like a lion in the bush stalking its prey. "You're going to die here today, Michael," said Bobby. "I'm going to make sure it's slow and painful."

Cardinal Washington reached into his crimson robes, holding up a small remote of some kind so they could all see. "If that touches me, I will target this entire complex with multiple orbital laser platforms —none of us will survive."

Without warning, the remote in the cardinal's hand started to smoke, tiny arcs of electricity snapping and popping all around it, and with a yelp, he dropped it. Rowen smiled to herself, guessing what had happened. "I don't think so," said a familiar voice, a voice she had always found arrogant, but in this moment, she never loved it more.

Arthur emerged from an alcove leading from the elevator in this section, Gibbs behind him. He had a long, glowing strand of what looked like water, oddly curving in on itself and floating above his open palm. "Cardinal Washington is right," said Arthur. "If that strand touches him and he dies, none of us will survive."

Rowen narrowed her eyes at him, looking for hints if he'd been infected. "Are you nuts?"

"A little," said Arthur, putting one hand behind his back, coming close to the webbing but not touching it. "We're all infected at some level. The virus is hidden in a single strand of RNA. All Cardinal Washington did was activate it, like flicking a switch. And even if we're cured today, in the long run it will come back because it will continue to spread, no matter what we do. Eventually, no one will be left."

"So, what, we let him live?" said Bobby, sounding incredulous.

The cardinal snorted, taking a step back. "You idiots are speaking like you've already won. I don't think so. You're the ones trapped in my web, and I have hundreds of thousands more infected at my disposal. No, I think I will leave you all trapped here and find another way on the base. It may take time, but I will have what I want."

Rowen narrowed her eyes, wondering what he was up to when Arthur raised his chin high, smiling like a Cheshire cat. "Gwen, Rodrigo, now would be a good time," he said, the slightly curved object in his hand glowing brighter. Behind the cardinal, a pool of shadow rippled into place, dark as night and almost invisible against the tram stations dark walls.

A man emerged from the pool first, olive skinned with a large beak of a nose and high forehead, dressed in red and black. Then to her surprise, a small blond girl emerged dressed in a long, white duster that looked like it had seen better days. "Holy shit! Gwen. She's alive." Before Cardinal Washington could react, Rodrigo put a transparent blade to his throat, and Gwen wrapped herself around his thick middle, whispering something in his ear that made him red faced, and even from across the tram station, Rowen could hear his ribs crack."

Nodding to himself, Arthur continued, "If you want to live to see the next few minutes, it would be a good idea if you remove the construct," he said, raising an eyebrow.

Rowen held her breath, watching the cardinal watching them, his dull silver eyes weighing and measuring them. At last, after a few moments, his shoulders fell, and the web constraining them vanished. "It doesn't matter what you do," he began, his voice sounding frail. "There is no way to stop the spread of it. I tried in the beginning, but..."

"You opened Pandora's box without even knowing it," said

Arthur, coming forward, "all in hopes of regaining your lost abilities, your powers."

"What is he talking about?" said Bobby coming forward, his gaze shifting back and forth from Arthur to the cardinal.

Arthur came to stand beside her, his voice taking on a lecturing tone. "The virus is a single strand of RNA that copies itself into the same set of genes that allow for Ascension. They're dormant in most people, but in us, it's active, using our RNA to copy and spread itself, and as a consequence it has the effect of supercharging our abilities, or in the case of the cardinal here, restoring what he'd lost."

Rowen braced herself with her one good leg, glancing around at everyone. "So, how do we stop it? Fix everyone?"

"We reverse the process," said Arthur. "We introduce this RNA strand into Cardinal Washington's genetic profile and get him to spread the cure."

"You want me to help you?" spat the cardinal, sneering at all of them. "You're stupider than you look, boy."

Bobby spoke up, his eyes never leaving Cardinal Washington. "You used to be a good person, Michael. You wanted to help people. Make up for all the terrible things your father did in the senate."

Cardinal Washington shook his head, looking away from Bobby's intense gaze. "That was a long time ago," he said finally.

"Uhh, excuse me," piped up Gibbs, glancing down at the tablet in his hand. "What're you talking about, getting the cardinal to spread the cure? It would take years; he would literally have to walk around the country breathing on people."

"I worried about that too," said Arthur, "until I saw Bobby and Jonah here, the way they combined their abilities...well, we can do the same with this...I think."

Rowen saw a smile come to Bobby's face as he crossed his arms over his thin chest. "You want to infect him with the cure then have me supercharge the replication process? Michael would be like a geyser: the cure exploding from every pore in his body."

"I won't stand for th—" began Cardinal Washington, only to be silenced by Gwen, brutally placing him in a stranglehold.

"I thought you had decided to serve your country, become someone with honor and decency," she said in a mocking tone, giving him a tight-lipped smile. "I've been waiting years to do that."

Rowen gave the blond a wink, strangely happy to know she survived after all. "So, how do we do this?" she said to Arthur, "Does Bobby here just wiggle his fingers, and presto chango, we're done?"

"Not quite. We would need a public area with a large number of infected to disperse the cure to the widest area possible, and we all need to be close, because we'll become carriers of the cure too. Would be nice to be up high also, for better airborne distribution."

Rowen's shoulders fell while he spoke, her mind quickly following his train of thought. "You gotta be kidding me," she said, burying her hands in her hair. "I really hate that place."

"What? Where?" said Bobby, his brows coming together.

"New York," said Rowen with a sigh. "He wants to distribute the cure in New York first. Fine...fine, let's go back to that hellhole that stole two years of my life—for what I hope is the last goddamn time!"

FORTY

IF YOU CAN MAKE IT HERE, YOU CAN MAKE IT ANYWHERE

Bobby pulled tight his long crimson coat, trying to control the chattering of his teeth. He had always hated the cold and having spent the last fifteen years frozen solid had only made him hate it more. "Can you tell me why we're not doing this somewhere warmer?"

"Well, it's a heck of a view," said Arthur, beside him, standing at a parade rest, seemingly unaffected by the cold. "That and it's one of the few places left in the city that's not run over or on fire." The view he was talking about was the view from the top of Empire State Building, and Bobby couldn't agree more: it was breathtaking. From this height, the city looked peaceful until you looked closer and saw the smoke billowing over a city that burned.

"I saved it once, you know," said Bobby, brushing a hand through his hair, somehow after everything, feeling optimistic. "I think it's one of the things I'm most proud of, not that anyone ever knew."

Arthur gave him a small smile, a twinkle in his deep-brown eyes. "Me too. Funny that we should have that in common."

Bobby was about to say more, was about to thank Arthur for giving him the chance to get to know him, despite the terrible things that were done to him by his clone, but when the shimmering shadow appeared, he prepared himself for an attack. Rodrigo appeared first, rippling into place, his features smooth, like he was uninterested. Bobby still found it odd that the man had no clue who he was, considering that Bobby had saved him from debtors' prison so long ago and given him his powers. But Arthur had explained that after he was gone, Cardinal Washington had cloned the tall Italian, more than once, but each time he had edited his memories, removing anything that would give him a conscience, and apparently, memories of Bobby were one of those things. Next came a trio including Gwen and Jonah, each of them on either side of Cardinal Washington, all of them half falling, stumbling, gasping, and choking when they fully materialized. Bobby could sympathize. Rodrigo's ability to teleport anywhere was a blessing, but the moments you spent in the place in between transport was a nightmare at best: dark and cold, with air that was unbreathable.

Bobby drew on his rage, dark shadows playing around his hands, ready to strike Michael down if he even looked like he was about to flinch, much less attack. Beside him, Arthur did the same: tensing.

"I shall return," said Rodrigo with a brief nod and then vanishing like he was never there.

Watching his former friend gasp for air, Bobby reached down and helped him to his feet, looking for a flicker of humanity left in his strange, dull gray eyes. He opened his mouth to say something, but Michael pushed him away, never looking up. "Just do what you have to do. Kill me and be done with it," he said in a voice that was tired, like he had aged in the last few minutes. At his side, Jonah and Gwen grasped his arms, holding him in place with a level of strength Bobby couldn't imagine.

"It's no less than you deserve," said Arthur. "But this won't kill you. You'll be back where you started: your powers faded with time, burned out."

Cardinal Washington spat on Arthur's boots, wiping his mouth with the sleeve of his robe. "Dying would have been better. I don't want to live in a world where you two idiots have any sway."

Sucking in a deep breath, Bobby moved in close enough that he could whisper in his ear. "You know, I can't wait because when this is done, you'll get your wish. I'll drain every last spark of life you have, leaving nothing more than a burned-out husk. You'll face justice for Elizabeth and for me, for all your myriad sins at last."

The cardinal's face contorted with rage, and he fought, twisted, and pulled against Jonah and Gwen, both of whom looked bored, being far stronger than the angry man they held in place.

"We should get ready," said Arthur, just as Rodrigo returned with Rowen, and her father. They had left Gibbs along with Blake to watch over the Ark, and they had asked Captain Young to fly the Odin back to the city on his own.

Bobby gave Michael one last smile before returning to Arthur's side. "So, what do you need me to do?"

Arthur raised a hand, and the glowing strand reappeared floating just above his palm. "When I tell you to," he began, looking around at all of them before continuing, "I'm going to need you to do exactly like you did with Jonah, like you did with Rowen when you Ascended her: pour as much energy as you can into the cardinal. I'll do the rest."

Bobby closed his eyes, feeling his way along slowly to that burning energy inside him, the blazing torrent of rage and pain that sat at the core of who he was. He was amazed at how much this well of power had grown, in the past he had compared it to a bonfire, growing and shrinking with how much energy he had consumed, but now. Now it was a tornado, a torrent of flame that extended as far as his metaphysical eye could see. Most times when he used this power, he just touched it, taking small portions, but today, without thinking of how, he plunged into it, wrapping his soul around it. Dominating it and bringing it to heel like the rabid dog it was. It had become easier to do this with time, but drinking in this much power, the pain was still beyond imagining, like his entire body had been submerged in lava. Trembling like a leaf he opened his eyes to see everyone shading their eyes, amazed that his glow was brighter than the noon day sun.

Looking over at Michael, he saw for the first time in all the years he'd known him, that telltale flicker in his eyes, the shortness of breath, beads of sweat rolling down his temples: he was afraid. Beside him, Arthur flicked his wrist, and the glowing strand of RNA floating above his hand shot out like an arrow, plunging into Michael's chest, washing over him like a wave. "Now!" shouted Arthur.

"Goodbye, Michael," whispered Bobby, releasing it all, every ounce of power, losing himself in the pain, his heart beating loud in his ears like a drum. In the distance, he swore he could hear someone start to scream, and then time stopped, and his world went white, and there was no more.

EPILOGUE

EPILOGUE: THREE MONTHS LATER

"What do you think he wants?" asked Rowen, threading the transport through the New York skyline.

"I don't know, kid, but given how much work they've been putting into rebuilding this city, rooting out the remaining infected and making sure they get the cure, I'm pretty sure that he wants to show off some ridiculous thing he made some poor schlub make," said Blake, scratching at his salt-and-pepper beard.

"He, of all people, should know that we don't have time for this. Half the country is still infected, and it's bad enough he tricked us, making us run around the damn country to spread the cure for him."

Blake put a booted foot up on the dash, smiling at her. "As long as Bobby keeps me up and running, I'm happy running errands. Hell, I haven't felt this good in years."

Rowen smiled back at him. "And to think you almost killed him...more than once," she said, laughing at him now.

"This is coming from a girl who's threatened to kill everyone she knows at least once," he grumbled.

"Keep it up, and I'll make good on my threats," she said, catching a glimpse at the coordinates Arthur had sent her yesterday. Rowen raised an eyebrow when she saw that she was headed for the reservoir in Central Park, where the Russian invasion once had their base and right where the glowing tower had once stood. In its place was a wide building just shorter than the tree line, made of clear crystal with a single tall spire down the center that reflected the noonday sun with an array of dazzling colors.

"Land at the back of the building. There's a set of doors; we'll be waiting for you there," said Arthur's voice over the comm, sounding almost giddy.

"We," said Rowen, blowing out her cheeks. "Sounds serious." She landed the small transport in the small area behind the building, and when she and Blake emerged, Arthur was waiting for them, wearing the silly black uniform he always wore, Gwen at his side.

"Hello, Rowen; hello, Blake," he said, putting his arms behind his back and puffing out his small chest. "Follow me, please."

Rowen gave Blake a look, rolling her eyes, but following. Arthur led them into the building proper, and she couldn't help but notice the construction reminded her of the Ark, with its smooth glasslike floor, highlighted by small illuminated crystals along the edges. "How is Gibbs?" she asked, breaking a promise to herself. Thinking of the Ark brought him to mind, and she wondered for the thousandth time how he was doing. He never called anymore. He was too busy delving into its secrets along with her father and Captain Young.

Arthur gave her a polite smile. "He's good, still speaking too fast, still obsessed. He helped me with the design and materials of this place, obviously."

"Arthur's just as obsessed," began Gwen, half dancing, half walking down the hall. "He just hides it better. Now, he just wants to show off."

Rowen was about to ask more questions, but when she walked into the circular room with the high glass ceiling, she was surprised to find her brother, Bobby, and even Rodrigo waiting for them around a large circular table. "What the hell is this?"

Arthur spread his arms wide, a smile on his face. "This is our headquarters, our base."

"Our base for what?" she asked, noticing the vast array of computers, holoprojectors, and communications equipment.

Arthur turned to her, his voice sounding serious. "If anything, the infection crisis taught me that I can't do it alone. None of us can. It was only when we banded together that we were able to stop it. So I'm proposing a permanent team, like the government had with the Divinity Corps project, but without all the bullshit. We can be ready to help people, save the world, if it needs it."

"This isn't some comic book, Arthur. We're not superheroes. We barely got through the crisis," said Gwen, looking at everyone. "We're not even adults; we're teenagers, children!"

"Children who have known war and violence, who have fought and bled, lived through more abuse and more pain than we should have at our young age, but we endured," said Arthur, his deep-brown eyes boring into her. "In ancient warrior cultures when kids were forced to fight, forced to die for the good of the tribe, they would call them spear children. Well, that's us! We're Children of the Spear. Children forced to live in a world where we can't be children, where we have to grow up fast, go into battle, and die young."

"Are you all in on this?" asked Rowen oddly, not finding any allies. She could tell he had already convinced them all. They were on his side. Bobby, at least, had the decency to blush and look away. One by one, they nodded, everyone in full agreement.

"C'mon, Rowen, we need you," said Arthur, offering his hand.

She stared at it for a moment as though it were a viper, before finally shrugging her shoulders and shaking it. "Fine, I'll join you morons. I'll be a child of the spear or whatever."

Gwen clapped excitedly and gave her a warm hug. "Welcome aboard!"

Arthur guided her to the table, pulling out a chair for her. "Now, let's make some plans for the future," he said smiling from ear to ear.

Rowen sat, a slight frown coming to her face. "Children of the Spear. Can we change the name at least? It sounds kinda silly."

The end...for now.

DID YOU ENJOY THIS BOOK? YOU CAN MAKE A HUGE DIFFERENCE

Reviews are the most powerful tool in my arsenal when it comes to getting attention for my books. As much as I'd like to, I don't have the muscle of a New York publisher. I can't take out full page ads in the newspaper.

Honest reviews of my books help bring them to the attention of other readers.

If you've enjoyed this book I would be very grateful if you could spend just five minutes leaving a review (It can be as short as you like) on the book's page. You can jump to the page by clicking on the link below.

Omega

ABOUT THE AUTHOR

Rhett's love for all things science fiction grew out of a Sunday morning family tradition of watching Star Trek re-runs on the CBC. His love of storytelling is the result of too many hours as a dungeon master trying to murder his players!

He lives in Pincourt Canada with his wife, daughter, and a crazy calico named Maggie.

If you like gritty, dark science fiction with deep characters you've found your author.

www.ingramcontent.com/pod-product-compliance
Lightning Source LLC
Chambersburg PA
CBHW030101260626
47156CB00008B/2478